MATT JENSEN, THE LAST MOUNTAIN MAN

DAKOTA AMBUSH

MATT JENSEN, THE LAST MOUNTAIN MAN

DAKOTA AMBUSH

William W. Johnstone
with J. A. Johnstone

PINNACLE BOOKS
Kensington Publishing Corp.

www.kensingtonbooks.com

PINNACLE BOOKS are published by

Kensington Publishing Corp.
119 West 40th Street
New York, NY 10018

PUBLISHER'S NOTE
Following the death of William W. Johnstone, the Johnstone family is working with a carefully selected writer to organize and complete Mr. Johnstone's outlines and many unfinished manuscripts to create additional novels in all of his series like The Last Gunfighter, Mountain Man, and Eagles, among others. This novel was inspired by Mr. Johnstone's superb storytelling.

All Kensington titles, imprints, and distributed lines are available at special quantity discounts for bulk purchases for sales promotions, premiums, fund-raising, educational, or institutional use. Special book excerpts or customized printings can also be created to fit specific needs. For details, write or phone the office of the Kensington special sales manager: Kensington Publishing Corp., 119 West 40th Street, New York, NY 10018, attn: Special Sales Department; phone: 1-800-221-2647.

ISBN-13: 978-0-7860-2344-8
ISBN-10: 0-7860-2344-9

First printing: February 2011

10 9 8 7 6 5 4 3 2 1
Printed in the United States of America

Chapter One

When Matt Jensen rode into Swan, Wyoming, few who knew him would have recognized him. He had a heavy beard, his hair was uncommonly long, and he looked every bit the part of a man who had not been under a roof for two months. Eight weeks earlier, he had said good-bye to Smoke Jensen back at Fort Collins, Colorado, arranging to meet him here in Swan on this date. Not since then had Matt seen civilization, having spent the entire two months in the mountains prospecting for gold.

The success of Matt's two months of isolation was now manifested by a canvas bag he had hanging from the saddle horn. The bag was full of color-showing ore. Prospecting wasn't new to Matt; he had learned the trade under the tutelage of his mentor, Smoke Jensen, so he knew the color in the ore was genuine. But exactly how successful he had been would depend upon the assayer's report.

Swan was a flyblown little settlement, not served

by any railroad, though there was stagecoach service to Rawlings, where one could connect with the Union Pacific. The town had a single street that was lined on both sides by unpainted, ripsawed, false-fronted buildings. It could have been any of several hundred towns in a dozen Western states. As Matt rode down the street, a couple of scantily dressed soiled doves stood on a balcony and called down to him.

"Hey, cowboy, you're new to town, ain't you?" one of them shouted.

"You gotta be new 'cause I don't know you," the other one added. "And I reckon I *know* just about ever' man in town if you get my drift," she added in a ribald tone of voice.

Matt smiled, nodded, and touched the brim of his hat by way of returning their greeting.

"Come on up and keep us company. We'll give you a good welcome," the first one shouted down to him.

"Ladies, until I get a bath, I'm not even fit company for my horse," Matt called up to the two women as he rode underneath the overhanging balcony where the two women were standing.

The second soiled dove pinched her nose and, exaggerating, made a waving motion with her hand. "Oh, honey, you've got that right," she teased.

Laughing, Matt rode on down the street until he reached a small building at the far end. A sign in front of the building read J.C. MONTGOMERY, ASSAYER.

Matt swung down from his saddle and tied his

horse off at the hitching rail. Hefting the canvas bag over one shoulder, he stepped inside, where he was greeted by a small, thin man.

"Can I help you?" the little man asked.

"Are you the assayer?"

"I am."

Matt laid the canvas bag on the counter, then took out a handful of rocks and lay them alongside the bag.

"I need you to take a look at this," Matt said.

Montgomery chuckled. "You want me to tell you if it is gold or pyrite, right?"

"No, mister," Matt said. "I know it is gold. All I want you to do is tell me how much money all this is worth."

The assayer picked up a couple of rocks and looked at them casually, before putting them back down. Then, taking a second look at one of them, he picked it up again, and this time he examined it through a magnifying glass.

"What do you think?" Matt asked.

"You're right," Montgomery said. "It is gold."

"You have any idea as to the value?"

"Do all the rocks have this much color?"

"I wouldn't have bothered carrying them in if they didn't," Matt replied.

"Well, then, I would say you have two or three hundred dollars here. In fact, I'll give you three hundred dollars for the entire bag right now."

Matt put the rocks back in the bag. "Would you now?"

"In cash," Montgomery said.

"You always cheat your customers like that?" Matt asked.

"What are you talking about?"

"What I have here is worth two thousand dollars if it is worth a cent," he said. "Thank you, Mr. Montgomery, but I believe I'll take my business somewhere else."

"I'm the only assayer in town."

"Perhaps. But Swan isn't the only town," Matt said as he left the office.

Just up the street from the assayer's office, Matt saw a sign that read HAIRCUTS, SHAVES, BATHS.

"Tell you what, Spirit, you've had to put up with my stink long enough," Matt said, speaking to his horse. "I think I'll go get myself cleaned up before I go looking for Smoke."

Dismounting in front of the building, Matt lifted his bag of ore from the horse, then went inside. Fifteen minutes later, he was sitting in a tub of warm water, scrubbing himself with a big piece of lye soap.

"Don't know if there is enough lye soap in all of Wyoming to get that carcass clean," a voice teased.

"Smoke!" Matt said, a big smile spreading across his face. He started to stand.

"No, no need to stand," Smoke said, holding his hand out, palm forward, to stop him. "You think I want to see that?"

Matt laughed. "How did you know I was in here?"

"We did say we were going to meet in Swan today, didn't we?"

"Yeah."

"I saw Spirit tied up out front. Did you think I wouldn't recognize him? He used to be my horse, remember?"

"I remember," Matt said.

"How did you do?" Smoke asked.

"See that bag there? It's full of ore. At least two thousand dollars worth, I would guess."

Smoke whistled. "That is good," he said.

"Tell you what, I'll be finished here in a bit. What do you say we go get us a beer? I haven't had a beer in two months."

"Sounds good to me. I'll go get us a table, and I'll even let you buy it, seein' as you had such a good outing," Smoke said.

A few minutes after Smoke left, Matt was out of the tub, had his shirt and trousers on, and had just strapped on his gun belt when three men burst unexpectedly into the room. All three had pistols in their hands.

"We'll take that bag of ore, mister," one of them shouted.

"Who are you?" Matt asked.

"We're the folks you're goin' to give that bag of ore to," one of the three said, and they all laughed.

While the three men were laughing, Matt was drawing his pistol, and while they were reacting to him drawing his pistol, Matt was shooting.

The pistol shots sounded exceptionally loud in

the closed room as Matt and the three men exchanged gunfire. When the shooting stopped, Matt had not a scratch, but the three would-be robbers lay dead on the floor.

Matt was still examining the bodies when four more men came bursting into the room. This time, three of them were carrying sawed-off shotguns. They were also wearing badges.

The fourth man with them was the assayer.

"There he is, Sheriff! He is the one who stole the bag of ore!" Montgomery shouted, pointing at Matt.

"What?" Matt asked. "What are you talking about? I didn't steal any ore from you!"

"He come into the office a little while ago," Montgomery said. "He had a bag of worthless rocks, usin' it as a way getting my attention. While I was looking at his rocks, he stole a bag of genuine ore. I didn't have no choice but to send my brother and two cousins to get the ore back. Didn't know it would come to this, though."

Montgomery looked down at the three dead bodies, then shook his head sadly. "If I had known they was goin' to be murdered like this, I never would'a sent 'em over here. A bag plumb full of gold nuggets isn't worth getting three good men killed."

"Come along, mister," the sheriff said, waving his shotgun menacingly at Matt. "You are about to learn that folks don't come into my town to steal and murder and get away with it."

"Sheriff, this man is lying," Matt said. "I brought

some ore in for him to assay, he tried to cheat me out of it, so I told him I would go somewhere else. You think I would stop to take a bath if I stole anything in this town?"

"I don't know what you would do, mister," the sheriff said. "But the thing is, I know Montgomery and I don't know you. So I reckon we'll let the judge sort it all out."

Matt looked at the three shotguns that were leveled at him. He was holding a pistol and he had a notion, but declined. He might be able to kill the sheriff and both his deputies before they realized what was happening, but then, he might not either. They were carrying shotguns, which gave them an advantage. It would also mean killing innocent men, and he couldn't bring himself to do that.

Matt turned the pistol around and handed it, handle first, to the sheriff.

"You are making a mistake, Sheriff," Matt said.

"You let me worry about that."

Montgomery reached for the sack of gold ore.

"Leave it," the sheriff said.

"Why should I leave it, Sheriff? This is the self-same sack of ore he stole."

"Leave it," the sheriff said again. "We'll let the judge decide whether or not that gold ore is yours."

Montgomery glared at the sheriff, then looked over at Matt. "I'll be standin' in the crowd watchin' you hang," Montgomery said.

"Let's go, mister," the sheriff said to Matt with a

wave of his shotgun. "I got a nice jail cell for you until the judge gets here."

Matt had been in jail for three days awaiting the arrival of the circuit judge so he could be tried. Smoke was just outside his cell, visiting with him.

"I shouldn't have left you," Smoke said.

"Why not? If you had stayed, you would be in jail with me right now," Matt said. "What good would that do?"

"I guess you have a point. I couldn't help you any if I were in there with you. At least, by being out here, if you can't convince the judge that you are innocent, I'll take matters into my own hands. I'll get you out of here, no matter what I have to do."

Matt was about to answer when he looked up to see the sheriff coming into the jailhouse, leading Montgomery. Montgomery was in shackles.

"What is it?" Matt asked. "What is going on?"

"You're free to go," the sheriff said as he opened the door to the cell. "Mr. Montgomery here will be taking your place."

"Sheriff, I have to hand it to you for doing your job," Matt said. "You've had a good three days of investigating."

"It wasn't me," the sheriff said. "It was John Bryce."

"Who?"

"John Bryce," the sheriff repeated. "Mr. Bryce is a newspaper writer for the *Swan Journal,* and he has been doing some, he calls it, investigative journalism. Here, read this," he said, handing Matt a newspaper.

An Innocent Man in Jail!

J. A. MONTGOMERY A CROOK
SHOULD BE CALLED TO ACCOUNT

We are under obligation to report to the public in general and to Sheriff Daniels in particular, the criminal activities of J. A. Montgomery, who has set himself up in Swan as an assayer. Montgomery is no such thing. Although he has hanging on the wall of his office a degree from Colorado School of Mines, this newspaper is in receipt of a letter from that institution claiming that no such person as J. A. Montgomery graduated, nor was ever a student there.

Further investigation has disclosed that Montgomery is wanted by the sheriff of Madison County, Montana, where, also fraudulently passing himself off as an assayer, he murdered and robbed a prospector. The circumstances of that event are so similar to the recent event between J. A. Montgomery, his brother Clyde, and two cousins, Drake and Birch, and a recent visitor to our town, Matt Jensen, that this newspaper believes Mr. Jensen, who is currently incarcerated, is innocent.

Should Matt Jensen be any longer detained, it would be a gross miscarriage of justice. Subjecting the county to a trial

> to establish his innocence would be a
> waste of time and taxpayers' money. The
> writer of this piece, John Bryce, is willing
> to stake his reputation upon the accuracy
> of this report, and urges Sheriff Daniels to
> act quickly to correct this error.

"After the paper come out, I sent a telegram to
the sheriff of Madison County, Montana, and he
answered that Montgomery was wanted for murder,
just like the newspaper article said. Then I went
over to talk to Montgomery and found that he was
tryin' to leave town."

"So I am free to go?" Matt asked.

"Yes, sir, you are free as a bird."

"Is this fella, John Bryce, in town?" Matt asked.

"Yes, sir, he's over to the newspaper office right
now," Sheriff Daniels said.

"I think I'll go look him up right now."

"Do you own this paper?" Matt asked when he
and Smoke found John Bryce hard at work in the
newspaper office.

"Oh, heavens, no, it takes a lot of money to own
and operate your own newspaper," John said. "I just
work here for Mr. Peabody as one of his journalists.
Someday I expect to own my own paper, though,"
he said.

Matt, who had had the ore returned to him,
reached down into his canvas bag and pulled out

four good-sized rocks. "Here," Matt said, handing the rocks to the newspaper man. "Cash these in and you may have your paper sooner than you realize. And if there is ever anything I can do for you, just let me know."

"Bless you, Mr. Jensen," John said, accepting the gold with a broad smile. "I'll never forget you for this."

Chapter Two

A brick had been thrown through the front window, and great jagged spears of the glass reached out from all corners of the frame. Two months earlier, John Bryce had paid a professional painter to come over from Bismarck to paint:

FULLERTON DEFENDER
John Bryce—*Publisher*
Millie Bryce—*Office Manager*

The letters were broad and black, outlined in white and gold. That sign, once a source of pride, was now no more than a few remaining letters on the remaining shards of glass.

LLE   ON   F   DER
J   y   *lisher*

Not one letter of Millie's name remained.

At the moment, John was standing just inside the office of the *Fullerton Defender*, surveying the damage. The perpetrators had done more than just break his front window; they had also trashed the office. His arm was around his wife, and he held her close to him as she sobbed quietly. Type had been scattered about the room, newsprint had been ripped and spread around, the Washington Hand Press, which John used to put out his weekly paper, was lying on its side.

They had come to the newspaper office directly from their breakfast table, having been told of the break-in by City Marshal Tipton. More than a dozen citizens of the town had already been drawn to the scene of the crime by the time John and Millie arrived, and they were standing in a little cluster out on the boardwalk, just in front of the building.

The perpetrators had left a note:

Don't be writting no more bad artacles about Lord Denbigh or we will kum back and do more damige to you nex time.

"Who would do such a thing?" Millie asked between sobs.

"It's fairly apparent, isn't it?" John replied. "Denbigh did it."

"We don't know that," Marshal Tipton said.

"The note doesn't suggest that to you, Marshal?" John asked.

"Just the opposite," Tipton said. "Denbigh is an educated man. Now, I'm not as smart as you are, but even I know how to spell the words come and damage."

"I don't mean Denbigh did it himself," John said. "I mean he had it done."

"Or maybe there are just some people in town who got upset with you because you've been coming down pretty hard on Denbigh in your stories. And Denbigh has done a lot of good for this town."

"Really? What good has he done?"

"Let's just say that he does a lot of business with the town."

"Yes, by allowing only the businesses he wants to stay, and squeezing out the others. He's killing this town, Marshal Tipton. And the people in town know it, only they are too frightened to do anything about it."

"So you plan to mount a one-person campaign do you, Bryce?"

"If I am the only one willing to do anything about it, then yes, I will mount a one-person campaign."

"Uh-huh," Tipton said, stroking his jaw as he surveyed the shambles of the newspaper office. "And look what it got you."

"It has set me back a bit, I'll admit," John said. "But it won't stop me. It'll take me a day to clean up. I'll have the paper out this Thursday, just as I do every Thursday."

"I'll help you pick up all the type, Mr. Bryce," a young boy of about twelve said.

"Thank you, Kenny."

"I can go get Jimmy to help too, if you want me to."

"That would be nice," John said. He turned toward the group of people who were still standing just outside the office, and seeing Ernie West-pheling, called out to him.

"Ernie, would you help me set the printing press back up?"

"Sure thing," Ernie said. Ernie, who had been a colonel during the Civil War, was now a local businessman who owned a gun store.

A couple of the other men also volunteered to help, and within a few minutes the printing press had been righted and was, once again, in its proper place. John surveyed it for a moment or two, then patted the press with a big smile.

"Not a scratch," he said. "It takes more than a few of Denbigh's hooligans to put ole George out of business."

"George? I thought your name was John," one of the men who had helped him, said.

"It is. George is the name of my printing press."

"You've named your press?"

"Sure. It's not only a part of this newspaper, it is the heart of the newspaper."

"What are you going to do about your window?" Ernie asked.

"I'll have to order a new glass from Bismarck," John said. "In the meantime, I guess I'll just board that side up."

"What are you going to do about this, Marshal?" Ernie asked.

"I'll look into it, see if I can find out who did it," Tipton replied. "But if I don't come up with any witnesses, I don't know what I can do."

"There has to be a witness somewhere," Millie said. "It had to make a lot of noise when they broke out the window."

"You live no more than a couple of blocks from here, Mrs. Bryce. Did you hear anything?" Tipton asked.

"No."

"And the newspaper belongs to you and your husband, so you would be even more attentive, I would think. You heard nothing, but you expect others in the town did?" Tipton shook his head. "No, ma'am, I don't expect I'm going to find anything."

"That's because you aren't looking in the right place," John said. "You and I both know who is behind this."

Tipton glared at John, but he said nothing.

Central Colorado

"Is the son of a bitch still following?" Cyrus Hayes asked Emmet Cruise. The two men had stopped for a moment in order for Hayes to relieve himself, and Cruise crawled up onto a rock to look back along the trail.

"Yeah, he's there," Cruise said.

"What the hell? Are we leaving bread crumbs or

something?" Hayes asked as he buttoned his trousers. "Who the hell is that, and how is staying on our trail?"

"I don't know who he is, but he's good," Cruise said.

"Yeah, well, let's go," Hayes said. "The more distance we can put between us and him, the better I will feel."

Earlier that morning, Hayes and Cruise had robbed the Rocky Mountain Bank and Trust in Pueblo, Colorado, and during the robbery, had shot down in cold blood a teller and two customers. The two customers, a man and his pregnant wife, had been friends of Matt Jensen. Because of that, even before the state got around to offering a reward for two bank robbers and murderers, Matt had gone after them.

Knowing they would be pursued, the two outlaws took great pains to cover their true trail, while leaving false trails for anyone who would follow. Then, reaching a stream, they started riding right down the middle of it, confident that they were erasing any sign that could possibly be followed.

For most trackers, that might work, but not for Matt. He had learned his tracking expertise from Smoke Jensen, who had learned his own skills from an old mountain man named Preacher. And Preacher was, arguably, the best tracker who had ever lived. Because that know-how had been passed down, Matt was almost equally as accomplished as Smoke or Preacher. He could even follow a trail through the water by paying attention to such things as rocks dislodged against the flow of water, or silt, which, when disturbed by horse's hooves, would leave a little pattern in the water for several minutes afterward.

Matt was tracking down the streambed when a rifle boomed and a .44-40 bullet cracked through the air no more than an inch from his head.

Matt leaped down from his horse and ran though the stream, his feet churning up silver sheets of spray as he ran. The rifle barked again, then, right on top of that, he heard the flatter sound of a pistol shot. Almost simultaneously, two bullets plunged into the water close by.

Reaching the bank on the opposite side of the stream, Matt dived to the ground, then worked his way toward a nearby outcropping of rocks. There, he sat with his back against the biggest of the rocks while he took a few deep breaths.

"Who are you?" one of the men called out to him.

"My name is Jensen," Matt called back.

"Jensen? Matt Jensen? Son of a bitch!" The outlaw had obviously recognized Matt's name and there was fear in his voice.

"Which one are you?" Matt called back. "Are you Hayes or Cruise?"

"What? I'm Hayes. How did you know our names?"

"Half the town saw you two boys riding away

from the bank, and half the ones who saw you knew who you were."

"What are you after us for, Jensen?" Hayes called. "I've heard of you, but I ain't never heard that you was someone who would chase a fella down for the reward. Is that why you are chasin' us?"

"I'm not after the reward."

"Then if you ain't after the reward, what the hell are you comin' after us for?"

"It seems the thing to do," Matt said, without being specific as to his reasons.

"Well, mister, you made a big mistake," Hayes shouted. "'Cause all you're goin' to do now is get yourself kilt!"

Hayes and Cruise fired again, and once more the bullets whistled by harmlessly overhead.

"You still there?" Hayes called.

"I'm still here."

"I tell you what, mister. Me and my partner here just talked it over, and we got us an idee. We have got us near 'bout five thousand dollars that we've taken from the bank. A thousand of it is your'n iffen you'll just go away," Hayes called.

"No deal."

There was a beat of silence, then Hayes called out again. "All right, how 'bout two thousand? We'll give you two thousand and all you got to do is let us ride away."

"You expect me to believe you two are willing to give me nearly half of what you took from the bank?"

"Why not? It's no big deal, we can always rob another bank," Hayes shouted back. "Two thousand dollars. You don't come across money like that very often, do you?"

"Not very often," Matt agreed.

"So, what do you think? You going to take us up on the offer?"

"Let me think about it," Matt said.

"You do that."

Matt had no intention of taking the two men up on their offer, but he responded in such a way as to enable him to stall for time until he figured out how best to handle this situation. He picked up a stick about two feet long, put his hat on top of the stick, then raised it slightly above the rock.

A rifle boomed, and the hat flew off the end of the stick.

"Ha! You got 'im, Cruise!" Hayes shouted.

"Whoa, I guess you two boys weren't really serious about giving me all that money, were you?" Matt called out.

"Son of a bitch, I missed!" Cruise said.

"Mister, you know what I said about givin' you that money? Well, you can forget about it, we ain't goin' to give you nothin'," Hayes said. "Except maybe a bullet right between your eyes."

Hayes's shout was punctuated with another rifle shot, this one hitting the top of the rock, then whining off into the valley.

After that there was silence.

The silence stretched into several long minutes. "Hayes? Cruise? You still up there?" Matt called.

There was another rifle shot, and this time the bullet hit the rock, not on the side facing away from Matt, but just to the right of him. One of them, the one with the rifle, had improved his position, and even as Matt scooted around to put the rock between himself and the shooter, there was a second shot.

This time, Matt saw the puff of smoke from the rifle, so he aimed at the spot and waited. Seconds later he was rewarded by seeing Cruise's face raise up.

Matt pulled the trigger, and Cruise fell forward, sliding belly-down until his face wound up in the stream. Matt watched for a moment longer to make certain Cruise was dead. Then suddenly, he heard the sound of a horse's hooves. Looking around he saw that Hayes had used the opportunity to get mounted, and was now galloping toward him. Hayes had his pistol in his hand and he was firing at Matt as he rode.

When Matt fired back, he saw a puff of dust rising from Hayes's vest, followed by a tiny spray of dust and blood. Hayes pitched backward out of his saddle, but one foot hung up in the stirrup and his horse continued to run, raising a plume of water as the outlaw was dragged through the stream. When the horse reached the other side of the stream and started up the bank, Hayes's foot disconnected from the stirrup and he lay, motionless, half in the water and half out, not more than ten feet from where the body of his partner lay.

Matt ran over to them, his gun still drawn, but the gun wasn't necessary. Because both men were dead.

Chapter Three

Hayes and Cruise were not the first outlaws Matt had ever tracked down. He was neither a lawman, nor someone who hunted other men for any reward the government paid for them, but he was always on the side of law and order, and sometimes, like this time, going after an outlaw just seemed to be the right thing to do.

He never sought trouble, but somehow, trouble had a way of finding him. As a result, Matt Jensen was one of a select company of men in the West whose very name could evoke fear among the outlaws and evildoers.

Matt took the bag of bank money from Hayes's saddle and started back to Pueblo, but just after noon, his horse stepped into an unseen prairie dog hole. The horse broke a leg and Matt had to shoot him. It was a hard thing to do; Spirit was only the second horse he had ever owned. Indeed, this horse had carried with him the spirit of his first horse, who was also named, not coincidentally, Spirit. There was nothing Matt could do now but take shanks mare, so, throwing his saddle, saddlebags, and the money bag over his shoulder, he began walking.

Matt Jensen dropped his saddle with a sigh of relief, then climbed up the berm to stand on the ballast between the railroad tracks. Just before him, the clear tracks of the Denver and New Orleans lay like twin black ribbons across the landscape, stretching north to south from horizon to horizon. For the moment, they were as cold and empty as the barren sand, rocks, and mountains that surrounded him, but Matt knew that a train would be passing through here sometime before sundown.

Since putting his horse down, Matt had walked for two hours, carrying his saddle with him, thus bringing him to his current position. He was, at the moment, standing alongside the railroad tracks some thirty miles south of Pueblo. Now all that was left for him to do was catch the train, so, using his saddle as a pillow, he lay down beside the tracks to wait. As he waited, he couldn't help but think of the horse he had just put down, and in order to combat the grief that threatened to consume him, he turned his thoughts to his first horse named Spirit, and particularly, to how he had come by him.

Right after the war, while still a boy named Matt Cavanaugh, the man now known as Matt Jensen made the trip west from Missouri with his father, mother, and sister. On the trail west, their wagon was attacked by outlaws, and all were killed but Matt. Matt escaped, managing to kill one of the outlaws in the process. The incident left Matt an orphan and shortly thereafter, he wound up in the Soda Springs Home for Wayward Boys and Girls. Rather than providing a refuge, though, the orphanage was so evilly run that eventually Matt escaped from the home.

A few days later, Matt, nearly dead from hunger and the cold, was found in the mountains by the legendary Smoke Jensen. Smoke took the boy in and raised him to adulthood. Out of respect and appreciation, Matt Cavanaugh changed his name to Matt Jensen, and though there was no blood relationship between the two men, they regarded each other as brothers. When it was time for Matt to go out on his own, Smoke surprised him with an offer.

"Why don't you go out to the corral and pick out your horse?" Smoke had asked.[1]

"My horse?"

"Yeah, your horse. A man's got to have a horse."

"Which horse is mine?" Matt asked.

"Why don't you take the best one?" Smoke replied. "Except for that one," he added, pointing to an Appaloosa over in one corner of the corral. "That one is mine."

---

[1] *Matt Jensen: The Last Mountain Man*

"Which horse is the best?" Matt asked.

"Huh-uh," Smoke replied, shaking his head. "I'm willing to give you the best horse in my string, but as to which horse that might be, well, you're just going to have to figure that out for yourself."

Matt walked out to the small corral that Smoke had built and, leaning on the split-rail fence, looked at the string of seven horses from which he could choose.

After looking them over very carefully, Matt smiled and nodded.

"You've made your choice?" Smoke asked.

"Yes."

"Which one?"

"I want that one," Matt said, pointing to a bay.

"Why not the chestnut?" Smoke asked. "He looks stronger."

"Look at the chestnut's front feet," Matt said. "They are splayed. The bay's feet are just right."

"What about the black one over there?"

"Huh-uh," Matt said. "His back legs are set too far back. I want the bay."

Smoke reached out and ran his hand through Matt's hair.

"You're learning, kid, you're learning," he said. "The bay is yours."

Matt's grin spread from ear to ear. "I've never had a horse of my own before," he said. He jumped down from the rail fence and started toward the horse.

"That's all right, he's never had a rider before," Smoke said.

"What?" Matt asked, jerking around in surprise as he stared at Smoke. "Did you say that he's never been ridden?"

"He's as spirited as he was the day we brought him in."

"How'm I going to ride him if he has never been ridden?"

"Well, I reckon you are just going to have to break him," Smoke said, passing the words off as easily as if he had just suggested that Matt should wear a hat.

"Break him? I can't break a horse!"

"Sure you can. It'll be fun," Smoke suggested.

Smoke showed Matt how to saddle the horse, and gave him some pointers on riding it.

"Now, you don't want to break the horse's spirit," Smoke said. "What you want to do is make him your partner."

"How do I do that?"

"Walk him around for a bit so that he gets used to his saddle, and to you. Then get on."

"He won't throw me then?"

"Oh, he'll still throw you a few times," Smoke said with a little laugh. "But at least he'll know how serious you are."

To Matt's happy surprise, he wasn't thrown even once. The horse did buck a few times, coming down on stiff legs, then sunfishing, and finally galloping at full speed around the corral. But after a few minutes, he stopped fighting and Matt leaned over to pat him gently on the neck.

"Good job, Matt," Smoke said, clapping his hands quietly. "You've got a real touch with horses. You didn't break him, you trained him, and that's real good. He's not mean, but he still has spirit."

"Smoke, can I name him?"

"Sure, he's your horse, you can name him anything you want."

Matt continued to pat the horse on the neck as he thought of a name.

"That's it," he said, smiling broadly. "I've come up with a name."

"What are you going to call him?"

"Spirit."

As Matt lay there alongside the track he continued to think about his two horses named Spirit. He had given them good lives, treated them well, always making certain they were well fed and cared for, but in the end, both had died before their time, precisely because by being his horses, they had been subjected to more danger than most other horses.

He thought about the expression in Spirit II's eyes just before he had pulled the trigger. It was as if Spirit II knew what was about to happen to him. Was he blaming Matt? Was he telling Matt he understood that it had to be done?

Fortunately, before Matt could sink any deeper into the morass of melancholy, he heard a distant whistle. Pushing the gloomy thoughts away, he got up from his impromptu bed and looked south, toward the train. When first he saw it, it seemed to be just creeping along, though Matt knew that it was doing at least twenty miles per hour. It was the distance that made it appear as if the train was going much slower. That same distance also made the train seem very small, and even the smoke that poured from its stack seemed but a tiny wisp against a sky which had now been made gold by the setting sun.

Matt could hear the reverberation of the puffing engine, sounding louder than one might think, given the distance. When the train came close enough for him to be seen, Matt stepped up onto the track and began waving. After a few waves, he heard the train begin braking, so he knew that the engineer had spotted him and was going to stop. As the engine approached, the train, which had appeared so tiny before, now appeared huge. It ground to a squeaking, clanking halt with black smoke pouring from its stack. Tendrils of white steam, escaping from the drive cylinders and limned in gold by the rays of the setting sun, wreathed the huge wheels.

The engineer's face appeared in the window.

"What do you want, mister? Why'd you stop us?" the engineer called down to him. He had to raise his voice over the rhythmic sound of venting steam.

"My horse stepped in a prairie dog hole and I had to put him down," Matt said. "I need a ride."

The engineer stroked his chin for a moment, studying Matt as if trying to decide whether or not he should pick him up.

"What's going on here? Why did we stop?" another man asked, approaching the engine quickly and importantly from somewhere back in the train. The man was wearing the uniform of a conductor.

"This fella needs a ride," the engineer said. "His horse went down on him."

"I'm not in the habit of giving charity rides to indigents," the conductor said.

"I can pay," Matt said. "I need to get to Pueblo."

"You can pay, can you? Well, let me ask you this. Does this place look like a depot to you? Do you think you can just flag down a train and board it anywhere you wish?" the conductor asked in a self-important and sarcastic voice.

"I don't know about you, Mr. Gordon, but I wouldn't feel right just leavin' him out here," the engineer said. "I mean, him losin' his horse and all kind of makes it like an emergency, don't it?"

The conductor stroked his chin and spent a long moment studying Matt. All the while, the pressure relief valve continued to vent steam, giving the engine the illusion of some great beast of burden, breathing heavily now from its exertions. Some distance away, a coyote barked, and closer in, a crow called.

"Hey! What's going on? Why have we stopped?" a passenger called, walking up toward the engine.

"Get back in the cars, sir!" the conductor shouted.

"You've got a trainload of people wondering why we stopped. We've got a right to know what is going on," the passenger said.

"Please, sir, get back in the cars," the conductor repeated. "I will take care of the situation." The conductor waited until the passenger reboarded the train, then looked up at the engineer.

"All right, Cephus, have it your way," the conductor said. He turned to Matt. "I don't like unscheduled stops like this, but I don't want it said that I left you stranded out here. It is going to cost you two dollars to go to Pueblo."

"Thanks," Matt said, taking two dollars from the poke in his saddlebag and handing it to the conductor.

"Sorry about your horse, mister," the engineer called down from the cab window.

"Yes, he was a good horse."

In an elaborate gesture, the conductor pulled a watch from his vest pocket, popped open the cover, and examined the face. The silver watch was attached to a gold chain, the chain making a shallow U across his chest.

"Cephus, we are due in Pueblo exactly one hour and twenty-seven minutes from right now," the conductor said to the engineer as he snapped the watch closed and returned it to his vest pocket. "I do not plan to be late. That means I expect you to make up the time we have lost by this stop."

"Yes, sir, Mr. Gordon, don't worry. If Doodle keeps the steam up, we'll be there on time."

"Don't you be worryin' none about the steam," Doodle, the fireman, said, stepping out onto the platform that extended just behind the engine. "You'll have all the steam you need."

"Come along," the conductor said to Matt. "You can ride in any car. There are seats in all three of them, and they are all day coaches."

"I'd rather ride in the express car, if you don't mind," Matt said.

"No, I'm sorry, I can't let you in there," the conductor replied.

"Maybe you haven't heard," Matt said, "but the bank in Pueblo was robbed this morning."

"Yes, I heard. What does that have to do with anything?"

Matt held up the canvas bag he had taken from Cyrus Hayes's body. "This is the money that was taken from the bank."

"What? What the hell, mister? Are you telling me you are the one who held up the bank?"

"No," Matt said. "I'm the one who is taking the money back to the bank. And I would just as soon not be riding in one of the passenger cars while I'm carrying this."

"Oh," the conductor said.

At that moment, the door to the express car slid open, and the express messenger looked down on them.

"He can ride in here with me, Mr. Gordon. It will be all right."

"I'll let him in there, but remember, it was your idea, not mine," Gordon replied.

"I'll remember. Hi, Matt," the messenger said.

Matt smiled up at a friend with whom he had played cards many times. "Hi, Jerry," he greeted.

Chapter Four

When Slater, Dillon, and Wilson tied their horses off in front of the New York Saloon, they saw a small, pasty-faced man sitting on a bench on the front porch.

"Howdy, Butrum," Slater said.

The little man nodded, but made no response.

"Want us to bring you out a beer?" Dillon asked.

"I don't drink," Butrum said.

"All right. Just thought I'd ask."

With an arrogance brought on by the fact that they rode for Nigel Denbigh, the largest rancher in Dickey County, the three men swaggered up to the bar and pushed aside some of the customers who were already there.

"Find another place to be, pilgrim," Slater said. "Me 'n my pards need this space."

The man Slater pushed aside worked as a clerk in the Fullerton Mercantile. Not wanting any trouble, he took his beer and retreated to the far end of the bar.

Ordering whiskey, the three men continued their conversation after their drinks were served.

"Do you really reckon Butrum don't drink?" Dillon asked.

"I don't think it's as much that he don't drink as it is that he can't drink," Wilson said.

"What do you mean, he can't?"

"Well, look at him. You ever see a fully grow'd man that was that little? Why, I bet one beer would just about make him drunker than a skunk."

The three men laughed.

"Maybe that's why Lord Denbigh hired him," Dillon said. "He has to sit out there on that porch ever' day, checkin' to make sure folks has paid their toll. Anyone else might be drinkin' all day, but seein' as Butrum don't drink, well, it ain't no problem."

"That's not the only reason he was hired," Slater said. "Don't you know who that is?"

"Yeah, I know who he is," Dillon said. "His name is Butrum."

"Yeah, Butrum. Ollie Butrum," Slater said. "He may be little, but don't let that fool you. They say he has kilt more than twenty men."

"Folks may say that, but has he really?" Wilson asked.

"I don't know," Slater admitted. "Do you want to try him?"

Wilson shook his head. "No, no," he said. "If

that's what folks say, then as far as I'm concerned, it's all true, ever' word of it."

Slater tossed his drink down, then called out to the bartender.

"Bartender, how about another whiskey down here?"

Without answering, the bartender brought the bottle down and refilled the three glasses.

"Hey, I hear tell the newspaper fella had hisself a little trouble the other night," Slater said. He laughed. "I hear tell they broke out his winder and messed up his place pretty good. Did you hear that?"

"I heard it," the bartender replied, keeping his answers as short and nonconfrontational as possible.

"It serves him right. Anyone who would write all those lies about Lord Denbigh deserves to have his place all torn up," Slater said. He laughed. "I'll bet he won't be writin' any more lies, seein' as how he can't get his paper out anymore."

"What makes you think he won't get the paper out anymore?" the bartender asked. "I understand he will come out this Thursday, same as always."

"How can he if his press is broke?"

"It wasn't broken," the bartender said. "It was pushed over, but it wasn't broken."

"I told you we should'a took an ax—" Wilson began, but Slater interrupted him in mid-sentence.

"Shut up, Wilson, you fool."

"Oh, uh, yeah, I was just sayin', we need to take

an ax back out to the ranch so we can get to work on some of them stumps," Wilson said in an attempt to minimize the issue.

Slater glared at him for a moment, then turned his back to the bar and studied the saloon. Seeing one of the bar girls occupied with a customer, he walked over to that table.

"Step aside, friend," he said to the man who had been laughing and joking with the young woman. "I'm taking your woman."

Slater reached out to take the girl by the arm. "Me and her is goin' to go up to her room for a bit." He continued. "Don't worry, though, I'll be finished with her soon," he added. "It's been a while since I had me a woman, so it ain't goin' to take me very long to get the job done, if you get what I mean."

"What makes you think that I'll go upstairs with you?" the girl asked.

"'Cause you're a whore," Slater said. "And that's what whores do."

"Other whores maybe, but not this whore," the bar girl replied. "I do what I want to do, and right now I am enjoying a conversation with my gentleman friend."

"Yeah, well, now you're going to enjoy that conversation with me."

"I don't think so," the girl said.

"Oh, I think you'll talk to me. Because, if you don't, I'm goin' to pistol-whip this here gentleman you was a' talkin' to."

The gentleman started to whimper, but the woman put her hand on his shoulder. "Don't worry." She looked at Slater, measuring the expression in his eyes. She saw nothing but evil, and she couldn't help but close her own eyes to blot it out. "Before I let him hurt you, I will go with him," the girl said.

Slater put his pistol away. "Yeah," he said. "I thought you might."

"Kaye," the bartender called to the soiled dove that worked for him. "Are you all right?"

"Yes, Paul, I'm fine," Kaye replied. "This won't be the first time I've ever had to deal with Mr. Slater."

"What makes you dislike me so?" Slater asked the woman.

"I don't like you because you have a very tiny pecker."

The others in the room laughed outrageously as Slater's face turned beet red. He vowed not to ask any more questions that might trip him up.

As the three men galloped out of town an hour later, they yelled and fired their pistols into the air. They were just passing a man and woman who were arriving in town in a buckboard, and the shouting and gunfire startled the buckboard team into a gallop. The woman hung on to her seat for dear life while the man fought to regain control of his team.

Most of the others, seeing the three cowboys

shouting and shooting as they rode their horses at an unseasonable speed, moved quickly to get out of their way.

In the office of the *Fullerton Defender,* John Bryce stood in the doorway and watched as the three men terrorized the town.

"What's all the noise?" Millie called toward the front. At the moment, she was in the back of the office, sweeping the floor.

"It's some of Denbigh's riders, razzing the town," John answered. "Slater, Dillon, and Wilson."

"It would be them," Millie said. "They are the worst of the lot."

John shook his head. "No. The little gargoyle that Denbigh keeps posted on the front porch of the saloon—Butrum—he is the worst of the lot."

"You would think Denbigh would have more control over his men."

"He does have control over them," John answered. "You think Denbigh didn't know his men were going to trash our office? He not only knew it, he ordered it done."

"Marshal Tipton says it could have been someone from town, either someone upset or someone doing it as a prank," Millie suggested.

"What sort of prank would tearing up some-body's place of business be?" John asked. "No, whoever it was did exactly what Denbigh wanted them to do. He wants, not only us, but the whole town to be intimidated. And he has about succeeded with the town. That's why he lets ruffians like Slater, Dillon, and Wilson act without restraint."

John walked back to the Washington Hand Press, put a sheet of paper onto the tympan, then moved the bed under the platen. "All right, George," he said, speaking to the hand press. "Do your stuff." John pressed it down with the bar, then used the rolling block to move the bed back out. Peeling off the first page of the newspaper, he held it up for just a moment to let the ink dry, then took it over to the light of the front window to read the copy.

The Northern Express Stage Company

Intelligence received from the above-mentioned company suggests that they would offer the best route from Fullerton south to Ellendale, the route bringing within easy reach the railroad, which, by connections, would provide our citizens with easy travel to all the great metropolises of America.

This company has plans to equip their line with twelve of the best and most comfortable Concord coaches, with one hundred and sixty horses, and would establish stations and supply ranches along the route at distances from twelve, and not to exceed fifteen miles apart. Though the Indians are believed to offer little or no trouble, The Northern Express Stage and Transportation Company has of late expressed some concern as to whether they will be able to put their plans into effect at all.

Mr. R. A. Weatherly, operations officer for the company, released the following statement. "It has come to the attention of this company that one individual has gained control of the Ellendale Highway and is imposing a toll upon all who make use of the road. We cannot, and will not pay tolls for the passage of our coaches, for to do so would render the profit so marginal as to be non-productive."

Though Mr. Weatherly mentioned no names, this newspaper feels an obligation to its readers to publish herein the name of the individual whose actions may cost our town this important transportation service. His name is Nigel Denbigh, and he has made the spurious claim that, because the road passes through his property, it is subject to a toll to be collected by him.

An appeal to Sheriff Hightower in Ellendale has availed us of no relief from this condition, and many of our citizens have already faced personal hardship because of the toll Denbigh has established on the Ellendale Road.

I am sending, by post, a copy of this newspaper to Governor Ordway in Bismarck, with the hope that he will see his way to right this wrong that is being perpetrated against us.

"Look at this, Millie," John said, showing the first printed page to his wife.

"I read it when I set the type," Millie replied. Millie was not only John's wife. She was also a valued employee, for she could set type, operate the press, and even write a column that was aimed specifically at the ladies of Fullerton. She had come to work for John when he started the newspaper some two years earlier, and the work relationship grew to something more. That was when John Bryce, who had thought that he would never be married, took her as his bride.

"Well, what do you think of it?" John asked.

"I don't know," Millie said.

"What do you mean, you don't know? You think it isn't a good story?"

"John, it is a wonderful story, and why shouldn't it be? You are, after all, a wonderful writer. But I don't want to see our place all messed up again. Or worse."

"What do you mean, worse?"

"You know what I mean, John," Millie said with a little shiver.

John walked over to Millie, put his arms around her, then pulled her to him. "Denbigh is an evil man, Millie, but he isn't dumb. And killing a public figure like me would be a dumb thing to do."

"I hope you are right," Millie replied.

"What I hope is that the effect of this article will be to galvanize the governor, the sheriff, the mayor, and the citizens of this town into action against the evil Mr. Denbigh."

"And I fear it will have just the opposite result," Millie said. "Already, some of the people are concerned over what happened here the other night."

"Concern? Nonsense, why should they be concerned?"

"They are afraid it might happen to them."

"That's nonsense."

"John, sometimes I feel as if you are trapped in a soap bubble. It is a wonderful soap bubble, filled with all the noble ideas of honor, truth, and justice, but you see nothing beyond that bubble. The people of town are afraid that Denbigh will react to your stories by stopping all business dealings with Fullerton. And whether you like him or not—"

"Not!" John interrupted, and stabbed his finger into the air. "Madam," he said, speaking as dramatically as if he were on stage. "I like him not!"

Millie laughed. "Whether you like him or not," she continued, "you must admit that he does a great deal of business with the people of the town. They are afraid they will lose that business."

"They are being foolish," John said, his voice returning to normal. "Don't they understand that without his interference, they would do even more business?"

"Nevertheless, the whole town is afraid, and I fear some may, out of their fear, stop doing business with us. I know you feel strongly about this, but we do have our own well-being to consider."

"Millie, you know yourself that if this town dies, we will as well. A newspaper can survive only as long at the public it serves survives. I am looking out for our own well-being."

"I suppose you are right," Millie acquiesced. "But I beg of you, John, to please exercise some caution."

At that moment, Kenny Perkins came into the office. Kenny Perkins was the twelve-year-old who had come to help pick up the scattered type. It was no accident he was there because Kenny worked for John. He was the son of Ma Perkins, a widow who owned a boardinghouse as well as a couple of other businesses. Kenny's father, Emil, had been killed three years earlier in a mining accident. Like his mother, Kenny had a nose for business, and he had convinced John that he needed a paperboy to deliver the *Fullerton Defender*. As it turned out, Kenny proved to be a very good paperboy, so the arrangement had a mutual benefit.

"Did you get the Thursday paper out, Mr. Bryce?" Kenny asked.

"Indeed I did, Kenny."

Kenny smiled broadly. "I knew you would. Are the papers ready to go yet?"

"That they are, Kenny, that they are. Go, quickly now, and wearing the shoes of Hermes, attend to your appointed rounds."

"I don't know what you are talking about. I'm not wearin' this fella Hermes' shoes. Heck, warm as it is today, I'm not wearin' any shoes a'tall. See?" Kenny held up one of his feet and wriggled his toes.

"The young man speaks the truth, Millie. His feet are as bare as the feet of a newborn babe."

Kenny laughed. "You're funny, Mr. Bryce." He

took the papers, then started up Monroe Avenue, which was the main street of town, with his delivery.

"Now there goes a good boy," John said.

"Yes, he is, and you shouldn't tease him so," Millie said.

"He enjoys it," John said. "Besides, without a father, he needs a man to joke with him now and then."

"I agree. But you can't say his mother isn't doing a good job with him. I've known Lucy for a long time. I just hope . . ." She stopped in mid-sentence.

"You hope what?"

"I hope the people who vandalized out newspaper office won't ever take it out on Kenny."

"I'm sure they won't," John replied.

"Yes," Millie said pensively. "I'm sure they won't either."

From out on the street, they could hear Kenny's call. "Paper! Get your paper here!"

John took a sheet of stationery from his desk.

"What are you doing?"

"I'm going to write a letter."

"To the governor?"

"No, I wrote to the governor once, and it didn't do any good. I'm writing this letter to Matt Jensen, but I'm going to send it to Smoke Jensen because he is the only one I know how to reach. If Smoke is still in contact with Matt Jensen, and I'm sure he is, I will ask him to forward the letter. I did a favor for Mr. Jensen once, and he said if there was ever anything he could do for me, to let him know. Well, there is something he can do for me now, and I'm about to let him know."

Chapter Five

At that moment, five miles out of town, Ian McCann, his son Leo, and McCann's two hands, Curly Dobbins and Slim Toomey, were moving thirty head of cattle along the Fullerton and Ellendale road when they approached a barrier—a gate that was stretched across the road. Leo, who was in front, stopped.

"What is it, boy? What did you stop for?" Ian called up to his son.

"Pa, the road is blocked!" Leo shouted back.

"What do you mean, blocked?"

"There's a gate acrost it!"

"Dobbins, Toomey, you two boys watch the animals," Ian said to his two riders, then, slapping his legs against the side of his horse, Ian rode past the little group of cows until he reached the front and saw the gate. There were two men standing in front of the gate.

"I'll be damned," he said. "What the hell is this, anyway?"

"What does it look like? It is a tollgate," one of the men said.

"Who are you?" Ian asked.

"The name is Bleeker. I'm in charge of the tollgate. You want to pass this way, you are going to have to pay a toll."

"What are you talking about? This ain't no toll road. I've done come this way dozens of times. It's a public road."

"It passes through Denbigh land. That makes it a toll road," Bleeker said.

"All right. How much are you talking about?"

"A dollar each for each one of you, and a dollar for each of the critters that pass through. Except your horses. We won't charge you nothin' for the horses," Bleeker added with an unpleasant laugh. The other rider laughed with him.

"Mister, are you out of your mind? I've got thirty cows and four men here. You're saying you want thirty-four dollars. I don't have that much money and I wouldn't give it to you if I had it."

"We can work something out," Bleeker said.

"Like what?"

"We'll take three of your cows."

"I'm getting twenty dollars a head for these animals from the Indian agent in Fullerton. That would be sixty dollars."

"Yeah, well, you ain't exactly in Fullerton now, are you? You are on Denbigh land. Here, your cows are worth ten dollars a head, and that means you are getting a bargain. You owe us thirty-four dollars, but I'm willin' to take thirty."

Ian shook his head. "The hell you are. We'll just find some other way."

"Too late," Bleeker said.

"What do you man, too late?"

"You don't understand. You've done come this far on Lord Denbigh's road. That means you already owe thirty-four dollars whether you go through the gate or not."

"You're crazy. I'm not going to pay you thirty-four dollars, and I'm not going to give you three cows."

Suddenly and unexpectedly, Bleeker drew his pistol.

"What the hell, mister!" Ian shouted in fear. "We ain't neither one of us armed!"

Bleeker pointed his pistol at the head of one of the cows and pulled the trigger. The cow dropped, and the others began bawling and milling about in fright, and if it had not been for Dobbins and Toomey, they might have scattered.

"If you had been reasonable about it, you could have given us three cows and gone on. Now it's still going to cost you three cows, plus the one you just lost."

"You're crazy!"

"Shall we cut out the three cows? Or do you want to choose?" Bleeker asked.

"I told you, I'm not giving you three cows!"

Bleeker shot a second cow and once again,

Dobbins and Toomey had to move quickly to control the remaining cows.

"Stop it!" Ian shouted. "For the love of God, man, what are you doing?"

"By your reckoning, you have just lost forty dollars, all because you would not pay the thirty-four dollars toll. Now, do I shoot another one? Or do you give up three cows?" Bleeker asked.

"Yes, yes, take them! Take them and be damned!" Ian said.

"Twenty-five head?" the Indian agent said when McCann brought in his herd. "I thought we agreed upon thirty head."

"I had thirty head when we left home," Ian said. He explained the run-in with Bleeker.

"Ah, yes, he works for Nigel Denbigh," the Indian agent said. "That explains everything."

"It explains nothing," Ian replied in frustration. "Who the hell is this Denbigh anyway? And what gives him the right to collect tolls on a public road?"

"You could say, I suppose, that might gives him the right," the Indian agent said. "Right now, he is not only the biggest and wealthiest rancher in this part of Dakota, but he also has the biggest army."

"Biggest army?"

"Yes. You would have to go all the way back to Fort Lincoln to find more men under arms than Lord Denbigh has on his ranch."

"Lord Denbigh?"

The Indian agent chuckled. "He's from England," he said. "I take it that over there he's a lord or some such thing."

"Yeah, well I don't like it," McCann said. "I don't like it one little bit. That son of a bitch cost me one hundred dollars today."

Prestonshire on Elm, the Denbigh Ranch, Dickey County, Dakota Territory

The bane of Elm Valley, in fact the curse of all of Dickey County, was Lord Nigel Cordell Denbigh, 6th Marquess of Prestonshire. Denbigh was a tall, slender man who was always fastidiously dressed. He kept his hair, which was brown and graying at the temples, perfectly coiffed, and his pencil-thin mustache well trimmed. The women of his social set back in England all agreed that he was handsome, though they also added that he was flawed in some way, rather like a stem of fine crystal, with a small imperfection that at first glance couldn't be seen. The more one saw of Denbigh, though, the more the imperfection, not of physical form, but of personal character, became evident.

It was because of that imperfection that Denbigh had been asked by his family to leave England. Having been challenged to a duel by a jealous husband, Denbigh exercised his right to choose weapons, selecting a dueling pistol. Most duels fought among gentlemen used the rapier, the reason being that the duels were rarely, if ever, fatal. It was understood among members of the peerage that the application of a dueling scar would be enough to satisfy the honor of the aggrieved. Using a dueling pistol turned the duel from a gentlemen's event to an act of murder by code.

Because of that, few gentlemen were skilled in the use of the dueling pistol. Denbigh, however, practiced constantly with the pistol, and on the day of the duel, killed his adversary, Lord Cedric Belford, with one well-placed shot. Denbigh was ostracized, not only for compromising Belford's wife, but also for taking unfair advantage of his prowess with a particular weapon when he was rightfully called to account. Wanting to avoid further embarrassment to the family, not only from the untidy effects of the duel, but from his other scandals as well, involving seduction, slander, betrayal, and personal greed, Denbigh was asked to leave England.

The pain of his departure was eased, however, by the provision of several thousand acres of land on the Elm River in the Dakota Territory, U.S.A., as well as a very generous yearly stipend. He had arrived in New York approximately two years earlier, accompanied by his manservant Tolliver and carrying a grip with thirty-five thousand pounds sterling. He was pleasantly surprised when he discovered that after the monetary exchange, he wound up with over a half million U.S. dollars.

At first, Denbigh had been bitter and angry about the expulsion, but as he grew more acclimated to the situation, he came to the belief that his being sent to the United States was the best thing that could possibly happen to him. He soon realized that he could have much more power, influence, and wealth here than he ever could back in England. Giving his ranch the grandiose name of Preston-shire on Elm, he began to expand his holdings, buying out land adjacent to his own until his ranch surrounded the only road into the town of Fuller-ton. Then, realizing it would take a veritable army to run his fiefdom, he began hiring men, not only workers for his ranch, but men with whom he could form his own militia.

For the moment, his rather large army was a drain on his resources, though he had so much money that he was in no danger of running out anytime soon. But despite the fact his private militia was costing him money, they paid their way by virtue of not only establishing but extending his personal power. And he also knew that they would, when all his plans were put into operation, pay for themselves.

It was Denbigh's dream—though it was a dream that so far he had shared with no one—to carve out a large, feudal estate, encompassing all the farms and ranches in the entire valley into his sphere of control, assimilating the land as his own, and employing the small landowners as serfs, beholden only to him. At the moment, he was examining a map of the valley with certain areas marked off, land that he owned, and land that he planned to acquire by whatever means possible.

He heard a discreet cough from behind him.

"Yes, Mr. Tolliver, what is it?"

Henry Tolliver, a short and rather rotund man with a bald head and protruding lips, was Denbigh's personal valet, the son, grandson, and great-grandson of maids and valets who had served the Denbigh family for nearly one hundred years. Tolliver had come to America with Denbigh.

"M'lord, Mr. Butrum wishes an audience," Tolliver said.

Butrum was one of the latest men to join his militia, Denbigh hiring him after reading an article in the San Francisco newspaper describing him as: "With a pistol, faster than thought, and in disposition, a man who can kill without compunction." As of now, Butrum was Denbigh's highest-paid employee.

Denbigh chuckled at the distaste Tolliver had for Butrum, most clearly demonstrated by the tone in his voice.

"Mr. Tolliver, why do I get the impression that you don't much like Mr. Butrum?"

"Perhaps, sir, it is because I do not like the man," Tolliver said.

"Why not?

"I find his demeanor most unpleasant."

"He kills people for a living, Mr. Tolliver," Denbigh said. "Someone who kills for a living can hardly be expected to have a very pleasant disposition now, can he?"

"No, sir," Tolliver replied.

"Henry, I find our Mr. Butrum unpleasant as well," Denbigh said, softening his words. "Not only Butrum, but every one of these cowboys, those who work for me and those who don't. You have to understand that they are not like you and me. Whereas we have generations of culture bred into us, these men are wild and uncouth, little more than animals really. But for now, I need them. I find myself in the unusual position of being dependent upon those who are far inferior. Now, if you would, please show Mr. Butrum into the study."

"Yes, m'lord," Tolliver replied.

Tolliver left the room and as he did so, Denbigh rolled up the map that he had been examining so that Butrum could not see it. He did not believe that Butrum was intelligent enough to discern the meaning of a map marked out with crosshatches, but he had no wish to discuss the matter with him.

Ollie Butrum had buck teeth, eyes so pale a blue that they were almost colorless, pale skin, and yellow hair. In a world of gentlemen, he would be marginalized, not only for his innate ugliness, but also because of his intelligence, which was minimal, and his demeanor, the antitheses of the proper etiquette and decorum that so occupied the world in which Denbigh was raised.

But the Dakota Territory was not a world of gentlemen, and if a gentleman wanted to survive in this world, he needed an ally like Butrum, either as a friend, or better in this case, as a loyal and subservient employee.

"Mr. Denbigh," Butrum started.

Denbigh said nothing, but held up his finger.

"I mean Lord Denbigh," Butrum corrected.

"Yes, Mr. Butrum, what is it?"

"The paper come out again."

"I expected that it would," Denbigh said. "Though he is a thorn in my side, one must confess that John Bryce has more courage than the rest of the town combined. He wrote another scathing article about me, I suppose."

"Scathing?"

"Bad."

"Yes, sir, he did," Butrum said. "But that ain't all he wrote."

"Oh? What else did he write about me."

"Well, nothin' else in the newspaper, but he did write a letter to someone and Clem Dawson, the fella that works down at the post office, he copied it down."

"Did he now? And where is the copy of the letter Bryce wrote?"

"I've got it," Butrum said. "Dawson give it to me 'cause he thought you might want to see it."

Denbigh took the letter from Butrum and began to read.

As Denbigh read the letter, doing so silently, Butrum walked over to the liquor cabinet to examine its contents. The cabinet was filled with bottles of various wines, liqueurs, and whiskeys. He started to reach for one of the bottles, but was stopped by Tolliver.

"The liquor in this cabinet is not to be touched, sir," Tolliver said. "That is a reserved cache."

"There is some rye whiskey in the cabinet, Mr. Tolliver," Denbigh said, not even looking up from the letter he was reading. "You may serve that to Mr. Butrum."

"Yes, sir."

Tolliver poured a glass of the rye whiskey, turning his nose up slightly at the aroma. Butrum took the glass, tossed it down, then held the glass out for a second serving. Tolliver poured another drink, then looked over at Denbigh, who had finished the letter and was now deep in thought.

"Is something troubling you, sir?" Tolliver asked.

"Mr. Butrum, have you ever heard of Matt Jensen?"

"No, I ain't," Butrum said as he turned the glass to his lips.

"Have you, Mr. Tolliver?"

"Only what I have read," Tolliver replied. "And from what I read, he must be quite a magnificent fellow."

Denbigh chuckled. "I suppose that's all in how you look at it," he said. "If he is on your side, he is magnificent. But if he is against you, it could be quite troubling."

"And is that likely to be the case, m'lord? Is Mr. Jensen likely to be against you?"

"If the newspaperman has his way, it might be."

"I can take care of the newspaperman for you," Butrum said. "And this time, there won't be no comin' back the way he did after Slater and the others did their little job."

"No, that's all right. We'll let him be for a while."

"Whatever you say. You're the boss," Butrum said. His voice had the high-pitched quality that was common in very small people.

"Don't leave just yet," Denbigh said. Pulling a piece of paper from his desk, he began to write. "See to it that this telegram is sent, will you?"

"Yes, sir," Butrum said.

After Butrum left, Denbigh returned to his map and began studying it again, though this time his mind was on something else. He was thinking about the man to whom he had just sent the telegram.

Lucas Meacham.

Denbigh had employed Meacham's services once before, and if there was anyone he had ever met, or even heard about, who was more deadly than Ollie Butrum, it was this man.

Meacham had once killed an entire family for Denbigh—father, mother, four kids, and a grandmother thrown in for good measure. He had a reputation for being deadly accurate with his shooting, and absolutely merciless with his killing. And though Denbigh had never met Matt Jensen, he knew it was going to take someone like Lucas Meacham to make certain that Jensen did not become a problem for him.

Chapter Six

Salcedo, Colorado

When Lucas Meacham struck the match, the flare of light made his piercing brown eyes, hawklike nose, and jutting chin even more prominent. Holding the match to his watch, he saw that it was almost ten o'clock. According to the information he had gotten, Bradley Keaton was supposed to appear on the corner under the lamplight at exactly ten o'clock.

Meacham was depending on that, because he had paid well to get it set up. And he knew that the person who was arranging this for him knew that if Keaton didn't show up, Meacham would be most unhappy. And people who met Meacham realized, very quickly, that he was not the kind of man one wanted to make unhappy.

A few minutes later, a man came out of the saloon, then stopped on the corner, under the street lamp. He stood there for a moment, looking in both directions. Meacham raised the rifle to his shoulder, but he lowered it when he saw a woman come out of the saloon to join the man. The man gave the woman some money; then the two of them hurried off to her crib.

Meacham blew his nose onto the ground, and waited.

Behind him, his horse whickered and stamped its foot.

From the saloon, a woman's high-pitched squeal of laughter was joined by a man's deep guffaw.

A back door slammed shut in one of the houses and, in the moonlight, Meacham saw a man heading for the toilet, carrying a wad of paper with him.

Another man approached the street lamp, this time coming out of the dark. The man stopped under the light of the lamppost, reached into his pocket to pull out a watch, then raised his hand to study it pointedly, as if waiting to meet someone.

This was the man Meacham had been waiting for, and once again he raised his rifle, then aimed at the easy target the street lamp provided for him. Once he had the sight picture lined up, he squeezed the trigger slowly, and was rocked back by the recoil of the exploding cartridge. Even from here, he could see part of the man's skull fly away as the heavy lead slug crashed through his head.

The heavy boom of the shot rolled back from the distant hills so that it sounded almost like a volley, rather than a single, exceptionally well-placed shot. Meacham mounted his horse and rode quickly toward the sprawled body of the man he had just shot. By the time he reached the corner, several others had gathered around the body.

"Who did this?" someone was saying. "Did anybody see anything?"

Meacham saw a star on the questioner's vest.

"I did it, Sheriff," Meacham said, swinging down from his horse.

"I'm the deputy, not the sheriff," the man said. "You're confessing to this, are you?"

"I'm not confessing, I'm claiming," Meacham replied.

"What do you mean, you are claiming? Who are you?"

"The name is Meacham. Lucas Meacham."

Meacham took a folded-up paper from his vest pocket and showed it to the deputy.

"This man is Bradley Keaton," Meacham said. "There's a thousand dollars reward out on him. Dead or alive," he added pointedly. "And as you can see, he is dead."

"Oh, yes," the deputy said. "He is definitely dead."

Meacham nodded toward the hotel. "I'm going to take a room in the hotel for tonight. I expect to have verification and payment by noon tomorrow."

"Yes, sir," the deputy said. "I'm sure you will have."

"Thank you."

The next morning, Lucas Meacham was awakened by someone pounding on the door of his hotel room. After shooting Keaton the night before, he had stayed up late drinking and playing cards, and now he felt as if every knock on the door had the effect of hitting him in the head.

"All right, all right!" he yelled, and even the sound of his own voice caused his head to hurt. Sitting up in bed, he saw the late-morning sun streaming in through the window, and he wondered what time it was. His throat was bitter from too many cigarettes, and sour with too much whiskey.

Whoever was outside the door pounded on it again.

"I said all right, I'm coming!" Meacham called out again. "If you pound on that door one more time, I'm going to shoot through it. Do you understand me?"

"Yes, sir," a muffled voice replied from outside the door. "Mr. Meacham?"

"What?"

"Are you Mr. Meacham?"

Wearing his long underwear, Meacham padded barefoot over to the door. He was carrying his pistol in his right hand, and with his left, he jerked the door open.

"What do you want?" he demanded. "And it better be good."

The man standing on the other side of the door was a small man, wearing a three-piece suit, bowler hat, and rimless glasses. He recoiled at the sight of the pistol in Meacham's hand.

"I have to make sure you are Lucas Meacham," the man said.

"Yeah, that's me."

"I have a telegram for you, Mr. Meacham," the man said, holding out a yellow envelope.

Meacham took the envelope from the small man's hand and, without a word, slammed the door. Walking back over to the bed, he sat down and pulled the telegram out to read.

REQUIRE YOUR SERVICES TO FIND MATT JENSEN STOP
ONCE YOU FIND HIM SPECIAL ARRANGEMENTS WILL APPLY
STOP YOU WILL BE COMPENSATED AS BEFORE STOP

N DENBIGH

Meacham had been tracking Keaton for nearly two months before finding him and killing him last night. He had nothing else planned, so this telegram came at a good time.

Denbigh wanted "special arrangements" applied to Matt Jensen. Special arrangements meant that he wanted this man Jensen killed. Denbigh always paid exceptionally well when he wanted someone killed. All Meacham had to do now was find Jensen, and that was going to be easy. As it so happened, Meacham had read about Matt Jensen just the day before, in the *Citizen's Monitor,* the Salcedo newspaper.

Matt Jensen To Be Feted in Pueblo

Bank Robbers Killed in Deadly Shootout

Stolen Bank Money Recovered

Matt Jensen, who is well known throughout the West as a champion for justice, will be honored Saturday next by the city of Pueblo. The celebration is in recognition of Mr. Jensen's daring pursuit and dispatch of the fiends Cyrus Hayes and Emmet Cruise.

The two outlaws, while perpetrating a bank robbery, did shoot and kill Joshua King, the bank teller, as well as two customers, Mr. and Mrs. Kyle Prescott, Mrs. Prescott being with child at the time. Upon learning of the robbery and murders, Matt Jensen began an immediate pursuit of the bandits and, on his own, tracked, located, and killed them. After he recovered the stolen money, Mr. Jensen returned every cent to the bank.

Mayor Robert McKay McClelland has declared Saturday next to be set aside so that honors may be paid to Matt Jensen. The editor of this newspaper wishes to take this opportunity to extend kudos to Mr. Jensen, whose sterling performance not only adds to his own considerable luster, but speaks well of the Western spirit.

When Lucas Meacham rode into Pueblo, he saw a huge banner stretched across Abriendo Street.

PUEBLO HONORS MATT JENSEN
FOR RECOVERING STOLEN BANK MONEY

It had not been hard to find Jensen. Stories of his running down the bank robbers and recovering the stolen money had appeared in nearly every newspaper in the West. This was going to be a lot easier than he thought, rather like taking candy from a baby.

As Meacham sat his horse, staring up at the banner, someone called out to him.

"Mister, you are going to have to get out of the street!"

"What do you mean get out of the street? What the hell for?"

"The parade is coming. The parade to honor Matt Jensen."

Meacham stared at the man for a moment, then expectorated a stream of tobacco juice before moving.

In a town as small and rural as Pueblo, any occasion for a celebration was a welcome event. The Pueblo Sons of Liberty Brigade were cooking a steer over a pit, and the aroma of the roasting beef permeated the whole town. Later, it would be served, along with baked beans, to all who would make a donation to the brigade. Firecrackers popped throughout the day as young boys would put them in places where they would cause the most mischief, then run away laughing at their own antics.

At one o'clock, there was a parade led by the city band, then the fire department's pumper, with all firemen in full uniform, followed by an open carriage in which Mayor Robert McClelland rode, waving at the people. The mayor's carriage was followed by a woman, leading a group of children. The woman was also carrying a sign, identifying the children as being students of Miss Margrabe's third-grade class.

The mayor had tried to talk Matt into riding in the carriage with him, but Matt was embarrassed by all the hoopla, and the last thing he wanted was to be riding in a carriage with the mayor. He managed to get out of it by explaining that he would much rather watch the parade than be in it.

After the parade there were games; the firemen defeated the Sons of Liberty in a spirited game of baseball, four to two, though the Sons of Liberty made up for it by winning the horseshoe-throwing contest. There was also target shooting, a three-legged race, and a tug-of-war.

Toward early evening, not being one to miss an opportunity to speak, Mayor McClelland mounted a speaker's platform and spoke for forty-five minutes, extolling the virtues of Pueblo and the progress the city had made under his administration. Not until the last minute of his speech did the mayor remember to thank Matt Jensen for recovering the money that had been taken from the bank.

* * *

Lucas Meacham sat at a table in the back of the Blue Star Saloon, nursing a drink and planning his job. He could hear the sounds from outside, the band music as well as occasional applause and cheers from the crowd.

"Honey, are you goin' to be a' wantin' me for anything?" the lone saloon girl asked him. "'Cause if you don't want me for nothin', I'm a' goin' to go outside and see what all is goin' on."

"No, I ain't goin' to be wantin' you," Meacham said. "If I was wantin' me a woman now, I'd get one a lot prettier than you."

The smile left the girl's face and her eyes reflected a moment of hurt, before she was able to file the insult away with all the other insults she had heard for most of her life. Turning from him, she walked quickly to the door, then outside.

With the departure of the bar girl, the only people left in the saloon were the bartender and two Mexican men who were sitting at a table near Meacham. It was obvious that the bartender didn't want to be here, as he was standing over by the door, staring out over the batwings at the activities outside.

One of the two Mexicans looked over toward Meacham. "Senor, you are not going to . . ." He turned to his companion. *"Celebrare?"*

"Celebrate."

"*Sí.* You are not going to celebrate the *grande* Matt Jensen?" This from the taller of the two men.

"I have no interest in Matt Jensen," Meacham replied. "As far as I'm concerned, Matt Jensen could fall off a horse and break his neck."

The two men smiled. "I think maybe we are amigos," the tall one said.

"What makes you think we are amigos?" Meacham asked. He wasn't the kind of man who would likely be friends with these two men, or any Mexicans for that matter.

"Because we do not care if he breaks his neck either," the tall one said.

"For two years we were in prison because of Señor Matt Jensen," the smaller of the two said.

Meacham took a quick glance toward the bartender and saw that he had not moved away from the batwing doors.

"So, because of Matt Jensen, you two were in prison, huh?"

"*Sí, señor,* for two years."

"How would you like to get revenge? And make some money besides?" he asked.

The two men looked at each other, then the smaller responded. "I think maybe we would like that very much."

Because of the many festivities and the dinner, it was late by the time Matt went to bed that night. He was staying in a room in the Railroad Hotel, the accommodations having been provided for him by the Colorado Bank and Trust. He fell asleep, not basking in the honors that had been bestowed upon him today, but feeling a sense of sorrow because it had been necessary for him to put Spirit down.

Later that same night, Lucas Meacham, Pablo Sanchez, and Enrico Gutierrez, the two men he had hired to help him, slipped through the dark shadows down the street to the Railroad Hotel. Although Lucas Meacham was a skilled gunman who believed he could take Jensen in a face-to-face gunfight, why take the chance? All he wanted was for the man to be killed so he could collect his fee from Denbigh, and if Sanchez and Gutierrez guaranteed that result, that was good enough for him.

Meacham, Sanchez, and Gutierrez moved in through the front door, then walked quietly over to the counter where the sleeping desk clerk was snoring loudly. Meacham turned the registration book around and, in the light of the quietly hissing kerosene lantern, ran his finger down the list of names until he found the one he was looking for.

"Room Two-oh-seven," he whispered.

Leaning over the counter, Meacham removed a key from a nail that was labeled 207.

"Let's go," he said.

Meacham led Sanchez and Gutierrez upstairs,

cautioning them to walk very, very quietly. When they reached the top of the stairs, Meacham held out his hand to stop them on the stairway, then leaned around the corner to look down the hallway toward Room 207.

The hallway was lit by four kerosene lanterns, two on each of the facing walls. The lanterns made hissing sounds, and occasionally the flame in one or another lantern would flicker for a few seconds, causing the shadows to dance. After making certain that no one was in the hallway and that all the doors were closed, Meacham pulled his pistol and, with his arm crooked at the elbow, pointed it straight up.

"Put out the lanterns as we go by," he whispered. "Let's do it."

The three men walked quietly, very quietly, down the hall, making certain they stayed on the hall runner, a long, narrow carpet that stretched from one end of the hallway to the other. As they passed each lantern they extinguished it so that the hallway grew progressively darker, until, by the time they were standing in front of Room 207, the only illumination was a dim, silver splash of light down at the far end of the hall, projected through the window by the moon.

Matt had no idea what time it was, nor how long he had been asleep, when something awakened him. He lay in the dark for just a second, fighting the momentary confusion of being unexpectedly awakened, when he heard, though it was barely audible, the sound of a key being inserted in the lock of his door. In one motion, he grabbed the gun from the holster that hung on the headboard, and rolled off onto the floor on the opposite side of the bed from the door.

At almost the same time as he reached the floor, the door to his room was opened and three guns began shooting at the bed. Because of his alertness, none of the bullets struck Matt, though he could feel and hear them hitting the bed.

Matt wriggled on his stomach to the foot of the bed; then, using the flame pattern of the muzzle flashes as his target, he shot back. He heard two of the men fall, followed by the sound of footsteps running down the hall. Matt got up and moved quickly to the door, hoping to get a glimpse of his attacker, but the hall lamps had all been extinguished, and he saw nothing.

Leaving Sanchez and Gutierrez lying dead or dying on the floor behind him, Meacham ran down the stairs and, seeing a startled desk clerk coming toward the foot of the stairs, shot him down.

Meacham left the hotel through a back door that opened onto the alley.

"What was the shooting?" he heard a voice call from the darkness.

"I think it was firecrackers. Kids have been setting them off all day," another voice replied.

"Damn fool kids," the first voice said.

A baby cried.

One dog began barking, and others took up the chorus as Meacham hurried quickly down the alley.

Chapter Seven

Fullerton, Dakota Territory

As the two cowboys rode into town, they were laughing and talking to each other. Three months earlier, they had left Texas riding in a generally northwestern direction with no particular destination in mind. But while they had no specific destination, they did have a purpose, for they sought not only to find work, but to experience new adventures.

"What do you think about this town, Billy?" one of them asked. "Think we might find work around here?"

"Maybe," Billy answered. "Hey, Jeff, what day is this?" Billy asked.

"I don't know. Thursday? Saturday?"

"You think it's close to June 30th?"

"I don't know," Jeff said. "Why are you askin' anyway?"

Billy pointed to a sign that had been posted on a kiosk that stood in the middle of the street just at the south entrance into town. "That's where I'm goin' to be on June 30th. I'll just bet you there will be some pretty girls there."

. The sign, neatly hand painted, read:

FIREMEN'S BALL
June 30th
Morning Star Hotel
Come One, Come All.

"Yeah, well, we won't be there if we can't find us someplace to work at. That's a month away. And if we can't get took on at a ranch or somethin', we won't have enough money to support ourselves for a month. Besides which, if there are any pretty girls there, you can bet they won't be alone," Jeff said. "Every cowboy within ten miles will be sniffing around them like bees on clover."

"But you forget you are talking about Dakota men," Billy said. "You know damn well that once a pretty girl gets a look at a Texas man, none of these Dakota fellas will have a chance."

Jeff laughed out loud. "You are full of it, Billy, anyone ever tell you that?"

"Yeah, well, like they say, they's some that's got it, and some that ain't. But don't worry, Jeff, you're with me, and I've got enough of it for both of us."

Jeff laughed again. "I'll give you that," he said.

"How 'bout we stop over there for a while?" Billy suggested, pointing to a building that was identified by a large sign up on the high false front as the New York Saloon.

"Sounds good to me," Jeff agreed.

Stopping in front of the saloon, the two young men dismounted, then began patting themselves down.

"Whoa, Billy, you're calling up a dust storm there," Jeff said.

"Well, you ain't no pretty clear day your ownself," Billy replied.

"You think we got dust on the outside, what do you think we got in our throats? I'll bet you that me and you done swallowed enough dirt to plant ourselves a hunnert acres of cotton," Jeff said.

Billy laughed. "We ain't in Texas no more. "What makes you think anyone up here has ever even seen cotton growin'?"

"I don't care if I don't never see any more of it my ownself," Jeff said. "I picked and chopped enough when I wan't nothin' but a young pup. Come on, let's go inside and get us a beer."

"Yeah, I can taste it now."

There was an ugly little man sitting on a bench just outside the door to the saloon, and he stood up and walked over to stand at the top of the three steps that led up to the porch.

"The name is Butrum," he said. "Ollie Butrum."

"Glad to meet you, Mr. Butrum. And not wantin' to be rude or nothin', but, how 'bout you step out of the way there?"

"Where do you fellas think you're a' goin'?" the ugly little man asked.

"Where's it look like we're goin'?" Billy replied, his voice showing his irritation. "Me'n my friend here is a' goin' in there to get us a drink, if it's any of your business. Which it ain't," he added.

"Oh, but it is my business," the ugly little man said. "You see, there don't nobody go into any buildin' in this town without I let them."

"Well, now, that's a hell of a thing," Billy said. "How come that is?"

"I don't let nobody in without I see their coupon. Let me see your coupon."

"Coupon? Now, just what coupon would that be?" Jeff asked.

"You did come through a toll gate, didn't you? The road leadin' into town has a toll gate down across the way, and you can't get through unless you pay the toll. Once you pay the toll, you get a coupon that says you can pass. My job is to check to make certain that ever'one who comes into town has that coupon."

"Ha! Well, there you go then," Jeff said. "We don't have no coupons, 'cause we didn't come in by no road."

"Then that's even worse," Butrum said. "That means you come across Denbigh land. So I'm goin' to have to charge you for that, same as if you had paid the toll like you was s'posed to. That'll be a dollar apiece."

"What?" Billy replied with an angry shout. Are

you tellin' us you expect us to give you dollar apiece just to go into the saloon and have us a drink?"

"I not only expect you to give me a dollar apiece, I intend to collect it. Now, hand it over."

The man who had identified himself as Ollie Butrum stood barely over five feet tall, and though he was scowling at the two cowboys, the scowl looked like nothing more than the petulant expression of an angry schoolboy.

The idea that a man so small had just told them that he intended to collect a dollar from each of them struck Billy as funny, and he laughed out loud.

The expression on Butrum's face grew angrier.

"You find that funny, do you?"

"Mister, ain't you got somethin' better to do, like sweepin' out a saloon or muckin' out a stall? I mean, what do little fellas like you do to make a livin' anyway?" Billy asked.

Now the expression on Butrum's face changed from a scowl to a caustic smile. "Funny you should bring that up, cowboy. I kill people for a living," he said.

"What?"

"Maybe you didn't catch my name. It's Butrum, Ollie Butrum."

"Is that supposed to mean something to me?" Billy asked.

"I take it that you aren't from around here."

"We're from Texas," Billy said. "And in Texas, scrawny little shits like you know their place. Now get out of the way before I knock you right on your ass."

Butrum stepped back from the steps, and his smile broadened, but still, there was no mirth in his expression.

"You want to fight me, do you, cowboy?"

Billy looked over at Jeff. "Which one of us is goin' to teach this little feller a lesson?"

"Billy, wait, I don't like the way this is goin'," Jeff replied.

"Better listen to your friend, Billy," Butrum said.

"Who told you you could call me by my first name?" Billy asked. "I sure as hell didn't."

"If we're goin' to fight, let's get to it," Butrum said.

"There's two of us, only one of you," Billy said. "So I'll give you your choice. Which one of us do you want to fight? And I sure hope you choose me."

"Oh, I want to fight both of you, cowboy," Butrum replied.

Billy whooped out loud. "Both of us? You want to fight both of us? Mister, your scrawny little ass couldn't handle one of us. Why would you want to fight both of us?"

"Oh, I'm not talking about that kind of fight," Butrum said. He stepped back a bit, then let his arm hang so that his hand was near his pistol. "The kind of fight I'm talking about is permanent."

"Gunfight?" Billy said, surprised by the announcement. "Wait a minute. Are you telling me you are wanting to have a gunfight over a dollar?"

"Two dollars," Butrum said. "One from each of

you. Now, you give me the dollars, like I said, and I'll let you live. Otherwise, I'll kill both of you and take the dollars from your dead bodies."

"Mister, you are crazy," Billy said.

"Billy, I told you, I don't like the looks of this. Let's give him the dollars," Jeff said.

"Don't go gettin' all scared on me now, Jeff. This little feller is as full of it as anyone I've ever seen."

"I don't like this. I got me a bad feelin'. Let's just give him the dollar and be done with it."

"Two dollars," Butrum said. "Each."

"What do you mean two dollars each?" Jeff said. "You said one dollar each."

"It cost you a dollar apiece to come into town, and it's goin' to cost you a dollar apiece to leave town, and you will be leaving town, so I might as well collect that now too. That'll be two dollars apiece."

"Mister, you done got into my craw somethin' fierce," Billy said. "We ain't givin' you one cent."

"Billy, I don't know," Jeff said.

"I ain't takin' nothin' more offen this little turd," Billy said. "Now if you ain't with me on this, get the hell out of the way and I'll kill him my ownself. Which is it?"

"I'm with you," Jeff said reluctantly.

"Draw!" Billy shouted as his hand dipped toward his pistol.

Billy had often practiced the quick draw, and he considered himself pretty good, but aside from taking a few shots at some cattle rustlers one night, he had never actually shot at a man before. Now he was less than ten feet away from someone who, though Billy didn't know this, had killed several men.

Even before he had the pistol out of his holster, Butrum fired, and Billy felt a heavy blow in the middle of his chest, then nothing. He fell back, the unfired pistol still in his hand.

Because Butrum had gone after Billy first, Jeff did manage to get off one shot, but his bullet hit the door frame in front of the saloon. Butrum's second shot hit Jeff between the eyes and he joined his friend in the dirt.

One block away from the confrontation, a farmer named Fowler pulled his team to a halt and sat in his wagon as he watched the drama play out before him. He had come into town for supplies, and his wife and young son were in the wagon with him.

"Wow! Pa, did you see that?" the boy asked.

"Yeah," Fowler answered. "I saw it."

"I ain't never seen nothin' like that before," the boy said excitedly.

"And I pray you never have to see it again," the boy's mother said. "E.B., let's get out of here. Let's go back home."

"No sense in doin' that, Sue," E.B. said. "We need the supplies, and we've already paid to come through the toll gate. We'd be foolish to go back home now."

The Fowlers sat in their wagon for a moment

longer as a crowd began to gather around the bodies of the two men Butrum had killed.

"Let's go to the store, get our goods, and then go home while everyone is distracted," E.B. said.

"He sure was fast," the boy said. "I bet there ain't nobody in the world faster'n him."

"I'll not hear another word about it," Sue said.

"But Ma . . ."

"You heard me. Not another word."

"John, what was the shooting about? Did you find out?" Millie asked when the editor came back into the newspaper office.

"Yes," John said. "Two young men were killed. Apparently they did not pay the toll when they came into town and Butrum was collecting it for Denbigh."

"Who were they?"

"Nobody knows who they were. From what I understand they were both strangers, never been here before. I imagine they were just cowboys come up from the States to look for work."

"Oh, how awful. They came into a town that is strange for them, and they are shot down in the street. You know they both have a mother somewhere who is worrying about them."

As E.B. Fowler started back home with the supplies in the back of the buckboard, he and his family were startled when they passed by the kiosk that stood in the middle of Monroe Avenue on the south end of town. There, they saw the two cowboys who had been killed earlier. They were standing upright by virtue of each of them having been tied to a six-foot-long one-by-six-inch plank that had been stuck into the ground. Each of the men had their arms folded across their chest, held that way by the same rope that tied them to the plank. One of the dead men had both eyes closed. The other had one eye closed and one open, the open eye bulging almost out of its socket. There were red splashes of blood on the first man's shirt, showing the entry wound of the bullet. The other had a hole, the blood almost black now, between his eyes.

Covering the sign that had been posted to invite all to the barn dance on Saturday night was another sign. This one, much more crudely lettered, read:

DO YOU KNOW THESE MEN?

"Pa! Look!" young Green called. "That's the two men that was killed, ain't it?"

"Oh, those poor men. Nobody even knows who they are," Sue said. "No, Green, don't look." Sue wrapped her arm around her son's head and pulled her to him.

"Ma, that ain't fair! Let me look!" Green protested.

"E.B., hurry on by."

E.B. slapped the reins against the back of his team, causing them to move more quickly, but he stared long and hard at the bodies of the two men as he drove by.

"They said in the mercantile store that Butrum shot those two men because they didn't have the coupon that showed they paid their toll," Sue said. "How can that be? Denbigh can't kill people just because they haven't paid the toll."

"That may have been what caused it," E.B. said, "but Marshal Tipton has already said there won't be any charges against Butrum."

"What? Why not? Butrum killed those poor men. We saw it ourselves," Sue protested.

"There were too many witnesses who saw the two cowboys draw against Butrum. Heck, we saw that, if you recall."

"It isn't right," Sue said.

"Them getting killed isn't right, the newspaper office getting messed up isn't right, and collecting tolls on a public road isn't right. Sometimes things happen that aren't right."

"Do you have the toll money ready?" Sue asked.

"Yes. Two dollars, one for you and one for me. I guess we're lucky that they don't charge for Green as long as he is in the buckboard with us."

"Two dollars to come to town and two dollars to leave town. That's almost as much money as we spent while we were in town," Sue said. "It isn't right. It just isn't right."

Chapter Eight

Pueblo, Colorado

Leaving the hotel after the shooting, Lucas Meacham went to the livery stable where he spent the night sleeping in the same stall as his horse. He heard one of the stable hands coming in the next morning and, though he was awake, he pretended to be asleep until the man walked by the stall.

"Good morning," the stable hand said. "Slept with your horse, did you?"

"Yes," Meacham said, sitting up and stretching. "Mr. Forbis, the livery owner, said it would be all right."

"Sure, he lets folks sleep with the horses all the time, saves them from having to pay for a hotel room. Hey, if you spent the night here, I bet you don't even know about all the excitement."

"You mean the parade and celebration over this fella, Matt Jensen? I thought that was all over yesterday."

"Nah, I ain't talkin' about that at all. I'm talkin' about the shootin' that took place in the hotel last night."

"A shooting?"

"Yes, sir. Seems that there was three men who tried to kill Matt Jensen while he was asleep in his hotel room last night. Only thing is, two of 'em got themselves killed instead."

"How do you know there were three men?" Meacham asked. "Maybe they were the only two."

The stable hand shook his head. "No, they was three of 'em. Dupree seen the third one as he was leavin'. He seen him shoot down Bubba James too. Onliest thing is, Dupree just seen him from the back, so he don't have no idee who it was."

"What about Matt Jensen? Was he hurt?"

The stable hand laughed. "Nah, he didn't get nary a scratch. I believe they're goin' to have a hearing about the shootin' this morning. It's goin' to be open to the pubic if you'd care to attend."

"No, I don't think so," Meacham said. "Shooting and all that? I don't like violence. I like to live as calm a life as I can."

"I don't blame you," the stable hand replied. "I'm a peaceable man too, don't like any kind of trouble. But I reckon Matt Jensen is just the kind of man that trouble follows around. Do you know anything about him?"

"Only what I read about him in the paper. I take it he saved the bank's money?"

"Chased down the outlaws, killed them, took

the money off them, and brought it back to the bank. But if you know anything about him, you'll know that ain't all that unusual for him. Jensen is the kind of man that's always doin' stuff like that. I'll just bet them three men didn't know who they was tanglin' with when they come after him last night. Oats?"

"What?" Meacham asked, surprised by the sudden change of subject.

"Do you want oats for your horse?"

"No, hay is good enough. I think I'll go find me someplace to have breakfast."

"You might try Little Man's," the stable hand said. "It's just down the street there on the right. You can't miss it."

"Thanks," Meacham said.

"Ha, you was just foolin' me, wasn't you, mister?" the stable hand said and Meacham started to leave.

"Fooling you? About what?"

"You say you don't like violence, but the way you're wearin' your gun, low and kicked out like that—seems to me like you might be a man who knows how to use it."

"I said I didn't like violence," Meacham said. "I didn't say I couldn't be a violent man if I needed to be."

The stable hand laughed out loud. "That's a good one, mister," he said. Yes, sir, that's a good one."

* * *

Just after noon on that same day, just as the stable hand had predicted, there was a preliminary hearing. The hearing was conducted by Judge Warren Phelps, circuit judge of Pueblo County.

His first witness was Anton Dupree, a notions salesman who called frequently on his customers in Pueblo and always stayed in the same room at the Railroad Hotel. He had been in that room last night, on the same floor as Matt. After the witness was sworn in, the judge questioned him.

"Tell me everything you can remember about last night."

"I heard what I thought were firecrackers coming from the other end of the hall. There had been a celebration yesterday with fireworks, so I thought maybe someone was just shooting them off in the hotel. But when I stuck my head out the door, I saw a man running down the stairs."

"Did you know him?"

"No, sir," Dupree answered. Then he shook his head. "Well, I can't really say as I know him because, truth to tell, I didn't get a close enough look at him to know whether I knew him or not."

"Why not? Did he not come close enough to you?"

"He was close enough, I reckon, but all the hall lamps was out so, except for a bit of moonlight comin' in through the window, the hall was totally dark. Also, by the time I seen him, he had already started down the steps, which meant that his back was to me."

"What happened next?"

"Next thing I know, Bubba James . . ."

"Bubba James would be the hotel clerk?"

"Yes, Your Honor. Bubba James come to the foot of the stairs and I heard him say, 'What's goin' on?' Then I seen this fella that had just run down the stairs shoot Bubba down."

"What did you do next?"

"I jumped back into my room," Dupree said. "I ain't no fool."

The others present for the hearing laughed, and Judge Phelps glared at them.

"How long did you stay in your room?"

"Not long. I listened at the door for a minute or two, and when I didn't hear nothin', I went on down the stairs. That's when I seen Bubba James, lying on his back on the carpet. I knew he was dead, but I bent down to check on him anyway."

"Did you go down to the end of the hallway where the earlier shooting had taken place?"

"Yes, Your Honor, I did. Then, after I seen for sure that Bubba James was dead, I went back up the stairs, and by that time someone had got a couple of the lanterns lit so I could see what was goin' on. There was two men lyin' dead on the floor, and lots others standin' around lookin' down at them."

"Were any of them armed?" the judge asked.

"Yes, sir, one or two of them were."

"Was Mr. Jensen there?"

"He was."

"Was Mr. Jensen armed?"

"Yes, Your Honor, Mr. Jensen, was armed. Fact is, he was holdin' a pistol in his hand."

"How do you know that the man you saw holding a pistol was Matt Jensen?"

"Oh, Your Honor, after all the hoopla and such about Mr. Jensen yesterday, it was easy to pick him out."

"Can you point him out now?"

"Yes, sir," Dupree said. He pointed toward Matt Jensen. "That's him, right over there," he said.

"Thank you. You are excused."

The hearings were open to the public because as one man had said, it was better than any stage play, for this was the drama of reality. As a result of public interest in the hearings, the courtroom was full.

After hearing testimony from Matt and the other residents of the hotel, Judge Phelps issued his ruling.

"This hearing finds that Pablo Sanchez, Enrico Gutierrez, and an unknown third party did, in the middle of the night, and with stealth and planning, enter the Railroad Hotel, ascertain Mr. Jensen's room number, ascend the stairs to the second floor, extinguish the hall lamps, and attempt, by the discharge of their weapons, to murder Matt Jensen. As Mr. Jensen was responsible for the incarceration of the two previously mentioned men, it is supposed that the motive for their attack was revenge.

"Subsequent to being fired upon, Matt Jensen returned fire, the balls of his pistol having devastating effect upon, and ending the lives of, Sanchez and Gutierrez. This act of homicide was in self-defense and, in all aspects, justifiable. No further investigation, trial, or hearing is deemed necessary."

Picking up his gavel, Judge Phelps slapped it loudly on his bench.

"This hearing is adjourned."

Immediately after the hearing, the sheriff, mayor, banker, and even the judge, along with several of the citizens of the town, came over to shake Jensen's hand.

"So, where are you going to go now?" the sheriff asked.

"Everywhere in general, nowhere in particular," Matt replied.

"Well, if you aren't in any hurry, you might stick around here for a couple more days. I know that the bank has your hotel room booked for three nights, and anytime I can see the bank spending money, it pleases me." The sheriff said, laughing at his own comment.

"Maybe I'll just do that," Matt said.

Because of his constant moving about, it wasn't every night that Matt got to sleep in a bed. However, as the bank had paid for three nights at the hotel, Matt was determined to take advantage of it.

The anchorless drifting had become a part of his heritage. He was a man defined by the saloons, cow towns, stables, dusty streets, and open prairies he had encountered. He could not deny them without denying his own existence and in fact, had no intention of ever doing so. At any given time, he was both a long way from home, and as close to home as the nearest hotel, or back room in a saloon. Most often, though, home was no more than a bedroll made from a saddle blanket and poncho.

When he left the courtroom after the hearing, he had nothing on his mind except to get a few days of rest and relaxation. And he intended to start that relaxation by finding a friendly card game in the nearest saloon.

Although the hearing had been open to the public, Lucas Meacham didn't attend it. He felt reasonably secure since the stable hand had told him that the only witness had seen him from behind and was, thus, unable to identify him. Meacham was in the saloon when, shortly after the hearing was over, two men came in.

"There ain't goin' to be no charges against Matt Jensen. The judge just dismissed the case," one of the men said.

"What did you expect?" his friend replied. "Jensen was just sleepin' in bed in the hotel room when the three come into his room to kill him. He didn't have no choice but to kill them, or else he would'a been kilt his ownself."

"Well, he only kilt two of 'em. The third one got away."

"Who was the third man, Gilley, do you know?"

the bartender asked as, responding to their silent signals, he began drawing two mugs of beer.

"No, sir," Gilley answered. "Don't nobody know who the third man was."

"Didn't Dupree see him?"

"You talkin' about the drummer? Yeah, he saw him all right, but he wasn't able to describe him at all. It was too dark and the man was goin' downstairs away from him. All he could say was that he did see the man kill Bubba James."

"So the third man got clean away, did he? I'll bet he's halfway to California by now."

"I don't think so," Gilley said.

"Why not?"

"Why would he have to run anywhere? Didn't nobody see him, which means there can't nobody identify him. Hell, he could be anywhere in town. For all we know, it could be that fella over there." Gilley pointed to Meacham.

Meacham cringed, and the hairs on the back of his neck stood up.

"No, that ain't him," the other man said.

"Really?" Gilley replied. "Now, tell me, Pollard, just how do you know he ain't the one?"

"Well, look at him," Pollard said. "Does he look Mex to you?"

"Mex? What does that have to do with anything?" Gilley replied in exasperation.

"Think about it," Pollard said. "The two that was

kilt was Mex, so don't it stand to reason that the third one would be Mex too?"

"So? Dupree didn't say the third man was Mexican."

"That don't mean nothin'. Dupree just seen the back of his head, is all, which means he wouldn't know if he was Mexican or not. No, sir, if them other two was Mex, then you know the third one was too. Look around. Do you see any Mexicans in this room?"

"No, I reckon not."

"Then you can bet that the third one ain't in this saloon."

Meacham relaxed a little. He had been cursing himself for selecting Pablo Sanchez and Enrico Gutierrez because they were so incompetent that they were unable to do the job, getting themselves killed instead. But because they were Mexican, it now appeared that everyone thought the third assailant was also Mexican, and that definitely kept him in the clear.

Meacham's confidence faded, though, when he saw Matt Jensen push his way through the batwing doors a few moments later. Last night, he had been standing in the doorway of Matt Jensen's hotel room, exchanging gunfire with him. It was dark, but there had been some light from the muzzle flashes of the three pistols. Was there enough light for Jensen to see? Had he gotten a good enough look at him last night that he could recognize him now?

"Beer," he heard Matt Jensen say to the bartender.

The bartender drew a beer and handed it to Matt.

"Congratulations on the hearing, Mr. Jensen. Course, we know'd all along that there wouldn't be no charge against you, seein' as how you didn't have no choice but to do what you done."

"Thanks," Matt said.

"And of course, getting the bank's money back, well, that was good too. Only, when you think about it, it wa'nt really the bank's money anyhow, was it?" the bartender asked. "That was money that belonged to all the people of town who had it on deposit there. I had a hunnert and seven dollars and sixty-three cents of my own money in the bank, so you might say you got my money back for me. Would 'a been hard for me to have to tell my wife that we'd lost a little better'n two months pay. Which is why this beer is on me."

"Thanks, and I'm glad I could be of help," Matt replied.

Matt raised the beer mug, blew off the head, then drank nearly three-quarters of it before he took it down. Then he wiped his mouth with the back of his hand and turned his back to the bar to look out over the patrons.

Damn! He's looking right at me! Meacham thought. *Did he see me? Does he know I was the third man?*

Jensen looked directly at Meacham, then passed his eyes around the rest of the room, showing no recognition whatever.

Meacham smiled broadly. *The son of a bitch didn't recognize me! There I was, in his room last night, and he doesn't even know who I am!*

Deciding not to press his luck any further, Meacham got up and left, leaving nearly a full glass of whiskey on the table behind him.

Chapter Nine

As Matt took a long look around the room, he saw Meacham leave. Because he had never seen him before, he didn't recognize him, but he did notice that the man left a full glass of whiskey on the table, and that was unusual enough to generate some curiosity about him.

Feeling no sense of imminent danger from him, however, Matt continued to peruse the room over his mug of beer. That was when he saw a few people sitting at one of the other tables enjoying a lively game of cards. There were two brass spittoons within spitting distance of the players, but despite their presence, the floor was riddled with expectorated tobacco quids and chewed cigar butts.

One of the players raked in his bank, then stood up. "I have to go, boys, or my wife will be comin' in here after me."

"Lord, get out of here quick, Arnie, I have no wish to be on your wife's bad side," one of the other players said, and the others laughed. The player who had spoken noticed that Matt was looking on.

"Mr. Jensen, the hero of the town," the man said in a welcoming voice. "And congratulations."

"What are you congratulatin' him for, Doc? For havin' the parade, for being acquitted by the hearing, or for not gettin' shot last night?" one of the other players asked.

"How about all of the above," the man called Doc replied, and the others, including Matt, laughed. Then, to Matt, Doc said, "We have an empty chair here and would be mighty proud and honored, if you would join us, sir." The player issuing the invitation was a rather tall, cadaverous looking man. He was wearing a black suit and string tie, in contrast to the other two players, who were wearing denims and cotton shirts.

Matt tossed the rest of his drink down, then wiped the back of his hand across his mouth. "Thanks for the invite," he said. "I'll be glad to join you."

"I'm Doc Mason," the spokesman for the group continued. "The fellow with the bush on his face is Clyde Hawkens, the other one is Sam Goodbody."

"Glad to meet you folks," Matt replied, shaking the hand of each of them in turn. "Any table rules I need to know?"

"You can take up to twenty dollars out of your pocket, but what you take out of your pocket and put in front of you is all the money you can play with," Doc Mason said. "You can't go back for more.

Even if you only take out ten dollars, you can't go back for more."

"Sounds reasonable," Matt said. "Who's been the winner so far?"

"Well, now, that would have to be Doc Mason here," Clyde said. "You'd better watch out for him. He's pretty good at the game. He says he is a dentist, but I think he's actually a professional gambler. He just claims to be a dentist so's he can get other folks to play cards with him."

The accusation was made in jest and the others, including Doc Mason, laughed at the good natured ribbing.

"Thanks for the warning," Matt said.

"He ain't a bad dentist," Sam, said. "But two weeks ago, he pulled the wrong tooth out of Harley Barnes' mouth."

"Yeah? Well, here's the thing, Sam," Doc Mason replied. "Have you ever noticed that all those teeth look alike? Sometimes, I just get them confused, is all."

Again, there was laughter around the table.

"How long you plannin' on stayin' in Pueblo, Mr. Jensen?" the dentist asked as he dealt the cards. It was easy to see why he was ahead. He handled the cards easily, gracefully, whereas the others around the table looked awkward, even when picking up the pasteboards. "The reason I asked, things seem to happen when you are around and I was just wonderin' when things are going to get back to normal."

"Depends," Matt replied.

"On what?" Clyde asked. "I mean, you ain't expectin' to have a parade in your honor every day, are you?"

"No, I don't need a parade every day. Why, do you think I'm that vain? One parade a week will do. Or I would even be satisfied with one a month," Matt teased.

"Lord knows, we need some substantial citizens around here to balance off these two degenerates," Doc Mason said, bantering.

The game continued for a couple of hours with Matt winning a little more than he was losing. He wasn't a big winner, but then there were no big winners or big losers. As a result, the game was played with comity and enjoyment.

After two hours, Matt laid down his cards and picked his money up from the table. "Well, gentlemen, I thank you for the invitation to play," Matt said. "It has made for a pleasant evening. But I think I will take advantage of the hotel room the bank has provided, for at least one more night."

"And we thank you for joining our game," Doc Mason said. "I hope you don't have any unwelcome visitors tonight."

"Wait a minute, Doc, how do you know he doesn't want a visitor tonight?" Clyde asked. "He's a young, unmarried man. He might want to have some young lady visit him."

"That's why I said 'unwelcome' visitors," Mason said.

Matt chuckled. "The only visitor I want tonight is Morpheus."

"Who?" Clyde asked.

"Morpheus," Matt repeated.

"Who is Morpheus?"

"Damn, Clyde, don't you know anything?" Doc asked. "According to Ovid, Morpheus is the god of dreams," Doc said.

Clyde shook his head. "I guess I never met either one of them," he said.

"Never met who?"

"Them two fellers you just mentioned, Ovid or Morpheus."

"Sure you have," Sam said. "Them's the two that used to work down at the locomotive shop."

"Oh, yeah, wait, I think I do remember them now. One of 'em had him a scar right here, didn't he?" Clyde asked, running his finger down his cheek.

"Yeah, but I don't remember which one it was, though," Sam said.

Doc looked up at Matt with a long-suffering sigh; then both of them smiled.

"Are you sure you want to leave me with these cretins?" Doc asked.

Matt chuckled. "I'm sure you'll manage, Doc. You seem quite capable."

"Thank you. Good night, Mr. Jensen," Doc said.

"Good night."

* * *

Across the street from the saloon, and tucked into the dark space between the apothecary and boot store, Meacham waited patiently for Jensen to leave the saloon. He had been waiting for about two hours now, and because he was growing increasingly impatient, he was just about to give up when he saw Matt Jensen push through the batwing doors.

"Well, it's about time you came out," Meacham said under his breath. He drew his pistol, and bracing it against the side of the apothecary building, took aim. Not wanting to hurry his shot, Meacham took a long moment, tracking Matt's walk by moving his pistol. Before he could pull the trigger, though, he heard a loud shout.

"Eeeyah! Eeeyah!"

The call came from the driver of a stagecoach who, by shouting and snapping the reins, was urging the team into a gallop so that the stagecoach would make a dramatic arrival in town. The sound of twenty-four hooves beating against the ground, as well as the creak and rattle of the coach and the singing of steel-rimmed wheels, filled the street with thunder.

The arrival of the coach caused Meacham to pull his pistol back until the coach had cleared the street. After the coach rumbled by, Meacham raised his pistol once more, but it was too late. Matt Jensen was no longer on the street. The coach had shielded him until he went into the hotel.

"Gramma!" a child shouted, and looking half a block down the street, Meacham saw a little girl run from the stage into the open arms of an older woman. There was a great deal of commotion around the arrival of the coach as the travelers stepped down to the welcome of those who had been waiting for the stage.

This was the terminus for the coach, and after all the passengers had debarked and the luggage, mail, and express packages had been taken off, the coach was driven around behind the depot, where the team could be unharnessed and the horses turned into the corral. Meacham waited until all the commotion had died down, then considered going into the hotel again tonight as he had last night. But whereas he'd had two others with him on the night before, plus the benefit of surprise, he had no such advantage tonight. If he went in tonight he would have to do it alone, and more likely than not, Jensen would be expecting him.

Meacham dismissed the idea. He was going to kill him, but he would just have to wait for a more favorable opportunity. He crossed the street to the saloon. He might as well have a few drinks before he went back to the livery to turn in for the night.

The bright sun, streaming in through his hotel window, awakened Matt the next morning. From somewhere nearby, construction was under way, and he could hear the sound of sawing and hammering.

Down the street from the hotel, the blacksmith was working at his forge so that the ringing sound of iron on iron could also be heard. There were other sounds as well: a freight wagon moving up the street and, irritatingly, the sound of a sign, squeaking in the hot dry breeze. From Wong Sing's Laundry, he could hear a couple of women, doing the wash and chatting loudly to each other in the melodic, but totally incomprehensible, Chinese language.

Matt got up, poured water from the porcelain pitcher into the basin, washed his face and hands, shaved, then got dressed. Checking out of the hotel, he walked down the street to Lambert's Café for breakfast, where he was greeted by several well-wishers.

"Any excitement last night, Mr. Jensen?" one of the other diners asked.

"All was calm," Matt said.

Others started asking questions as well, until the café owner himself, Joe Lambert, intervened. "For crying out loud, will you people let him eat his breakfast in peace? Eggs ain't good when they get cold."

Matt nodded his thanks at Lambert, then finished his breakfast undisturbed.

It was almost by accident that Meacham saw Matt Jensen go into the depot later that morning. He followed, and when he heard Matt buy a ticket to Salida, Colorado, Meacham waited for a few minutes, then he stepped up to the ticket agent's window, made arrangements for his horse to be taken on the train, and bought a ticket for himself to Salida.

The train was not due to leave Pueblo until ten o'clock that night, and wasn't due to arrive in Salida until seven the next morning. Meacham would have all day to plan his operation, and all night to carry it out.

Chapter Ten

Fullerton, Dakota Territory

John Bryce discovered the identity of the two slain cowboys by following up on the only clues he had available to him. Witnesses had heard the two men address each other as Billy and Jeff, and in Billy's pocket there had been a receipt for a saddle purchased from Dockum's Ranch in Crosby County, Texas. An exchange of telegrams had established the identity of the two men, along with a request to please give the two men a Christian burial. John wrote about it in the next issue of the *Defender.*

Murdered Men Identified

Cowboys From Crosby County, Texas

The two young men murdered in the street three days previous, have now been identified as Billy Gilbert, age 23, and Jeff Hodges, age 20. Strangers to our town, for the last three years they have been riders for Merlin Dockum, owner of Dockum's Ranch in Northwest Texas. "They are as fine a couple of young men as I have ever had ride for me," Mr. Dockum told this newspaper in an exchange of telegrams. He also asked that Mr. Gilbert and Mr. Hodges be given Christian burials, and I replied that the good people of Pueblo would do just that.

I am now calling upon the citizens of Pueblo to make a donation to a fund that will pay any expenses as may be incurred by providing a decent burial for these two fine young men. It is the least we can do now, for we all bear some guilt of their murder, if not by commission, then by omission. We have allowed the psychopath, Ollie Butrum, to live among us with neither question nor challenge.

John and Millie stood in the pastor's study of the Good Hope Baptist Church. As it happened, the Reverend Bertis Landers was Millie's father, and he was about to conduct the funeral for Billy Gilbert and Jeff Hodges. Mrs. Rittenhouse, the organist, was playing a funeral dirge as citizens of the town filed by the coffins. The plain pine coffins were now sitting on sawhorses at the front of the nave. They were open for viewing and the two cowboys, cleaned up by the undertaker Tom Lisenby, were wearing suits that neither of them had ever seen in their lifetime.

"John, it was very good of you to find out who these

two young men were, and to write an article that would pay for the funeral," Reverend Landers said.

"It was good of you to agree to conduct a funeral for someone you didn't even know," John replied.

"They are children of God," Landers replied. "That's all I need to know."

Recognizing that the music was nearly completed, Landers nodded at his daughter and son-in-law, and they left the pastor's study to take a seat in the congregation. Shortly after they were seated, Landers stepped up behind the pulpit.

The church was completely full, and Landers glanced out at them, silent for a long moment. Then he began to speak.

"These two young men, Billy Gilbert and Jeffrey Hodges, are a long way from their homes, and some may lament that they are away from their families as well. But I say no, they are not away from their families. We are all brothers and sisters in the sight of God, and no more is that evident than here, today, when so many of you have come here to share the love and brotherhood we feel for these two young men."

After the church service, the two coffins were carried out to the cemetery, one stacked on top of the other inside the hearse. At least half of those who had come to the funeral service in the church went out to the cemetery for the interment, and John was surprised to see that Denbigh had come into town as well. He told him so when he greeted him.

"I have not only come to town, Mr. Bryce. I have

also made a donation to the Reverend Landers, equal to the amount of money the town raised for the funeral. I told him to use the donated money for the church."

"Surprisingly decent of you," John said.

"I am glad you appreciate my effort," Denbigh replied. "I just wish you would be somewhat more circumspect in the provocative articles you write."

"Sometimes the truth is provocative," John said.

"Oh, but I beg to differ with you, sir," Denbigh said. "You have falsely accused one of my employees of murder."

"It *was* murder."

"All who witnessed the shooting testified to the contrary. They all say that the two cowboys drew their guns first."

"They also say that Butrum goaded the young men into drawing."

"You can't kill someone just by goading them," Denbigh said. "No, sir, it is quite clear. Mr. Butrum did not draw until he was forced to do so to defend himself."

"You can say what you want, I'll say what I want," John said.

"Yes, but the only difference is, when you talk, you do so in your newspaper, and that gives you a distinct advantage over everyone else."

"I am speaking for everyone else, Mr. Denbigh. My newspaper is the voice of the people."

"A word of advice, Mr. Bryce. Use some caution in exercising that voice, or I fear you may lose it.

Next time one of your irate readers takes umbrage with one of your inflammatory articles, he may do more than just a little vandalism."

"Is that a threat?"

"Not a threat, just a little friendly, but cautionary, advice."

"I will not be shut down, sir, do you hear me? As long as there is breath in my body, I will fight for the people of this town, and against you," John said.

Denbigh applauded lightly. "How very noble of you, Mr. Bryce. Now, if you will excuse me, I must return to my ranch."

John watched Denbigh walk back to his coach, where a liveried footman held the door open for him.

The graveside services were finished, and as the grave diggers shoveled dirt down onto the two plain wooden coffins, the people of the town started leaving the cemetery.

"What was all that about?" Millie asked, coming up to stand beside her husband.

"Nothing much," John said. He was well aware that he had just been threatened, but he had no intention of letting Millie know about it. Millie worried enough already.

"It was a nice funeral," Millie said. "I know their families would be pleased to know that so many strangers turned out just to bury them. I'm proud of you."

"Proud of me for what?" John replied. He was still distracted by the warning Denbigh had given him.

"I'm proud of you for making all this possible. Instead of being dumped into some unmarked grave, they now have a nice plot and a tombstone that identifies them by name," Millie said. "You know what I would like to do? I would like to have Mr. Ludwig take a picture of the tombstones, and have you send the picture back to Texas. I'll bet they would appreciate that."

"I'm sure they would," John said. He put his arm around his wife's shoulder as they started out of the cemetery, back toward the newspaper office. "I'll get in touch with Mr. Ludwig, and we'll just do that."

Pueblo, Colorado

At nine forty-five that evening, Meacham had a moment of concern. It was nearly time to leave, but Jensen had not yet shown up at the train station. Had he changed his mind? Had he left town by stage? Meacham's concern was eased, though, when he saw Jensen arrive in the mayor's personal carriage.

"Mr. Jensen, next time you are in this part of the country, do visit us here in Pueblo again," Mayor McClelland said. "You are always welcome."

Matt stepped down from the carriage, then threw the saddlebags, his only luggage, over his shoulder. "Will I get another parade?" he asked.

"Well, I don't know," the mayor replied.

"It would give you another opportunity to make a speech."

Mayor McClelland laughed out loud, then reached out to shake Matt's hand. "In that case, Mr. Jensen, I will guarantee you another parade. Good-bye, Mr. Jensen, do have a pleasant trip. Driver," McClelland said with a little wave of his hand.

"Where to, Mr. Mayor?" the driver asked.

"Home. Heavens, at this hour, I dare not go anywhere else. Not if I want to stay on Mrs. McClelland's good side."

Matt went into the depot to make certain that his saddle had been checked through. Then he stepped out onto the depot platform to wait for the train.

Meacham waited on the platform as well, though he stayed on the opposite side from Matt.

"Here comes the train!" someone shouted, and those waiting on the depot platform, which, even at this hour of the night, were a rather significant number of people, moved toward the track for a better view.

The kerosene headlamp that sat just in front of the bell-shaped smokestack was but a small light in the distance. The headlamp, Matt knew, was not to light the track in front of the train, because the distance the light would illuminate was less than the distance it would take to stop the heavy train. The sole purpose of the headlamp was to warn others of the approaching train.

As the train grew closer, the light became more prominent and the sound of the engine louder.

Finally, the engine rushed in with white wisps of steam escaping from the thrusting piston rods, sparks flying from the pounding drive wheels, and glowing hot embers dripping from the firebox. The train was so heavy that it caused the wooden depot platform to shake, and Matt could actually feel the vibrations in his stomach. Then came the yellow squares of light that were the windows of the passenger cars, slowing, and finally grinding to a halt with a shower of sparks and a hissing of air from the Westinghouse air brakes.

Even after it came to a complete stop, the train was still alive with the gurgling of boiling water, the hiss and puff of vented steam, and the snap and pop of overheated bearings. A dim glow of orange shone through the window of the locomotive, and those who ventured close enough to peer inside were baffled by the maze of pipes, levers, and gauges.

Matt waited as the arriving passengers stepped down from the train. The three lady passengers were helped down the boarding steps by the solicitous conductor.

As soon as the last arriving passenger had detrained, the conductor pulled out his watch and examined it, snapped the cover closed, then put it away.

"All aboard!" he called.

That was the signal for the departing passengers to board the train, and Matt started toward the train with the others.

* * *

Lucas Meacham made certain to select the same car as Matt Jensen, and when Jensen took a seat toward the front of the car on the left-hand side, Meacham sat on the right-hand side, toward the rear. The juxtaposition of their seats gave Meacham the opportunity to keep an eye on Matt.

Although this would be an all-night trip, the car in which they were sitting was a day car with no provisions for berths. That meant that if anyone did any sleeping, they would have to do so by accommodating themselves as comfortably as they could to the seat, awkward though it may be. Meacham was sure that he would have ample opportunity during the night to kill Matt Jensen.

Three times during the night, Meacham got up from his seat and went to the front of the car, but each time he passed Matt Jensen, Jensen looked up at him. Each time, Meacham nodded, then went to the water scuttle at the front of the car.

The first time Meacham passed his seat, Matt nodded politely, then watched as the man unfolded a paper cup and used it to take a drink of water. The second time the man passed, Matt became a little curious, thinking it unusual that someone would have such a thirst, but he brushed it off. The third time the man passed by, Matt was intensely alert. He remembered now having seen this man in the saloon back in Pueblo. This was the same man who had walked out of the saloon, looking nervous and leaving behind a full glass of whiskey. Matt didn't know who this person was, but was reasonably sure he wasn't just someone who was made uncommonly thirsty by train travel.

Although Matt had dozed a few times when the train first left the station, he had no intention of sleeping anymore. He stayed awake for the rest of the night, keeping a wary eye on the man at the rear of the car.

When the train pulled into the Salida station the next morning, Meacham watched in frustration as Matt Jensen got off the train. He had missed his opportunity to kill him during the night.

It was still early in the morning, but Meacham had been awake most of the night, so he was more in the mood for a beer than he was for a cup of coffee. Fortunately for him, the Pair-o-Dice Saloon was already open, so he went inside.

"Well, now, I ain't seen you in coon's age," someone said, and looking toward the speaker, Meacham recognized Angus Witherspoon. The two men had been bounty hunters together for a while.

Meacham took his beer over to the table to join him.

"Witherspoon," he said. "Where have you been keeping yourself?"

"Here and there. You?"

"Here and there," Meacham answered. "What are you doing here? You on someone's trail?"

"No, I got no prospects at the moment," he replied. He was drinking coffee, and he took a sip, eyeing Meacham over the rim of his cup. "You taking to drinking beer for breakfast, have you?"

"No. I was up on the train all night," Meacham replied.

"Following a prospect?"

For a moment, Meacham wasn't going to answer; then he decided that Witherspoon might come in handy. They had worked together before, and Jensen was proving to be a little more difficult than Meacham had expected.

"As a matter of fact, I do have something going," Meacham said. "Are you interested?"

"I might be. How much is the reward?"

Meacham shook his head. "Huh-uh, it ain't that kind of a deal. This is what you might call a private job."

"But it is a paying job, right?"

"Oh, yes, it is a paying job all right."

"How much?"

"Five hundred dollars."

"You mean two hundred fifty apiece?"

"No," Meacham said. He took a swallow of his beer, then smiled across the table at Witherspoon. "I mean five hundred dollars for you."

"Really? How much are you getting?"

"What difference does it make to you how much I'm getting, as long as you get your five hundred?"

"It don't make no difference, I don't reckon," Witherspoon said.

"It involves killing," Meacham said.

"I don't mind killin' as long as I'm the one doin' the killin', and not the one getting' killed," Witherspoon replied with a little chuckle.

"Then you're in?"

"I'm in," Witherspoon said. "Who are we killin'?"

"Matt Jensen."

"Matt Jensen?"

"Yeah. Do you have a problem with that?"

"No, I don't have no problem with it. But I'm wonderin', do you know who Matt Jensen is?"

"I know him when I see him. We aren't what you would call pards or anything. Why do you ask? Do you know him?"

"Yeah, I know him. Well, what I mean is, I've never met him, but I know about him. And I know enough to know that he ain't goin' to be all that easy to kill."

"If he was easy, I wouldn't have even asked you to join in. Are you still in? Or does Jensen scare you?"

"Hell, yes, Jensen scares me. He scares anyone who has any sense. But yeah, I'm in. When do I get the five hundred dollars?"

"You ain't goin' to get the money till the job is done," Meacham said.

Chapter Eleven

As soon as Matt left the train, he walked down the street to the J.C. Jones Corral where he was met by a tall, very slender man with a large nose and a pockmarked face. The man was smoking a pipe, and he pulled it from his mouth as he greeted Matt.

"Yes, sir, what can I do for you?"

"Are you Mr. Jones?"

The man shook his head. "Jones died a couple of years ago and I bought the place from his widow. I kept the name 'cause folks knew it that way. I'm Keith Collins."

"Mr. Collins, I'm looking to buy a horse," Matt said.

"Are you now? Well, sir, you have come to the right place, I can tell you that." He stuck his hand out. "And you are?"

"Jensen. Matt Jensen."

"Matt Jensen, is it? I believe I just read about you, Mr. Jensen. Are you the same Matt Jensen who recovered the stolen bank money for the Bank of Pueblo?"

"Yes, I am. Unfortunately, I lost my horse while doing so."

"That's a shame. I know how much store a man can put in his horse. And I can see why you need a replacement right away. I tell you what, why don't you come around back and take a look at the livestock? That's where I keep the horses that I have for sale."

There were about a dozen horses in the paddock, and Matt pointed to an Appaloosa. "How about that one?" he asked.

"Yes, sir, I can tell that you have an eye for horses," Collins said. "He is the best one I have. Would you like to take him for a ride?

"If you don't mind."

"No, sir, I don't mind at all," Collins said. "Do you have your own saddle?"

"Yes, it's back at the depot."

"Well, you can go get it, or I can supply you with one."

"I prefer to use my own," Matt said.

"Can't say as I blame you. If you're buyin' this horse for your use, might as well get him used to the saddle he'll be wearin' right away," Collins said. "I'll move him out front and have him waiting for you when you get back."

"Thanks," Matt said.

* * *

"Looks like he's renting a horse," Meacham said to Witherspoon. "I wonder where he's goin'."

"Only one road out of here and it goes toward Cleo," Witherspoon said. He smiled. "And I know just where we can go to wait for him."

Matt was about half an hour out of Salida when he decided to go back into town. He had twisted around in his saddle to look back when a rifle cracked, and he heard the deadly whine of a bullet frying the air right by his head. Luckily, he had just changed positions in his saddle at almost exactly the same moment the rifle was fired. Had he not done this, he would be dead.

Matt leaped out of the saddle, snaking his rifle out of the boot as he did so. He slapped the horse on the rump to get it out of the line of fire; then he ran, zigzagging, toward a little knoll. Another bullet hit the dirt just after he zigged, and it whined away into the desert. Matt dived for the top of the knoll, then rolled over to the other side. He turned around then, and inched back up to peek over the top.

He saw no one.

Matt slipped back down, then put his hat on the end of his rifle and poked it up over the edge of the knoll. He held it there for a long moment, hoping to draw fire, but nothing happened. Then, when he was absolutely certain that there was no one there, he moved cautiously to where the ambusher had been.

Whoever had been there was gone, but Matt found the remains of a cigarette, and the spent brass casing of a couple of .44-40 shells, jacked out of the rifle by the assailant after firing. He also found tracks, indicating that there had been two men involved in the ambush, though as both shell casings appeared to come from the same rifle, only one had fired at him.

Who was trying to kill him? And why?

Matt chuckled as he considered the question. With as many enemies as Matt had made over the years—a better question might be, who wasn't after him?

Looking around, he saw the Appaloosa he had been riding, standing about a quarter of a mile away. Matt put his fingers to his lips and whistled. Such a whistle would have brought either of his previous horses trotting toward him, but this horse stood still.

"Well, at least you didn't run away," Matt said aloud, as he started toward the animal. It took him a couple of minutes to cover the distance between the horse and himself and, fortunately, the horse stayed in place for the entire time.

"You had a clear shot and you missed," Meacham said as he and Witherspoon rode back into town.

"The son of a bitch moved just as I fired," Witherspoon said.

"You missed," Meacham said.

"I'll get him next time."

"There won't be a next time."

"What do you mean?"

"I'll take care of him myself."

Though he was very alert on the ride back, there were no other attempts on his life. Matt returned to the corral, dismounted, and was patting the horse on the neck as the owner came out to greet him, a wide, salesman's smile spread across his face.

"So, what do you think, Mr. Jensen? Is this a fine horse, or what?"

"He's a good horse," Matt said.

Collins's smile broadened, and he rubbed his hands together in anticipation.

"So, I guess we need to talk price now," he said.

Matt patted the horse again, then began to remove his saddle.

"Oh, there's no need for you to remove your saddle," Collins said. "As soon as we close the deal, you can ride him away from here. Yes, sir, you are getting yourself one fine animal."

Matt looked at the horse, and thought of him standing there, even though he had whistled for him. It hadn't been that important today, but suppose it had been a matter of life or death. What, then, if he had a horse who could not respond to his whistle? And, he realized, it wasn't a matter of training. He had never trained either one of the Spirits—they had both possessed an innate understanding, a quality that, obviously, this horse did not have.

"I don't think I want him," Matt said.

The proprietor's smile was replaced by an expression of disappointment and surprise.

"What are you talking about? He is the best horse I've got, and you said yourself he was a good horse."

"He is a good horse," Matt said. "He just isn't the right horse."

"He's not? What is the right horse? Tell me, and I'll make sure you get one that is right."

Matt held the saddle draped over his shoulder.

"How are you going to do that?" Matt asked. "You just told me this was the best horse you had."

"Well, I—" The proprietor started to say, then changing his thought in mid-sentence, went on. "I'll tell you right now, you ain't goin' to find yourself no better horse in Salida. No, sir, nor none better in Fremont County, I'm a' thinkin'."

"I think you may be right," Matt said.

The proprietor, thinking he had won Matt over, smiled again. "Well, then, you need a horse and I've got a horse, so let's do a little business."

"Thank you, no, I believe I'll go somewhere else."

"Where? You just now agreed with me that there ain't no better horse in the whole county."

"I did, didn't I? I suppose that's why I'm going up to Eagle County."

"Eagle County? What's up there?" the perplexed proprietor asked.

"Sugarloaf Ranch," Matt replied.

Leaving the livery stable, Matt returned to the depot, where he bought a ticket for Big Rock. Then, with three hours to kill before the train was due to leave, he crossed the street to the saloon.

"Son of a bitch, that's him!" Meacham said when he saw Matt come into the saloon. He and Witherspoon were sitting at a table on the opposite side of the stove from the bar.

Witherspoon turned in his chair and saw Jensen order a beer.

"Will he recognize you if he sees you?"

"He saw me on the train coming up from Pueblo," Meacham said. "But I don't think he knows I'm the one that's been trying to kill him."

"Been trying? You mean there was another time before we tried out on the road?"

"Yeah, back in Pueblo," Meacham said. He told of trying to shoot Matt in his bed in the hotel, only to get the two men who were with him killed.

"I planned to kill him on the train," Meacham said, "but I never got the chance."

"You know your problem?" Weatherspoon asked.

"What?"

"You've been sending boys to do a man's job." Meacham stood up.

"What are you going to do?" Meacham asked.

"I'm goin' to kill Matt Jensen, and make myself five hunnert dollars," Witherspoon said.

"Not in here, you ain't."

"You want him dead, don't you?"

"Yes, but this ain't the place to do it."

"Dead is dead, and one place is as good as another," Witherspoon said as he slipped a knife from a sheath on his belt.

Meacham shook his head. "No, I don't have a stake in this," he said. "Not in here."

"Oh you'll have a stake in it, all right," Witherspoon said menacingly. "In fact, you have a five-hundred-dollar stake in it."

Witherspoon moved to the middle of the saloon floor, then stopped about twenty feet behind Matt.

Matt had just taken a drink of his beer when suddenly a knife flashed by in front of him. The blade buried itself about half an inch into the bar with a thocking sound. After that, the handle vibrated back and forth.

Instantly, Matt dropped his beer and, turning toward the direction from which the knife had come, drew his pistol even before the beer mug hit the floor. There was only one man standing behind him, and even if he wasn't reaching for his own pistol, Matt would have known that he was the one who threw the knife.

When the man saw how quickly Matt had drawn

his gun, he let his pistol fall back into his holster and held his hands up in the air.

"No, no," he said. "Don't shoot, Jensen. Don't shoot!"

"Why the hell not?" Matt replied coldly. "If you were a little better with that knife, it would be sticking out of my back right now."

"I was just—I was just tryin' to get your attention," Witherspoon said weakly.

"Yeah, well, you got my attention, all right."

"I didn't mean nothin' by it. It was just a bet, is all."

"Nobody is foolish enough to do something like that for a bet," Matt said.

When Witherspoon didn't answer, Matt asked, "You the one that's been dogging me?"

"What do you mean?"

"Someone took a couple of shots at me out on the road today."

"What makes you think it was me?"

"Because whoever it was wasn't much better with a rifle than you are with a knife."

"It wasn't me," Witherspoon lied.

"All right, it wasn't you. But this was. Why did you try to kill me? And don't tell me again that it was a bet. That will just get me riled enough to shoot you where you stand."

"All right, I was after you," Witherspoon said.

"Why?"

"You may not know this, Jensen, but you've got a price on your head."

Matt shook his head. "No, I don't," he said. "There is no paper out on me anywhere. I'm not wanted by the law."

Witherspoon smiled. "I didn't say nothin' about the law. I just said you got a price on your head. Someone wants you dead."

"Who?"

"I don't know."

"You must know. If you don't know, how do you expect to collect your money?"

"I won't be collectin' any money," Witherspoon said. "I'm through with it now."

"You expect me to believe that?"

"I'll give you my pistol," Witherspoon said. "That will prove to you that I'm out of it."

Holding his left hand out, palm facing Matt as if pleading with him to hold back, Witherspoon reached for his pistol with his right hand, moving very slowly.

"I'm just going to pull my gun out real slow now," Witherspoon said. "Don't go getting all excited or anything."

Matt watched as his adversary pulled his pistol from the holster. Then he turned the pistol around so that the butt was pointing toward Matt.

"See what I mean?" he said. "I ain't puttin' up no fight now, and this here saloon is full of witnesses who'll swear I was handin' you my gun. You can't shoot me now. If you do, you'll hang, sure."

"Who the hell are you?" Matt asked.

"The name is Witherspoon. Angus Witherspoon."

"Witherspoon? Yeah, I've heard of you."

Witherspoon smiled. "You have heard of me? Well, now, I'm just real flattered. I must be doin' pretty good for the great Matt Jensen to have heard of me."

"All right, Weatherspoon, hand me your pistol," Matt said, holding out his left hand.

In a totally unexpected maneuver, Weatherspoon executed a border roll, as fast as if he were drawing the pistol from his holster. Matt suddenly found himself looking down the business end of a Colt .44.

Matt had relaxed his own position to the point where he let the hammer down on his pistol, and had even lowered his gun. Now he had to bring his pistol to bear, while at the same time drawing back the hammer. And the fact that Weatherspoon had already started his own action, put Matt at a distinct disadvantage.

The quiet room was suddenly shattered with the roar of two pistols and the saloon patrons yelled and dived, or scrambled for cover. White gun smoke billowed out in a cloud that filled the center of the room, momentarily obscuring everything.

From his position at the far side of the room, Meacham was as surprised as everyone else. He hadn't been surprised by Weatherspoon throwing his knife; Weatherspoon had all but told him he was going to do that. But he was surprised by the way things had developed. Now, like everyone else in the saloon, Meacham stared at the cloud of smoke, waiting for it to clear enough for him to see what happened.

Finally, the smoke drifted away, and Meacham saw Weatherspoon standing there, a broad smile on his face.

Damn! Meacham thought. He did it! The son of a bitch did it!

Weatherspoon opened his mouth to speak, but the only sound he made was a gagging rattle, way back in his throat. The smile left his face, his eyes glazed over, and he pitched forward, his gun clattering to the floor.

Matt looked down at Weatherspoon for a moment, then holstered his pistol.

After that, bedlam broke out in the saloon as everyone hurried over to congratulate Matt, to shake his hand and to build a memory they could share with their grandchildren many years from now.

Conspicuously absent from the crowd of well-wishers was Lucas Meacham. And though Matt didn't know Meacham's name, he was quite familiar with him by now and he watched as Meacham hurried away from the saloon. He couldn't help but wonder if Meacham wasn't somehow involved in all this.

Chapter Twelve

The McCann Ranch, Dickey County, Dakota Territory

When the Fowlers arrived at the McCann place in their buckboard, they saw several other rigs already there, from surreys to buckboards to wagons. There were a number of children outside the house playing various games, and Green jumped down even before the buckboard came to a stop to join in.

"Green, be careful!" Sue scolded. "Don't jump down before we've even come to a halt. You can hurt yourself."

"I'll be careful, Ma!" Green shouted over his shoulder as he ran to join the others.

"Oh, the McCanns have such a beautiful place," Sue Fowler said as E.B. parked among the other vehicles. "Why, did you know that stained-glass transom above the door came all the way from St. Louis?"

E.B. chuckled. "Yes, so Ian has told me, more than once."

"Well if he is proud of it, I don't blame him."

Yesterday, Ian McCann had sent his son Leo, and his two riders, Dobbins and Toomey, to all the neighboring ranches inviting them to his house today for a meal and a discussion.

"Discuss what?" E.B. had asked Toomey.

"Mr. McCann didn't tell us that," Toomey replied. "All he said was to ask if you would come for a discussion and a meal." Toomey smiled. "And I'll tell you the truth, Mr. Fowler, when Mrs. McCann cooks up a big meal for company and all, it ain't somethin' you want to miss."

Cora McCann came out onto the front porch to welcome them, inviting Sue to join her and the other women in the kitchen, while E.B. was directed to the parlor.

"So, what are we going to do about Denbigh?" Curt Jennings was asking, just as E.B. stepped in through the door.

"Nothin', if you ask me," Louis Killian answered. "I mean, do you have any idea how many men he's got workin' for him? The best thing to do, I believe, is let Sheriff Hightower or Marshal Tipton handle it."

"Sheriff Hightower never comes up here, and you know it. You also know that neither Marshal Tipton nor any of the folks in Fullerton are goin' to do anythin' about it," McCann said. "Denbigh has them all buffaloed."

"Maybe the Petersons have the right idea," Donovan suggested.

"Peterson sold out to Denbigh," McCann said.

"Yeah, that's what I'm talkin' about."

"So did Thompson and Pratt," Putnam added.

"I talked to Don Peterson just before he and Marian left," Donovan said. "He went two years without making a crop. He said he couldn't hang on anymore, so he went back to Kentucky."

"Don't you see? That's what Denbigh wants," McCann said. "He wants us all to sell out to him."

"That would be better than just leaving," Donovan said. "And if we get squeezed down so much that we can't make it, the only thing we can do is leave our property for Denbigh to grab."

"If you ask me, this whole business about collecting a toll on the road is just a way of forcing us to leave," Byrd said.

"Which is why we're holding this meeting now, to figure out what is the best way to handle it," McCann said.

McCann was the one who had called all of his neighbors together to discuss the "Denbigh" problem. And though it was a serious meeting, it had turned into a social event as well, as evidenced by the gathering of wives in the kitchen putting together a meal that everyone would enjoy later in the day.

"Ian, is it true that the son of a bitch actually killed two of your cows for no reason?" Frank Tanner asked.

"Yes," McCann answered. "Well, it wasn't actually

Denbigh that done it. It was a fella by the name of Bleeker."

"That don't matter none whether it was Bleeker that killed your cows, or Butrum that killed them two strangers that come to town," Tanner said. "Both Butrum and Bleeker work for Denbigh, which means he was behind it, so as far as I'm concerned, he is as guilty as they are."

"Butrum isn't guilty," E.B. said.

"What do you mean he isn't guilty? You said yourself you seen him kill those two men," Jennings said.

"I didn't say he didn't kill them. I said he wasn't guilty. At least that's what it says in the paper." E.B. began to read from the latest copy of the *Fullerton Defender.*

"Displaying a total lack of moral courage, Marshal Tipton has refused to even hold a hearing on the terrible events so recently transpired.

"Ollie Butrum, a man who is known not only for his prowess with a firearm, but a willingness to use it, demonstrated his skill and callousness when, with but little provocation, he shot down Billy Gilbert and Jeff Hodges, the two cowboys who now lie buried in the Fullerton Cemetery, many miles from their home."

Putting the paper down, Fowler looked at the others. "Gentlemen, like it or not, this is what we are going to have to deal with, and we are going to be on our own. I'm afraid that it is exactly as Ian said. We aren't going to be able to count on either Sheriff Hightower or Marshal Tipton for help."

"Sounds to me like that newspaper fella—what's his name?" Killian asked.

"Bryce. John Bryce," Fowler replied.

"Yes. John Bryce. Sounds to me like he's the only fella in town who has any gumption in him at all," Killian said.

"Maybe so, but just talkin' about all this ain't gettin' us nowhere," Jennings said. "What we need to do is, we need to put our heads together and come up with an idea of what to do. We need some sort of a plan."

"Well, ain't that why we're here?" Killian asked.

"Yeah, McCann, you called this meeting," Tanner said. "Just what is it you have in mind? Or do you have any idee a' tall?"

"I've been thinking about it," McCann said, "and yes, I think I do have an idea. I believe we should all go into town at the same time, and when we come to the toll gate, refuse to pay the toll. If all of us stick together, they won't be able to do anything about it," McCann said.

"Now you're talkin'," Tanner said. "I've been sayin' all along that if we was to all go together, there wouldn't be nothin' Denbigh could do to us."

"I don't know," E.B. Fowler said. "I've been through the toll gate and the one thing I've noticed is, all the guards there have guns. I don't have to tell you that, Ian, seeing as they killed two of your cows."

"That's not a problem. We'll carry guns as well,"

Frank Tanner said. He smiled, and rubbed his hands together

"No, Frank, no guns," Ian said.

"No guns? What do you mean no guns? If they are armed, how are we going to fight them if we don't have guns?" Frank asked. Frank Tanner pulled his pistol out and showed it to the others. "They don't call the Colt an equalizer for nothin', you know."

"McCann is right. If we carry guns, there is sure to be shooting," E.B. Fowler said. "And if there is shooting, someone is goin' to get killed."

"Yes, well, that's generally what happens when you have a war," Frank said. "And this is a war as sure as the one we just come through. I was at Antietam, Chancellorsville, and Gettysburg, and by God, we showed those Rebels a thing or two. If I wasn't afeared of the Rebels, I ain't about to be afeared of some Englishman and the polecats he's got workin' for him."

"You forget, Frank, some of us were in those same battles," Killian said.

"Then you know what I'm talkin' about."

"Only we was on the other side," Killian added.

Tanner was quiet for a moment, then he nodded. "Yeah, well, we're all on the same side now, ain't we? All I'm tryin' to say is, when the killin' starts, we just need to make certain that nearly all the ones getting' kilt are the ones on the other side."

"It doesn't have to be a war," McCann said.

"Then you tell me what you're talkin' about,

Ian," Frank said. "Did you or did you not call this meeting after what happened to you when you tried to take your cows into the Indian agency?"

"I did."

"And did you not just say that we should all go together?"

"Yes."

"And what, exactly, are we supposed to do when we get to the tollgate? Get down on our knees and say, 'Please, sir, can we pass?'"

"Not quite like that," McCann said. "But I do think that if we present a united front, a group this large all refusing to pay the toll, there won't be anything they can do about it. I don't believe they would just start shooting us in cold blood."

"What makes you think that?" Tanner asked. "They kilt them two cowboys for purt near no reason a' tall. And don't forget they kilt your two cows, and while it's not the same thing as killin' a person, it sure shows what kind of people they are."

"Frank may have a point, Ian," Jennings said. "I mean, more than likely Denbigh's men wouldn't start shootin' us down in cold blood, but if they did take a mind to do it, oughten we to have some guns to defend ourselves?"

"If we have guns, it wouldn't be in cold blood, would it?" McCann replied. "I know it takes some courage for you to do what I'm askin' you to do, but I do believe our best chance is just to call their bluff."

"Ian, let me ask you this," Tanner said. "Did you think they would shoot your cows?"

"No, I didn't have no idea a' tall they would do somethin' like that," McCann admitted. "But cows aren't people. I don't think they would shoot a person down in cold blood."

"Oh, no? What about what happened in town?" Killian asked. "Didn't Butrum shoot those two strangers down in cold blood?"

"It wasn't exactly cold blood," E.B. said. "I was there, I saw it. The two strangers were armed. They were not only armed, they went for their guns first. I'm not saying Butrum didn't prod them into drawing, but they did draw first. And if they had not gone for their guns, I don't think Butrum would have shot them. Not in front of the whole town."

"The newspaper said Butrum drew with no provocation," Jennings said.

"No, it says that he had little provocation," E.B. corrected. "We don't know what kind of provocation they might have had. And, like I said, the two men were armed, and they did draw first. Or at least, they tried to draw first."

"That is exactly why I don't want us to go armed," McCann said.

"Who put you in charge?" Frank demanded.

"I put myself in charge," McCann said. "I'm the one that called this meeting, and I'm the one who suggested that we all go together next time we go to town. So if you are going to be a part of this, then I am in charge."

"I have no problem with Ian being in charge, whether self appointed or not," E.B. said. "But just to make it official, I say we vote on it. I nominate Ian McCann as head of our group."

"I second that," another said.

The vote was unanimous, including even a belated vote from Frank Tanner.

"Yeah, all right, I figure when you come right down to it, especially since you got the biggest ranch of all of us, that you are the one should be in charge," Tanner said.

"Good. If that's all settled, then I think we should go in next Saturday morning," McCann said.

After that, the meeting broke into several conversations, some about what was going to happen on Saturday, but several others of a more personal nature.

"Ian," Cora McCann said, sticking her head into the parlor. "I don't want to break up your meeting, but we can eat anytime you are ready."

"I was born ready to eat," Dennis Donovan said and the others, looking at his rather corpulent frame, laughed as they all started toward the dining room.

Of all the ranchers present, Ian McCann was the only one who could host such a meeting, because he was the only one who had a house large enough to accommodate so many people. Though there were too many people to sit at the table and eat, the table did serve a useful purpose by being filled with dozens of dishes of meats, vegetables, and bread, along with cakes, pies, and cobblers.

As the guests filed by the table, even the shiest among them had no trouble in filling their plates.

Ralph and Amanda Putnam, who were the Fowlers' nearest neighbors, found a place near them to sit and eat.

"Tell me, E.B.," Ralph said. "Do you really think we will be able to force Denbigh to take down that tollgate by doing this?"

"I don't know," E.B. answered truthfully. "But we've got to start somewhere. We can't just sit back and let him run roughshod over us like this."

"Maybe Frank is right," Ralph suggested. "Maybe we should all go armed."

E.B. shook his head. "I don't think so. Not yet anyway."

"Not yet?"

"Let's face it, Ralph. There may come a time when this develops into a shooting war. I hope it does not, but I will fight before I completely surrender to him."

"Yeah," Ralph said. "Yeah, I guess I will too."

Chapter Thirteen

Fullerton, Dakota Territory

As a newspaperman, John Bryce spent a lot of time visiting with the good citizens of the town of Fullerton, not only to sell advertising and subscriptions to his paper, but also to gather news and run down rumors. Following up on a few leads, John learned that the small ranchers and farmers of the valley were planning to gather into one large group to come into town on Saturday, hoping by sheer numbers to force their way through the gate. He decided that he would ride out to the gate to witness the confrontation.

"John, no," Millie said. "There's no telling what might happen out there. It's too dangerous."

John chuckled. "Darlin', Shiloh was dangerous, I was there. Fredericksburg was dangerous, and I was there too. What happens today will be newsworthy, but it won't be dangerous. And I wouldn't be much of a newspaperman if I let a little danger keep me from going out there to cover the story."

"All right, but please be careful," Millie said.

Realizing that the tollgate across the Ellendale Road would be the point of confrontation between the small ranchers, farmers, and Denbigh's men, John approached from Fullerton, which put him on the north side of the tollgate. He came to within sixty feet of the gate, then stopped. One of the gate guards, a man that John knew only as Bleeker, called out to him.

"You comin' through the gate, newspaperman?"

"I don't think so," John replied.

"Then what are you doing out here?"

John dismounted, tied off his horse, then climbed halfway up the side of a small hill and sat down. "I'm just taking the air," he said.

"Taking the air, you say? Well, my advice to you is, not to get in the way."

"Get in the way of what?"

"A bunch of pig farmers are going to try and surprise us, only we ain't the ones goin' to get surprised, if you get my meanin'. So, like I said, just don't get in the way," Bleeker repeated.

John wasn't all that surprised that Bleeker knew about what the farmers and small ranchers had planned. After all, *he* knew about it, so it wasn't that much of a secret. But exactly what that would portend, he had no idea.

The elevated area where John chose to wait did give him an excellent view of the tollgate, as well as the road on the other side, so he settled in to watch, not having any idea as to what might transpire. Shortly after he sat down, he saw someone else come up to join the two gate guards. He felt a start when he recognized that the new man was Ollie Butrum. Butrum was easy to recognize, because he was head and shoulders shorter than the other two men.

Although Butrum had killed the two young men in town a few days earlier, he was a fairly recent addition to Denbigh's company. But even before the shootout the other day, Butrum's reputation with a gun had become well known throughout the Dakota Territory.

For a moment, John wondered what Butrum was doing here; then he realized that Denbigh had probably decided to send Butrum to the tollgate to deal with the farmers and ranchers, rather than let Bleeker and Carver deal with them. That wasn't good. Bleeker and Carver were bad enough by themselves, but the addition of Butrum could only make the situation much more volatile.

Even as John was contemplating Butrum's presence, he saw, approaching from the south, a rather substantial body of men. The ranchers and farmers were coming, and John felt a sense of foreboding. He had come out here thinking the challenge to Denbigh's right to charge a toll might be newsworthy. But now, with Butrum standing alongside the gate guards, he feared it could turn into something much worse.

John wanted to yell at them, to tell them to go back, and he actually stood up, preparatory to doing just that, when Bleeker called out to the approaching riders.

"Hold up there!" Bleeker shouted, stepping out into the middle of the road in front of the gate.

The natural formation of the terrain amplified the voices so that from John's viewpoint he could hear, as well as see, everything that was going on.

"Where do you think you are going?" Bleeker's voice was challenging, almost taunting.

"We are going into town," McCann replied, his voice coming to him, a little more subdued by distance than was Bleeker's, but clearly defiant. The farmers and ranchers continued to approach the gate. That they were able to do so without further challenge emboldened them, and they came all the way up until stopped by the gate itself.

"Open the tollgate, Bleeker," McCann demanded.

"Are you in charge of this group?" Bleeker asked.

"I am."

"How many of you are there?"

"There are twenty-three of us."

"Then the toll will be twenty-three dollars."

"Bleeker, you can tell your boss that we don't intend to pay the toll," McCann said. "Not now, not ever again. And as you can see, we got no cows with us for you to kill. Now, kindly step aside and open that gate."

"I'll open the gate when you give me twenty-three dollars."

"And if we don't give you twenty-three dollars, what are you going to do? Do you plan on shooting two or three of us like you did my cattle?" McCann asked. "I don't think even you would shoot a man in cold blood, so I'm asking—no, I'm demanding, that you open that tollgate."

"Mister, you ain't in position to demand nothing. And you ain't goin' through the gate without paying the twenty-three dollars," Bleeker said.

"Yes we are, and by God you ain't stoppin' us," Frank Tanner said, moving away from the rest of them. That was when John saw that Tanner was holding a gun in his hand, and he was pointing it at Bleeker, who, so far, had not drawn his own pistol.

"Frank! I said no guns!" McCann shouted.

"I know what you said," Tanner called back. "Maybe the rest of you are afraid to face these people, but I ain't. No, by God, I ain't scaired at all."

Tanner turned his attention back to Bleeker. "And I'm tellin' you right now, mister, if you don't open that gate I'll shoot you as dead as McCann's cows."

Ollie Butrum stepped out in front of the other two guards and, though he had not drawn his pistol, it loomed large and ominous from his side.

"Put that gun away, cowboy," Butrum said.

"Oh, my God, Frank, do what he says!" McCann said. "That's Butrum, the one we were talkin' about."

"I don't care who it is," Tanner replied. "Maybe

the little turd ain't noticed that while his gun is still in his holster, mine is in my hand."

"You ain't afraid of me?" Butrum asked.

"Why should I be afraid of you? Like I said, your gun is in your holster, my gun is in my hand."

"So it is," Butrum said. "So it is. But your gun isn't pointed at me, is it?"

"No, it ain't. It's pointed at this feller, and you've just give me an idea. Iffen you don't unbuckle that gun belt and let it fall, I'll just have to blow this fella's brains out."

"Go ahead," Butrum said.

Tanner was a little surprised by the unexpected answer, and he blinked a couple of times.

"What? What did you say?"

"I said, go ahead, shoot him," Butrum said.

"Maybe you think I ain't serious," Tanner said.

"No, you told me you are goin' to do it, so I figure you are serious, but I don't care. Go ahead, kill him. He don't mean nothin' to me. I don't even like the son of a bitch," Butrum said.

With a loud yell, Tanner suddenly swung his pistol toward Butrum but, as he did so, Butrum drew, the gun appearing in his hand so fast that John wasn't certain it hadn't already been there. Butrum pulled the trigger and Tanner, with a look of shock on his face, dropped his pistol, then slapped his hand over a chest wound. Blood began spilling through his fingers as he fell back onto the road.

After the shot, at least ten men, all armed, came out of the trees alongside the road. John recognized

Slater, Dillon, and Wilson, but there were also some he had not seen before. That was when he realized that Denbigh, having heard of the plans of the small ranchers and farmers, had put into operation, a plan of his own.

"Well, now," Bleeker said. "It looks to me like Mr. Butrum just saved you boys a dollar. With that feller dead, that means you only owe me twenty-two dollars, and you can either pay me now, or you can turn around and go back home." He paused for a moment, then added, "Or you can try and force your way through and wind up just like your friend there. Which will it be?"

"Come on, men," McCann said, turning his horse. "We're goin' home."

A couple of the men with McCann dismounted and picking up Tanner's body, laid it belly-down over his own horse. Then, remounting, they rode off with the others.

"If any of you folks want to come through here on your own and pay the toll, why you'll be mighty welcome," Bleeker called out to them as they rode away. He, and the men with him, laughed out loud.

John Bryce had not shown himself throughout the entire event. Now, sick at heart over what he had just witnessed, and angry to his very core, he remounted his horse and rode back to Fullerton.

As the newspaper editor rode back to town, he began composing the article he was going to write.

His newspaper was a weekly, and the next issue wasn't due until Thursday, but he had no intention of waiting that long. He was angry, and he wanted to take advantage of that anger in order to give the story the piquancy it needed.

John Bryce was forty-five years old, and had been in the newspaper business for twenty-five years. A bad leg had kept him from the war, but he had become a correspondent for *Harper's Weekly*, covering the war from battlefield and campground, facing the same dangers and hardships as if he had been a soldier.

After the war he came West, working for one newspaper after another until his chance encounter with Matt Jensen enabled him to buy a press and start his own newspaper. Before coming to Fullerton, he had published newspapers in four other towns. He had named his newspapers *The Avenger, The Crusader, The Monitor,* and *The Guardian*, choosing such names in keeping with his philosophy of being an investigative journalist, always ready to crusade for truth, right, and justice.

Oftentimes, he would attach himself to the fortunes of a particular town, moving on when the town itself went bust. But sometimes, he was forced to leave when his method of crusading journalism stepped on too many toes. Two years ago, which was one year after he'd arrived in Fullerton, Dakota Territory, he'd met and married, Millie, the daughter of Reverend Landers, the preacher of the only church in Fullerton. On their wedding night, he took an oath to quit moving from town to town, promising her that the *Fullerton Defender* would be his last newspaper.

He had been here for a little over three years now, and in that time had built up quite a loyal following. But a newspaper could only be as successful as the town it served, and that was becoming a problem. Fullerton had once shown great promise of developing into a productive city—there had even been talk of building a spur railroad to connect them to the Chicago and Western at Ellendale. But now the town was dying, and the cause of the demise of Fullerton was Nigel Denbigh.

John had already written a few articles about Denbigh, and though he knew that most of the citizens of the town agreed with him, a few had asked him to tone it down a bit.

"Why be such a crusader?" Doc Purvis had asked. "You are just going to get yourself on Denbigh's bad side, and he doesn't seem to me to be the kind of man you want to anger."

"I don't have any choice, Doc," John had told him. "Denbigh is killing this town and if this town dies, so does my paper. I promised Millie I would stick it out here, and I don't intend to let some English son of a bitch take over this town without a fight."

John's wife, Millie, was cleaning the newspaper office and arranging the type for Thursday's issue when she heard John come in.

"Well, was your ride out there newsworthy?" she asked.

"Yeah, it was newsworthy," John replied. The tone of his voice was flat, and pained, and Millie picked up on it immediately.

"What happened?" she asked.

"They killed Frank Tanner, Millie. They shot him down in cold blood."

"Oh, John, no," Millie gasped. "His poor wife. Amy will be lost without him."

"Yes," John said.

"And he was shot down in cold blood, you say? Who did it?"

John sighed. "Actually, it wasn't really cold blood," he said. "Tanner had his pistol out and was threatening to use it. He always was pretty much of a hothead; you remember how he got into a fight with that miner at the dance that night, just because he asked Amy for a dance."

"Yes, I remember. Who shot him, do you know?"

"Oh, yes, I know. It was Butrum, the same person who shot those two cowboys."

"And you say Frank already had his gun out?"

"Yes."

"Then that means there won't be anything done about this killing either, will there? Butrum will just go on killing with impunity, backed by Denbigh and tolerated by the marshal and this town. Nobody will do anything about it."

"No, that's not true. I'm going to do something about it."

"Do what? I don't like it when you talk this way."

"I'm going to put out an extra."

"An extra? Oh, John, I don't know. So many people have pulled their advertising from us that we barely have enough money to put out our regular paper. Do you really intend to do an extra?"

"Millie, the name of this newspaper is the *Fullerton Defender. Defender,*" he repeated. "If I don't do something to defend the rights of the people of this town, then the paper is not worthy of its name."

"What will an extra do but get more people upset with you?"

"A strongly written article can do much to arouse an oppressed people. You have heard of Thomas Paine, haven't you?"

"Yes, of course I've heard of Thomas Paine," Millie said.

"You might call me the Thomas Paine of the West. Only, instead of a broadside, I'll be putting out an extra."

Before starting, John walked over to the front door, turned the sign around to read CLOSED, and pulled down the long, green shade that shut off the door window. "Now, you set the type, I'll dictate the story."

Millie walked over to the type trays. Placing the line sticks on the press form, she looked up at her husband.

"I'm ready," she said.

"These are the times that try men's souls," he began.

* * *

It took but one hour to print five hundred newspapers, that number being sufficient to supply a paper to virtually every family in the county. Once the print run was completed, John stepped out onto the front porch of his office, put his fingers to his lips, and gave a loud whistle.

Hearing the whistle, Kenny Perkins came out of his ma's boardinghouse, and when he did so, John waved him over.

"I have some papers for you to deliver," John said when Kenny arrived.

"Today? But this ain't paper day," Kenny said.

"I put out an extra. Don't worry, you'll get paid extra to deliver it."

"Yes, sir," Kenny said.

After Kenny delivered all the papers to the subscribers, he stood out on the street corner shouting "Extra" until the rest of the papers were sold. Less than an hour after he left the office, he came back with the collected money, wearing a broad smile.

"Here you are, Kenny, fifty cents," John said, counting out the pennies. "You did a good job. Thank you."

"Yes, sir, and thank you," Kenny said. "Mr. Bryce, everyone is talkin' about your paper today. I didn't get a chance to read it, but you must've said somethin' important, 'cause whatever you wrote got 'em all riled up. But riled up in a good way," he added quickly.

"I hope it did, Kenny. I sure hope it did," John said.

Shortly after Kenny left, Mayor Adam Felker came into the office, clutching a copy of today's extra.

"John, are you crazy?" he asked.

"I don't think so, Mayor," John said.

"Well, I think so. Writing this article isn't going to do a thing in the world but make Denbigh mad."

"Good, that's what I set out to do," John said. "And if you are honest with yourself, Adam, you will agree with me."

"Well, what if I do? The point is, Denbigh has us between the rock and the hard place. Why, do you know that right now almost eighty percent of all business done in this town is through Denbigh? If he was to pull his support away from Fullerton and take it somewhere else, say up to Lamoure, or Penequa, or down to Emma, where do you think that would leave us?"

"Free of him, I would hope."

"Bankrupt, that's where," Mayor Felker said. "Now, I think you ought to write a retraction and put it in Thursday's newspaper."

"A retraction?" John laughed. "What good would that do? And what would make anyone believe me anyway?"

"You could say you've been thinking about it,

and you have second thoughts," Felker said. "You're a good writer, John, you could make it just real believable."

"Tell me, Adam, do you think the rest of the town thinks just as you do?"

"I know they do," Mayor Felker replied.

"Has a citizens' committee come to you and asked you to come talk to me about this?"

"Well, no, but . . ."

"John!" someone shouted from the street. "Excellent story! You said what is on everyone's mind! Keep up the good work, the whole town is behind you!"

"Thank's, Ernie!" John replied, shouting his answer over the mayor's shoulder. He turned back to Felker. "Well?" he said.

Felker started to say something, and though his jaws worked, nothing came out. Finally, and in obvious anger and frustration, he turned to leave, finding his voice just before he stepped down from the porch.

"This is going to mean trouble, John," he said. "You mark my words, this is going to mean trouble."

Chapter Fourteen

Prestonshire on Elm

"Yes, Mr. Tolliver?" Denbigh asked, looking up from the book he was reading.

"Mr.—Butrum—is here to see you, sir," Tolliver said, as always setting Butrum's name apart to show his disdain for the man.

"Show him in, please."

"Yes, m'lord," Tolliver said with a respectful dip of his head.

Denbigh put a bookmark between the pages he was reading, then closed the book and set it aside. Before Tolliver returned with Butrum, Denbigh poured whiskey into a glass, and he handed it to the little man when he came in.

"Thanks," Butrum said. He took a drink.

"What is it, Mr. Butrum?" Denbigh asked. "Why have you left your post in town?"

"I came out here 'cause that newspaper editor has done wrote another one of them articles. He put it out in somethin' that's called an extra. All the folks in town is talkin' about it."

"Well, what does he say?"

"It's all full of highfalutin talk, so it's kind of hard for me to understand all that much, to tell you the truth. But I figure a smart man like you can most likely read it and figure it out all right. So, that's why I brung one of them papers with me for you to see."

Denbigh cringed, and ground his teeth at the fractured grammar, but he said nothing, realizing that a silk purse could not be made from a sow's ear.

"So, Mr. Bryce put out an extra, did he? And it is all about me?"

"Yes, sir. And it ain't just about the shootin'. It goes on about the toll and the like. Like I said, it's got a lots of folks in town talkin'."

"Let me read it," Denbigh said, reaching for the paper.

Butrum had the paper folded up and stuck inside his shirt. Reaching in between the buttons, he pulled out a folded sheet of paper and handed it to Denbigh.

Denbigh turned his nose up slightly as he took the paper from him. Then he read aloud, the first line.

"These are the times that try men's souls." He stopped reading then, and laughed out loud. "Oh, good one, Mr. Bryce, very good. Don't you think so, Mr. Butrum?"

"I don't know," Butrum said. "I don't know what that means."

"You've never heard that line before?"

"No, sir, I ain't."

"Well, Mr. Butrum, it is a line that is borrowed from one of your own treasonous rebels."

"Who would that be?"

"Thomas Paine."

Butrum shook his head. "No, sir, I don't reckon I ever met nobody by that name," he said. "Least-wise, not that I can recall."

Denbigh chuckled softly, then continued. "I believe you said that all the people in town are talking about this article?"

"Yes, sir, ever'where you go, you hear folks talkin' about it," Butrum said.

"What are they saying?"

"Well, sir, they're sayin' they don't think it's right for you to be a' collectin' a toll like you're doin'. And they are wonderin' why no one is doin' nothin' about it."

"I see."

"But then some of 'em is worried about it and say they don't think the newspaper fella should be writin' articles like that." Butrum chuckled. "They don't want to make you mad."

"Sensible people, I would say," Denbigh said.

"If you ask me, Mister, uh, that is, Lord Denbigh. The fella that is causin' all the trouble is this here newspaperman."

"I would say that you are right," Denbigh said.

"Just messin' up his office like Slater and them boys done ain't goin' to stop this man. No, sir, he's got more gumption than just about anyone I've ever seen."

"I suppose that is right," Denbigh said. "He is a troublemaker."

"Iffen you want me to, I can fix it so he won't be givin' you no more trouble," Butrum suggested.

"How?"

"I'll kill him for you, if you want me to."

"I wouldn't say we are ready to go that far yet," Denbigh said. "You just keep doing what you are doing. Make certain nobody gets in or out of town without paying the toll."

"I may have to kill a few more people," Butrum suggested. "I hope that don't bother you none."

"Mr. Butrum, other than your unique talent for killing, can you think of any other reason I might have hired you?" Denbigh asked. "Why should that bother me?"

"Just so's you know," Butrum replied, not entirely sure that he understood what Denbigh just said.

"I don't care how many people you kill," Denbigh said. "As long as you manage to keep it legal. If your activities result in your being indicted for murder, you are on your own. I will neither defend you, nor will I pay a lawyer to defend you. Do you understand that, Mr. Butrum?"

"Yeah. All I have to do is make them draw first."

"Now, I want you to wait around for a moment or two. I'm going to write a letter to Mr. Bryce, and I want you to take it in town to the post office."

"No need to do that, Mr. Lord Denbigh. I can just take the letter directly to Bryce his ownself."

Denbigh shook his head. "No," he said. "No, I do believe the letter will have more effect if you take it to the post office. It will be more official that way."

"Yes, sir, whatever you say," Butrum said.

Butrum waited quietly until Denbigh finished the letter. Once he finished, Denbigh folded it, put it into an envelope, then sealed it.

"This feller you got workin' for you, Tolliver?" Butrum said as Daveport handed him the envelope.

"Yes, what about Mr. Tolliver?"

"I get the opinion he don't care much for me," Butrum said.

"Your feeling is accurate. He doesn't like you."

"Why not? I ain't never done nothin' to him."

"No, and you never shall," Denbigh replied. "Not if you intend to remain in my employ."

Fullerton, Dakota Territory

John Bryce was setting type for the regular weekly newspaper when Millie came into the newspaper office. Smiling, she held out several envelopes.

"Look at this!" she said enthusiastically.

"What is it?"

"It's mail, silly. Mail from people about the extra edition we put out."

"Ha! I thought you said you were opposed to the extra edition."

"I was then, because I thought it was a waste of money. But if we get this many letters in response, that means it has struck a resonant cord. And that has to convert into more business for us. Why, I'll bet we get half a dozen new advertising accounts from this."

John chuckled. "Accounts. Is that all you think about? Don't you care a whit about the responsibility of a newspaper to look out for the public?"

"We can't very well look out for the public if we don't have enough money to publish," Millie said.

"Touché, my dear. I suppose you do have me there," John said. He finished setting the line in a composing stick, then fit the stick into the printing bed.

"Listen to this letter, from the fire chief, Walter Bowman," Millie said. "'In times of trouble the people of our great nation have always been able to count upon the valor and industry of its most courageous citizens. You, sir, have the soul of a crusading journalist, and our fair community is blessed to have you as our advocate.'

"And this one from Paul Deckert," Millie continued. "'Keep up the good work, John, the whole town is behind you.'"

Millie picked up the next letter, but didn't open it. "Oh," she said, the tone of her voice changing. "This one can't be good."

"Why not? Who is it from?"

"It is a letter from Mr. Denbigh."

"Read it."

"I'd rather not. You read it."

Millie handed the unopened envelope over to

John. He opened it, then pulled out the single page. He read for a moment, then smiled.

"All right," he said. "Now we are getting somewhere."

"Getting somewhere? What do you mean? What does the letter say?"

"He says that I may have had a point with my article, that perhaps he is hurting business in town. He also says that he would not want to kill the town as it serves a necessary function. He asks me to come talk with him."

"Are you going to go see him?"

"Yes. After all, I'm the one that organized the ball. I at least owe him a dance," John replied, chuckling at his own joke.

Two miles south of Fullerton, on the Fullerton-Ellendale road, John reached the tollgate. Bleeker and Carver were sitting on the side of the road, and Bleeker, sucking on a long stem of grass, got up to approach him.

"You know the rules, newspaperman," Bleeker said. "It's going to cost you a dollar to get through."

"I will not pay one dollar to pass through here," John said. "I received a letter from Denbigh asking me to come speak with him. I will not pay a dollar merely for the privilege of speaking with a despot."

"What is a despot?" Carver asked.

"It means someone who is assuming more power

than is rightly his, someone like Denbigh who is acting like a tyrant."

"A what?"

"Never mind," John said. "I'm afraid you lack the necessary intelligence to comprehend the meaning. Open the gate."

"Not without you pay the dollar."

"Let him through," Bleeker said.

"You know what Lord Denbigh said. He said ever'one has to pay."

"But the newspaper editor here is goin' to see the boss. I say let 'im through."

Carver thought for a moment, then swung the gate open. "All right, mister, you can go on through."

John nodded, but said nothing as he rode by the open gate, heading toward Denbigh's house.

Ten of the several thousand acres of Preston-shire on Elm had been set aside and exquisitely landscaped. These were the grounds on which Denbigh's house, Denbigh Manor, was situated. It was a house one might expect to see in the English countryside, but scarcely on the range in Dakota Territory. Three stories high with a mansard roof and corner towers. Nigel Denbigh had gone all out to create the most grandiose home he could. The house was approached by a long, wide avenue, paved with white limestone and lined with aspen trees. The avenue ended at a large, circular drive in front of the house, the centerpiece of which was a dramatic statue of Denbigh himself.

John was met by a uniformed groomsman, who held the horse as the newspaper editor dismounted.

"I'm here to see Denbigh," John said.

"Yes, sir," the groomsman said. "If you will avail yourself of the bell pull at the front door, someone will see to you."

"Avail myself of the bell pull," John repeated. He chuckled. "Someone teach you to say that?"

"Yes, sir, Mr. Tolliver, he taught us all to say that whenever someone comes up," the groomsman said. "I will give your horse food and water," he added as he led John's horse away.

John climbed the broad steps up to the porch, then, crossing the porch to the huge carved oak door, he pulled on a rope that hung alongside. He could hear the melodic chimes echoing from within the house, and a moment later, Mr. Tolliver answered. John recognized Tolliver, because he had seen him in town before.

"Denbigh invited me to come visit with him," John said, purposely using his last name only.

Tolliver winced at the disrespectful tone, but he invited John into the house.

"Wait here, sir, I will see if the master of the house is receiving," Tolliver said.

This was the first time John had ever been in the house, and he looked around at what he could see as he waited, taking in the dramatic ceiling heights, the white oak flooring, the custom moldings, and the decorative architectural columns, as well as a grand, sweeping elliptical staircase.

A moment later, Tolliver returned.

"Lord Denbigh is in the library," he said. "If you would follow me, sir?"

The library, as John knew it would be, was a beautiful room of rich mahogany, lined with book-shelves that were filled with books of various sizes and hues. Denbigh was standing in the middle of the room, wearing a white robe that featured upon the left breast the Denbigh family crest, a black lion with red claws, rampant against a white shield, filled with stars of black *fleur-de-lis*.

"Mr. Bryce," Denbigh said. "I am pleased that you accepted my invitation."

"I'm here," John said. "What do you want to talk about?"

Denbigh walked over to his desk, then picked up a folded copy of the *Fullerton Defender.*

"These are the times that try men's souls," Denbigh said, reading aloud the opening line of John's extra edition. He laid the paper back on the desk. "You are quite the crusading scribe, aren't you?"

"It's called freedom of the press. While we don't have titles in America, we do have freedom of the press. It's in our Constitution. You have heard of our Constitution, haven't you?"

"What would it take, Mr. Bryce, to hire your services?"

"Hire my services? What do you mean, hire my services? Hire my services for what?"

"I would like to hire your services to be my advocate, rather than my adversary," Denbigh said. "Such things are done, I know. It would not be unprecedented, nor would it be unsavory to hire you to write something favorable about me."

"It would be more than unsavory, it would be absolutely dishonest," John replied.

"Would it?" Denbigh picked up an earlier copy of the *Defender*, and began to read. "Fuller and Simpson, men's furnishing goods, shirts and underwear of all kind, the finest men's furnishing goods store in America."

Denbigh put the paper down and smiled at John. "Really, Mr. Bryce. Are you telling me that there is no other men's furnishing goods store anywhere in America that is as good as Fuller and Simpson?"

"That is merely an advertisement, sir," John explained. "A certain degree of hyperbole is allowed, indeed is expected, in advertisements."

"Well, then, that should ease your conscience," Denbigh said. "I will hire you to write favorable advertisements about me."

"No," John said. "I cannot, and I will not. I believe that your actions are stifling, indeed, killing, not only Fullerton, but nearly all of Dickey County. I will not support you. On the contrary, I will fight you as hard as I can."

"I'm sorry to hear that, Mr. Bryce. I'm just real sorry to hear that," Denbigh said. "I had hoped that you and I could come to some sort of an accommodation."

"That was my hope as well. You said in your letter that you thought I had a point in my article. In fact, I believe you said you would not want to kill the town as it serves a necessary function."

"Did I?"

"You did. I took that to mean that you were willing to discuss removing the toll from Ellendale Highway."

"You took it wrong," Denbigh said. He made a motion with his fingers toward Tolliver.

"Yes, m'lord?"

"Do show Mr. Bryce out, will you, Mr. Tolliver?"

"Yes, m'lord."

"That's it?" John said. "This is the end of our conversation?"

"Mr. Bryce, do be careful on your ride back to town," Denbigh said ominously.

Chapter Fifteen

Big Rock, Colorado

When Matt stepped down from the train in Big Rock, he waited on the platform until his saddle and saddlebags were off-loaded. Then, picking them up, he walked across the road from the depot to Mercer's Corral where, according to a professionally lettered sign, one could RENT HORSES, BUCKBOARDS, AND WAGONS.

"Yes, sir, I'll be right with you," the proprietor said when Matt walked into the barn through the wide-open double doors. The proprietor was putting a horse into a stall.

"No big hurry, Bob, I never like to disturb a man at his work," Matt said.

Hearing himself addressed by a familiar voice, Bob turned, then, smiled broadly.

"Well, Matt Jensen, as I live and breathe," he said jovially, hurrying toward the opening with his hand extended.

Matt shook his hand.

"What can I do for you?" Bob asked.

"I just came in on the train," Matt said. "I'd like to rent a horse for a while."

"Yes, sir, I'll pick out a good one for you," Bob said. "Are you going to be here long?"

"Not too long," Matt said. "I thought I'd ride out and visit with Smoke for a spell."

"Yes, I thought that might be what brought you here. Is Smoke back?"

Matt looked confused. "Back? I don't know— I didn't know he was gone. This wasn't a planned trip, I just happened by."

"Well, he may be back, I don't know. All I know is he left a few days ago, for who knows where. You never know with Smoke, he is one travelin' man. Oh, but this time Sally didn't go with him, so even if he isn't here, you can say hi to her."

"Yes, I'll do that," Matt replied, disappointed that his old friend Smoke might not be home.

Sugarloaf Ranch

"Miss Sally?" Cal called in through the back door of the main house. "Miss Sally?"

"Yes, Cal, what is it?"

"There's a rider a' comin'."

"Oh, is it Smoke?"

"No, ma'am, it ain't him. I don't know who it is."

"Oh!" Sally said, seized by a sudden fear. "Oh, God in heaven, Cal, you don't think . . ." She let the sentence die in her throat, too frightened to give words to the terrible thought that maybe something had happened to Smoke and this was someone who had come to tell her.

"No, ma'am, I don't think that," Cal said, understanding what she meant. "If somethin' had happened to Smoke, it would more'n likely be Sheriff Carson comin' to tell us, or maybe Mr. Longmont. It wouldn't be no stranger."

"Yes," Sally said. "I'm sure you are right."

Sally walked out onto the porch and looked toward the rider. For a long moment, the anxiousness did not leave her face. Then, suddenly, she relaxed and broke into a great smile.

"Well, I'll be. It's Matt," she said. "My goodness, I haven't seen him in ages."

"Matt who?" Cal asked. "Who is Matt?"

"An old friend," she said as she stepped down from the porch and hurried to meet the rider with a welcome wave.

Fifteen minutes later Matt, Pearlie, and Cal were sitting around the kitchen table. Sally was in the kitchen as well, but at the moment she was standing by the stove, with the oven door open. The kitchen was redolent with the sweet aroma of freshly baked bear claws.

"You should'a seen 'im," Cal said. "Pearlie hung on to that bull like a tick on a dog, an' no matter what that bull did, goin' this way and that, humpin' up in the middle, kickin' out his hind legs, he couldn't shake Pearlie."

"Cal didn't do bad his ownself," Pearlie said. "He won the calf-ropin' and the bull-doggin' contest."

"I'm sure Smoke will be proud of both of you," Matt said. "I'll tell you the truth, Miss Sally, that smells mighty good," Matt said.

"Sally makes the best bear claws in Colorado," Pearlie said.

"Sally makes the best bear claws in the world," Cal added, not to be outdone.

"You boys don't have to butter me up," Sally said. "I'm baking enough bear claws to satisfy even your appetites."

"Too bad Smoke isn't here to enjoy them," Cal said.

"Yes, I had hoped to see Smoke," Matt said as he took a bear claw from her. "Where is he anyway?"

"He is in Nevada," Sally said. "Nicole's brother, Bobby Lee Cabot, got himself into some trouble, and Smoke went to help him out."[2]

"Really? What sort of trouble has Bobby Lee got himself into? I haven't seen him in a long time."

"Wait a minute, you know this fella, Bobby Lee, do you?" Cal asked.

"Sure do."

"How come you know him and we don't?"

"Cal, Matt knew Nicole, Smoke's first wife," Sally said.

---

[2] *Shootout of the Mountain Man*

"Wow, I had no idea you had known Smoke that long," Cal said.

"Oh, I knew Smoke long before he ever thought about marrying Nicole," Matt said. "But yes, I knew Nicole. I also knew Art, their baby."

"Yeah, I know about Smoke's first wife and his kid," Cal said. "And I know they was both kilt, and Smoke kilt the ones who done it. Didn't know you knew them, though."

Sally laughed. "That's understandable, Cal, since you didn't even know about Matt until a few minutes ago."

"When did you first meet Smoke, Matt?" Pearlie asked.

"You might say that Smoke met me," Matt replied.

"What do you mean?"

"I was nothing but a kid, starving and freezing to death in the mountains, when Smoke found me. If he hadn't found me when he did, I would've been dead within another few hours."

"You might say that Smoke's finding you was quite fortuitous," Pearlie said with a broad smile.

"Why, Pearlie," Sally said. "Fortuitous? I'm impressed."

"Yes, ma'am. I learned that word while I was at the rodeo in Denver, and I've been lookin' for a chance to use it."

"Speaking of that, Matt, one might also say that your stopping by is quite fortuitous."

"Fortuitous in what way?" Matt asked.

"Yesterday, I received a letter for you. I was going to give it to you before you left, but this seems as good a time as any."

"A letter for me?" Matt asked, surprised by the statement.

"Yes. Well it was addressed to Smoke, but when I opened it, I saw that it was actually meant for you."

"Who is the letter from?"

"It is from a man named John Bryce. Do you know him?"

"John Bryce?" Matt thought for a moment. Then he smiled and nodded. "Yes, I remember John Bryce. Smoke and I met him a long time ago. I was about to be tried for robbery and murder, the charge lodged by a crooked assayer. And since I was a stranger to the town, the sheriff took his word over mine. I hadn't been tried yet, but it wasn't looking good for me, and Smoke had already determined to break me out of jail if need be. Of course if he had done that it would have made criminals out of both of us. But, just before the trial, John Bryce, who was a journalist for a local newspaper at the time, wrote a story that cleared me. And I have a letter from him, you say?"

"Yes. Just a moment, I'll get it for you."

Dusting a residue of flour from her hands, Sally walked over to a secretary/bookcase, opened the curved-glass door, and took out an envelope, which she handed to Matt.

Matt remove the letter from the envelope, then turned it slightly to catch the morning sunlight.

The cursive letters were formed by neat and even strokes on the stationary.

"He sure has a neat hand, doesn't he?" Matt said.

"He certainly does," Sally agreed. "I taught school for seven years and never encountered anyone with such penmanship."

Dear Mr. Matt Jensen,

I do hope you remember me, though as our paths crossed so long ago, I would not be at all surprised if you have forgotten the humble journalist whose investigative reporting once freed you from the unjust accusation of murder and robbery.

Although I intend this letter to be for Matt, I am addressing to Smoke, because whereas I know that Smoke Jensen can be reached at Surgarloaf Ranch, I do not know how to get in contact with Matt. I feel some degree of confidence that this will reach Smoke, and I ask, if you are still in contact with Matt Jensen, that you forward this missive to him.

Matt, I recall that you once promised to come to my aid should I ever require it. I require it now, though I am ever mindful of the fact that any obligation to me, if it had ever existed at all, would have been totally satisfied by your generous donation of money by which I was able to start a newspaper. I hasten to add, however, that it is not for me alone that I seek help, but rather for the people of the town of Fullerton, and the county of

Dickey, in Dakota Territory. The hapless citizens of this fair community are sorely in need of justice, that commodity being denied us by the nefarious operations of an evil Englishman who, by stint of wealth and land holdings, holds us all in his grip. The person of whom I speak is Nigel Cordell Denbigh.

I have no wish to make a request that would be a disruptive imposition, but if you are available, and if you would be so inclined as to pay a visit to the offices of my newspaper, The Fullerton Defender, in Fullerton, Dakota Territory, I would be eternally grateful. I must tell you, though, that any help you might supply us would have to be gratis, for I can offer you nothing but the guarantee of good home-cooked meals prepared by my wife, Millie, an uncomfortable bed in our spare room, and the undying gratitude of a newspaper editor who is giving test to the adage "The pen is mightier than the sword."

> *Your friend,*
> *John Bryce*

When Matt finished the letter, he folded it, returned it to the envelope, then handed it to Sally.

"How long have you had the letter?" Matt asked.

"Just since yesterday," Sally replied.

"That means it is still timely."

"I would think so. Are you going to answer his request?"

"Yes, I'll go. I would be honored to go. I'll leave right away."

"I don't know the man, but if he is responsible for saving you from hanging, then I am glad you are going to help him," Sally said.

"Now I need to ask a favor of you," Matt said.

"Of course," Sally said.

"I need a horse," Matt said. "Spirit broke his leg and I had to put him down."

"Oh, Matt," Sally said, reaching her hand across the table to rest on his arm. "I know what Spirit meant to you."

"Yes, ma'am," Matt said. "He sort of carried on the spirit of the first Spirit, if you know what I mean. I'd like another horse that can do that as well, and seeing as I got Spirit One from Smoke, I think it would be really good if I could get Spirit Three from him as well. Of course, I intend to buy him, not take him as a gift the way I did the first one."

"Smoke took Seven with him, but he left Drifter behind. You can have any horse but Drifter. Cal, take Matt out to the corral."

"Yes, ma'am," Cal said. "Uh, Miss Sally, does that mean *any* horse?"

Reading the expression on the young man's face, Matt knew what was troubling him.

"Cal, point out Drifter, also the horses you and Pearlie are riding. I'll pick from the rest."

A wide, relieved smile spread across Cal's face. "Yes, sir, come on out. Smoke has some really great horses."

After looking through the horses in the Sugar-loaf stable, Matt saw one that appealed to him. Examining the horse carefully, he saw a coat that glistened like burnished copper, though his long tail was somewhat lighter. The horse was just under seventeen-and-a-half hands at the withers, completely blemish free, and a model of conformation

"What do you think about that one?" Pearlie asked.

"Do you know the horse?" Matt asked. He rubbed the horse behind his ear, and the horse dipped his head in appreciation.

"I know him. He's a good horse," Pearlie said. "He can run like the wind and he'll hold to a good trot all day without tiring."

"What do you think, Spirit?" Matt asked. "You want to come with me?"

"You're going to name him Spirit?"

"That is his name," Matt said.

"I thought you said your other horse was named Spirit."

"Both my other horses were named Spirit."

Pearlie chuckled. "You're just like Smoke. He names all his horses Seven or Drifter."

"I find nothing strange about that," Matt said. "If you find a good name, why give it up?"

Walking over to the rental horse, he removed the saddle, then put it on Spirit Three. Spirit stood tall and proud, accepting the saddle without the slightest complaint.

"Yes, sir," Matt said. "We're going to get along just fine."

As Matt tightened the saddle cinches, Cal and Pearlie stood with him. He finished, just as Sally came out of the house, carrying a small sack.

"You didn't have to come out here," Matt said. "I was going to come back in to pay you for the horse, and to tell you good-bye."

"If I took money for the horse, Smoke would be all over me," Sally said. "He's yours."

"I don't feel right about just taking him without paying you."

"Then take it up with Smoke next time you see him." Sally held out a little sack. "I thought you might enjoy these. I'm sending some bear claws with you," she said.

"Thanks," Matt replied. "I know that I will enjoy them."

"But you kept some behind, didn't you, Miss Sally?" Cal asked.

"I kept some behind," Sally said.

Matt took the bear claws, shook hands with Cal and Pearlie, then swung into the saddle. Pearlie had put a lead bridle on the rental horse, and he handed it to Matt.

"You can just leave this lead bridle with Mr. Mercer at the livery in town," Pearlie said. "One of us will pick it up, next time we go in."

"Thanks," Matt said. He touched the brim of his hat. "Tell Smoke I'm sorry I missed him, but I'll drop back by sometime in the not too distant future."

"I will," Sally said. "Be careful, Matt. I don't know what was behind this letter, but I've learned, since living with Smoke, that most of the time when someone sends a letter like that asking for help, it's not just a walk in the park."

Smoke nodded, then slapped his legs against Spirit's side, riding out at a gallop. This was as good a time as any to see what the animal had in him.

Chapter Sixteen

Prestonshire on Elm

"Excuse me, m'lord," Tolliver said, stepping into the study of Denbigh Manor.

Denbigh, who was cleaning his dueling pistol, looked up when Tolliver came in.

"Yes, Mr. Tolliver, what is it?"

"There is a—gentleman—by the name of Lucas Meacham who wishes to have an audience with you." Tolliver showed that he did not believe Meacham was actually a gentleman by the way he sat the word apart from the rest of the sentence.

"Meacham is here?" Denbigh asked, surprised by the announcement. "What is Meacham doing here? I thought he was . . . never mind, show him in."

"Yes, sir."

Denbigh did not put the pistol away but was, instead, aiming it at an imaginary target when Tolliver showed Meacham in to the study.

"Ha!" Meacham said. "What the hell is that?"

"This is a single-shot percussion dueling pistol made by A. Kehlner of Prague. It is a .58-caliber, eight-and-seven-eighths-inch ribbed round barrel, exquisitely made, and perfectly balanced," Denbigh said.

"What do you think somethin' like that can do?" Meacham asked. "Especially since it only has one shot."

Denbigh aimed the pistol at Meacham, and pulled the hammer back. "One shot is enough," Denbigh said, his words cold, quiet, and calculating.

"What? Look here, what are you doing?" Meacham asked, putting his hands out in front of him. "Point that thing somewhere else."

Denbigh held the pistol steady for a moment as Meacham squirmed; then, with a smile, he lowered it, and eased the hammer back down.

"Evidently, you think it quite capable of killing someone as well," Denbigh said.

"Did you say that was a .50-caliber?" Meacham asked.

"It is a .58-caliber."

"That's the size of a small cannonball. Hell, yes, it can kill someone."

"Why are you here, Mr. Meacham? Am I to gather by your presence that you have dealt with Matt Jensen?" Denbigh asked.

Meacham rubbed the back of his hand across his mouth. "Uh, no, not exactly," he answered.

"What do you mean, not exactly? You have either taken care of the matter, or you have not," Denbigh said. "Which is it?"

"I have not," Meacham replied.

"Then I will ask you again. Why are you here?"

"Mr. Denbigh, do you know this man Jensen?"

"You will address me as Lord Denbigh."

"What? Oh, yeah, Lord Denbigh. I'm sorry, I forgot."

"To answer your question, no, I do not know anything about him."

"Yes, sir, well, you said you had never heard of him, so I guess you don't know, but he is one of the best known pistoleers in the West. His name is practically legend, and he is one hard son of a bitch to kill."

"Why? Won't a bullet kill him, just as it would any other human being?"

"Yes, sir, that's not what I meant. What I meant was, getting that bullet into him. It's like he has nine lives or something. And like I said, he is damn good with a gun."

"I thought you were good with a gun," Denbigh said. "Isn't that why I hired you?"

"Yes, sir, I am good with a gun, but this man, Jensen, well, sir, he's about as good as they come. I don't reckon there's more'n two or three people in the country who are as good as he is."

"Would you be one of those two or three?"

"As a matter of fact I am," Meacham said.

"Then, what is the problem?"

"The problem is, we ain't talked about money."

"Of course we have. In the telegram I sent you, I

clearly said that you would be compensated as before," Denbigh said.

"Yes, sir, but what I want to know is, how much money are we talking about? Because the, uh, compensation you give me last time, well, that was for someone who barely knew which end of the gun a bullet come out of. It's different with Jensen, and what you paid last time ain't enough for this job."

"How much do you think this job is worth?" Denbigh asked.

"Three thousand dollars," Meacham said.

"Three thousand dollars?"

"Yes, sir."

"That's twice as much as I gave you for your last job."

"Yes, sir. But like I said, Jensen is twice as hard to kill."

"All right. If you get the job done, I will pay you your price."

"Good," Meacham said.

"Unless Mr. Butrum kills him first."

"Wait a minute. You have hired someone else to kill Matt Jensen?"

"Not specifically," Denbigh said. "But I have hired someone who is quite skilled in the use of firearms, and has demonstrated to me a willingness, no, I daresay an eagerness, to ply his trade. If he encounters Matt Jensen before you do, then he may kill him. That would save me the three thousand dollars I just promised you."

"Who is this Butler person anyway?"

"Oliver Butrum."

Meacham snorted.

"You have a comment?"

"Yeah, I ain't worried, 'cause he ain't goin' to kill Matt Jensen."

"How do you know he won't?"

"'Cause I've never heard of him. And if I've never heard of him, he damn sure ain't goin' to be good enough to kill Matt Jensen."

"We will just have to see, won't we?" Denbigh said.

By way of dismissal, Denbigh picked up an oiled cloth and began cleaning his pistol again. When he saw that Meacham had not yet left, he looked up.

"You have something else?"

"Yes, sir."

"What?"

"I, uh, don't know where Matt Jensen is. I mean, I found him, but before I could do anything, I sort of lost track of him."

"Well, Mr. Meacham, you can't very well kill him if you don't know where he is, can you?"

"No, sir."

"Hadn't you better be looking for him?"

"Yes, sir, but the thing is, seeing as you are the one who wants him dead, well, I was thinking that maybe you might know where he is."

Denbigh chuckled. "Most astute of you, Mr. Meacham," he said. He lifted his pistol and Meacham grew tense, but relaxed when he saw Denbigh aim the gun at something outside the window.

"The truth is, I do not know where he is at this exact moment, but I have a pretty good idea of where he will be soon."

"Where?"

"Here, Mr. Meacham. Or at least, in Fullerton. It would seem that Fullerton has a crusading journalist, and that journalist has written a letter to Matt Jensen, inviting him to come to town. I don't think it will be for a social visit."

"Do you know when he is coming to Fullerton?"

Denbigh looked at Meacham with an expression of annoyance. "No, I'm afraid he did not clear his itinerary with me."

"Well, then, I'll just go into town and wait on him," Meacham said.

"Yes, you do that," Denbigh replied.

Denbigh loaded his pistol, then fit it with a percussion cap. "I'll walk you outside," he said.

Meacham was visibly nervous at seeing Denbigh with a loaded pistol, but he walked outside with him. Once outside, Denbigh pointed to a prairie rose. The small, pink wildflower was some thirty yards distant.

"Would you like to see a demonstration of the Kehlner dueling pistol?"

Meacham chuckled. "You ain't goin' to tell me you can hit that flower from here with that thing, are you?"

Denbigh didn't answer. Instead, he aimed, and pulled the trigger. The percussion cap popped, then concurrent with the boom of the pistol, there was a flash of smoke and light. The heavy-caliber bullet destroyed the prairie rose.

"As I said, Mr. Meacham, one shot is enough," Denbigh said.

"Yes, sir, I reckon it could be," Meacham said.

The groomsman who had taken Meacham's horse from him earlier now came toward him, leading the animal.

"Mr. Meacham?" Denbigh said as Meacham swung into the saddle.

"Yes, sir?"

Denbigh gave Meacham a dollar. "You will come to a tollgate on the road between here and town. Give the men who are manning the gate this dollar, and they will give you a coupon. When you get into town you will encounter Butrum. Butrum will ask you to show him a coupon, proving that you paid the toll. Show him that coupon."

"Since I'm workin' for you, won't they just let me through? Especially if you give me a letter or something?" Meacham asked.

"Yes, I'm sure they would," Denbigh replied. "But I don't want anyone to know you are working for me, not the men at the gate, and not Mr. Butrum. When you get to town, try and remain as inconspicuous as you can until you get the opportunity to attend to your task."

"All right, whatever you say, Mr. Denbigh."

Denbigh glared at Meacham.

"Lord Denbigh," he reminded him.

* * *

Meacham had been on the road for about half an hour when he saw the tollgate. Someone stepped out into the road in front of him. For a moment he contemplated telling them that he worked for Denbigh, and keeping the dollar. After all, a dollar was a dollar.

But for some reason, Denbigh didn't want anyone to know that Meacham was working for him, and he didn't want to anger Denbigh, because he didn't want to take a chance on losing the three thousand dollars he was going to get for killing Jensen.

"Where you headed?" the man at the tollgate asked.

"What difference does it make to you as long as I pay the toll?" Meacham asked.

"No difference at all, I reckon. That will be . . ." Bleeker started to say, but when he saw Meacham extending a dollar to him, he stopped in mid-sentence. "A dollar, yes," he said. "Well, good for you, you had the money all ready. How did you know how much the toll was?"

This would be his opportunity to say that Denbigh told him, but he restrained himself.

"I'm not here to palaver with you. Just open the damn gate and let me through," he said.

Bleeker took the dollar. "Well, it's good to see that you are a good citizen. Oh, and if you are goin' into town, more'n likely you are going to run into a sawed off runt of a fella, a real little man by the name of Butrum. He's goin' to want to see this coupon, so it's best you don't lose it. Oh, and when he asks you to see it, you show it to him, you hear? Butrum might be a little fella, but he ain't the kind of man you want to piss off."

"I'll keep that in mind," Meacham said.

Chapter Seventeen

Denver, Colorado

Matt had a six-hour layover in Denver, which was plenty of time for him to take care of something he needed to do. After making certain that Spirit was taken off the train and secured in the depot stable, Matt went out front of the depot and caught a ride on one of the horse-drawn trolleys. He stepped off the trolley ten minutes later in front of the Federal Building. The office of the man he was looking for was on the second floor, and when Matt opened the door to the office, he was greeted by an officious-looking young man.

"Yes, sir, may I help you?"

"I would like to speak with Marshal Connors," Matt said.

"May I tell the marshal who is calling, and the subject of the visit?"

"You don't need all that, Simmons, I recognize the voice," a loud, gruff voice called from behind the frosted-glass window of a door. The door was jerked open and Matt saw a giant of a man standing there.

"Matt Jensen, you reprobate, come on in here," he said, greeting him effusively. "What brings you to Denver?"

"Hello, Charley. I have a favor to ask," Matt said.

Connors chuckled. "Doesn't everyone? But Lord knows, I owe you a favor or two."

Three days later

Matt had been dozing in his seat when he felt the train beginning to slow. The change in the train's velocity caused him to wake up, and when he looked out the window, he saw nothing but rolling prairie and distant mountains.

"Ellendale," the conductor called as he walked through the car. "We're comin' into Ellendale. Unless you're going back with us, folks, you are all going to get off here because this is where the track ends."

The conductor's announcement galvanized all the passengers into action and, bracing themselves against the movement of the car, they began removing their personal belongings from the overhead rack.

After three days of travel, and having changed trains three times, Matt was now on the Northern Pacific, the final leg of his journey. He continued to stare through the window as the train slowed even more for its entry into the town of Ellendale. As had been the case in every town they had passed through, there were several people standing on the platform, not as potential passengers, nor even to meet arriving passengers, but just to be present for the most exciting event of the day, the arrival and departure of the train. The train lurched to a stop alongside the small depot, and everyone in the car prepared to disembark since, as the conductor had explained, this was the final stop.

Stepping down from the train, Matt walked forward to the stock car, where he waited as his horse was off-loaded. He walked up to it, then rubbed it behind the ears.

"I'll bet you've been wondering what was going on," he said. "Well, it's over now. What do you say you and I take a long ride?"

A quick perusal of the county map inside the depot showed him that Fullerton was about twenty miles northeast of Ellendale.

"Just keep that low-lying range of hills to your right," the stationmaster told him. "You can't miss it."

"Thanks," Matt said.

It was nearly noon when Matt saw a boy standing out behind a house, drawing water from a well. Matt's canteen was low, and Spirit was thirsty, so he sloped down the hill and headed toward the compound, which consisted of a house, barn, what appeared to be a granary, and an outhouse.

Seeing him approach, the boy called over his shoulder.

"Pa! Pa! Stranger's a' comin'!"

So as not to appear hostile, Matt swung out of the saddle about thirty yards before approaching the yard. Then he led Spirit and walked the rest of the way, reaching the yard at about the same time a man came out onto the porch. The man had a rifle in his right hand, though at the moment, he was holding it low, by his knees.

"Good afternoon," Matt said, touching the brim of his hat.

"Can I do something for you, mister?" the man on the porch asked. The boy, who was about twelve, moved around behind the well, obviously schooled by his father to be in position to get down behind the well if necessary.

"The name is Jensen, Matt Jensen," Matt said. "I'm on my way to Fullerton and I saw the boy at the well. The truth is, my canteen is empty, and my horse is thirsty. I was wondering if I could trouble you for some water? I would be glad to pay you for it."

"Pay for it, you say?"

"Yes, sir."

"You don't ride for Denbigh, do you? He owns just about everything you can see around here except for the hills. And if he had his way, he would own them too."

Matt shook his head. "I don't ride for Denbigh."

"I didn't think so. Not if you offered to pay for the water. Neither Denbigh, nor anybody who works for him, would pay for anything if they could get away with it. Help yourself to the water."

"Thanks. And I'm serious about paying for it."

"No need for that. The Lord put the water in the ground, doesn't cost me anything to take it out, and it don't seem to me that it would be Christian for me to charge for it. What did you say your name was again?"

"Jensen. Matt Jensen."

"My name is Fowler, Edward B. Fowler, but most folks just call me E.B. That's my boy, Green."

"Green?"

"Back in Texas we had us a two-year drought before he was born," E.B. said. "My wife took it real hard, thought maybe she wasn't ever goin' to see anything green again, so when the boy was born, we named him Green just so she could see green anytime she wanted."

E.B. laughed, and Matt laughed with him. He dipped the dipper into the bucket, then glanced up at E.B.

"Sure, go ahead, take a drink," E.B. invited. "I'll wager it'll be about the best-tasting water you ever put in your mouth."

Matt drank deeply and the water was cool and sweet. E.B. was right about the water. If it wasn't the best water he had ever tasted, it was certainly equal to it. He began pouring it into his canteen and as he did so, Spirit started pawing at the ground.

Matt looked around at his horse, then back toward E.B. "Do you have a watering trough somewhere?"

"Just inside the corral fence," E.B. said. "Your horse can drink all he wants."

"Thanks," Matt said. "And you were right about the water. It is very good."

"Would you like me to lead your horse to the water, Mr. Jensen?" Green asked.

"Why, thank you, Green, I'm sure Spirit would appreciate that."

"Spirit?"

"That's my horse's name."

"Come along, Spirit," Green said, taking the reins. Spirit looked at Matt.

"It's all right, you can go with him," Matt said.

Spirit followed the boy easily.

"That's a good-looking horse," E.B. said. "Well trained too."

"He's not trained," Matt said. "He's just smart."

E.B. chuckled. "I hear you," he said.

"E.B., who are you talking to?" a woman asked, coming out onto the porch then. The woman was younger than Matt would have imagined E.B.'s wife to be, and very attractive, though rather tired looking. She was wearing a white apron over a dark gray dress, and though most of her hair was covered by an unattractive bonnet, Matt could see by the tendrils that hung from the bonnet that her hair was a rich, chestnut color. She was holding a long-handled wooden spoon in her right hand, while with her left arm she was cradling a large wooden bowl.

"Sue, this gentleman is Matt Jensen. He stopped by for water."

"Mrs. Fowler," Matt said with a slight nod of his head. He touched the brim of his hat in a salute.

"Why don't you invite him for dinner, E.B.?" Sue said. "It's about ready."

"Of course. Won't you stay for dinner, Mr. Jensen?"

"Oh, I don't know, I certainly would not want to intrude on your family," Matt said.

"It's not an intrusion," Sue Fowler said. "We get company so rarely here that your presence would be most welcome."

Matt smiled. "The thought of a home-cooked meal does beat eating jerky," he said.

"If you want, I'll have Green take the saddle off your horse and let him loose in the corral," E.B. said. "No doubt he needs a break too."

"Thanks."

"Green, unsaddle Mr. Jensen's horse and put some fresh hay out," E.B. called over to his son. "If we're going to feed Mr. Jensen, we may as well feed his horse as well."

"All right, Pa," Green called back.

"Better let me unsaddle him," Matt said. "Spirit is still new, and I don't know but what he might get spooked if someone else took the saddle off."

Matt walked out to the corral and removed the saddle. Spirit dipped his head a few times, then trotted once around the corral before coming back to the trough where Green had put fresh hay.

When Matt returned to the house, Green was pouring warm water into a basin. The boy handed Matt a bar of soap and a washcloth.

"Ma says you have to wash up, before you can eat," he said.

"Green!" Sue called from inside. "I said no such thing! I said he could wash up, not that he had to."

"You always tell me I have to wash up," Green replied.

"That's different."

"What's different about it? Don't adults get dirty too?"

Matt chuckled. "We do indeed," he said. "I think I have to wash up."

A few minutes later, Matt was sitting at a table that featured fried chicken, canned string beans, mashed potatoes, gravy, and biscuits.

"Oh, my," Matt said as he looked over the food. "And to think I almost turned this down."

Green reached for a drumstick, but Sue glared at him and he pulled his hand back.

"Not before your father says grace," she said.

Green bowed his head, as did Matt, while E.B. blessed the meal.

"Bless this food to our use, and ourselves to your service, amen."

"Amen," Sue and Green said.

"Out here, we don't get to church all that often," E.B. said after the blessing. "I reckon blessing the meal is about as close to churchifying as we can get."

"We used to go into Fullerton ever' Sunday just to go to church," Sue said. "It's a Baptist church. We were Methodists before we came up here, but it's the only church in town, so that's where we go.

At least, that's where we used to go. We don't go anywhere now."

"Yes, well, we can't do it now, Sue, and you know it. It costs us two dollars to go into town and another two dollars to come back home. We can't afford to go to church anymore."

For a long moment, Matt had been aware of Green staring at the pistol strapped to his side, so when Green asked the question, Matt wasn't surprised.

"Mr. Jensen, why do you wear a gun?" Green asked.

"Green! What sort of question is that to ask a guest?" Sue scolded.

"I just wondered why he was wearin' a gun is all," Green said. "Pa don't wear no gun. And Mr. Byrd and Mr. McCann, they don't wear a gun neither. Mr. Tanner used to wear a gun, but he got killed by Mr. Butrum, who is the same one we saw kill those two cowboys, remember?"

"It's not something I want to remember," Sue replied.

"But you do remember it, Ma. How could you forget it? We seen him shoot down them two cowboys."

"Hush now," Sue said. "I told you it wasn't something I want to remember. It's not something I want to talk about either."

"I was just wonderin' why Mr. Jensen is wearin' a gun, is all."

"Mr. Jensen is a traveling man," E.B. said. "I

expect it's some comfort to wear a gun when you travel."

"Are you a good shot?" Green asked Matt.

"Tolerable," Matt answered.

"I'd sure like to see you shoot it sometime."

"Green, that's enough. Mr. Jensen didn't come here to be pestered by the likes of you," E.B. said.

"I didn't mean to be pesterin' you, Mr. Jensen," Green said by way of apology.

"I don't feel pestered, Green," Matt said. "And your pa is right. I'm wearing a gun because I travel a lot, and that means I take most of my possessions with me. My gun is one of my possessions, and the easiest way to take it with me is to wear it."

"There now. Are you satisfied?" E.B. asked his son.

"Yes, sir," Green answered contritely.

"Good. Perhaps we can eat the rest of our meal in peace," Sue said.

They talked during the meal. E.B. and his wife were originally from Texas. "After I come back from the war, well, the Yankees was comin' down with a pretty heavy hand, and even heavier taxes. It finally got to where I couldn't take it anymore. Then I read that there was good land for home-steading if you was willing to come up here to the Dakota Territory. So, we decided to sell everything we had and come up here."

"We decided?" Sue asked.

"Now, Sue, you know very well that if you had

said you didn't want to come, that we would have never left Texas."

Sue reached across the table to lay her hand on E.B.'s hand. "I knew that you wanted to come," she said softly. "And wherever you go, that's where I'll be.

Matt ate with great relish. When he finished, he pushed back from the table and rubbed his stomach appreciatively.

"Mrs. Fowler, I cannot remember when I had a better meal. You are a wonderful cook."

"Why, thank you, Mr. Jensen. Thank you very much."

Matt stood. "I need to be going on, but I do wish you would let me pay for this wonderful meal."

"Nonsense, what sort of hostess would I be if I charged my guests?"

"Then I will sing your praises, not only as a gracious hostess, but a wonderful cook," Matt said. "Mr. Fowler—"

"E.B., please."

"E.B., it has been a pleasure and I hope to meet you again sometime soon."

"Well, if you stay in these parts for a while, I'm sure we will meet again," E.B. said. "Will you be staying here for a while? Uh, not that it is any of my business," he added quickly.

"I'm not sure how long I will be here," Matt said. "But I would like to ask you something. You mentioned a man by the name of Denbigh. Who is he?" Matt remembered that Denbigh was the name mentioned in John Bryce's letter.

"He is an Englishman, Lord Nigel Cordell Denbigh," E.B. said.

"*Lord* Denbigh? I thought there were no titles in America."

"There aren't. But he makes anyone who works for him call him Lord. And if you want to do business with him, you also call him Lord."

"When I first rode up, you asked if I rode for Denbigh. What made you think that?"

"I'm sorry I accused you. Just a little spooked, I guess."

"Have you had any run-ins with him?"

"Not directly," E.B. said.

"Except for what happened when you joined Mr. McCann and the others to try and force your way through the tollgate," Sue said. "Frank Tanner was killed."

"Like I said, that wasn't a direct run-in with Denbigh. That was a run-in with some of his men."

"It's the same thing," Sue said. "And after all, his collecting a toll is why we don't go to church anymore," Sue said.

"You said something a moment ago about it costing you two dollars to go to town and another two dollars to come back," Matt said. "Is that what you were talking about? A toll?"

"In order to go into town you have to take the Ellendale Road and it goes right through the middle of Denbigh's property," E.B. said. "He has men positioned there to charge you a toll."

"It isn't his road," Sue said. "Ellendale Highway

is a public road, laid out by the Territory of Dakota. Mr. Bryce wrote about it in his paper. He said the road was constructed by the Territory of Dakota as a public thoroughfare to which people should have clear and unfettered access. I guess we should be thankful to him that he doesn't charge a toll for the young people who have to go into town to go to school. If he did, that would be two dollars per day, and we couldn't afford it."

"Oh, yes, Denbigh is a very compassionate man," Sue said sarcastically.

"I'm not takin' up for him, Sue. I'm just sayin' we should be thankful he doesn't charge the kids who are going to school."

"We don't need to be thankful to him for anything," Sue replied resolutely.

"If the road is public, Denbigh has no right to charge anyone a toll, even if the road does run through his property. Why doesn't the sheriff do something about it?" Matt asked.

"The sheriff is down in Ellendale, and he doesn't pay that much attention to what goes on in Fullerton. Fact is, he doesn't pay that much attention to anything that goes on in the whole valley. Denbigh pretty much has Elm Valley all staked out for his ownself. In fact, he not only controls the valley, he just about controls the whole county."

"How can he do that? Doesn't Fullerton have a mayor, city council, or marshal?"

"Mayor Felker is a businessman and so are all the people who are on the city council, and Denbigh bein' their biggest customer, they don't want to do anything that would piss him off."

"E.B., mind your language!" Sue said sharply.

"Sorry, Sue, but that's the way it is, and you know it. Like I said, the sheriff don't pay no attention to what goes on up here, and Marshal Tipton isn't goin' to do anything unless he has the backin' of the mayor and the city council. What we need is someone with a little gumption."

"Like the newspaperman," Sue said.

"Yes, but all he has done is write articles about it. We need more than words. Words don't mean anything to someone like Butrum."

"Butrum? Who is Butrum?" Matt asked.

"Ollie Butrum is the one who killed Frank Tanner, and the two cowboys that Green was talking about a moment ago," E.B. said. "He is a paid killer for Denbigh. He is the ugliest, most dried-up little runt you ever saw in your life. In the real world, he would be someone you wouldn't give a second look to. But this isn't the real world, and Butrum has everyone terrified."

"We seen him kill the two cowboys," Green said.

"Green is right," E.B. said. "We went into town for supplies and were unwilling witnesses to it. Two young men challenged Butrum and he killed them both."

"He's real fast," Green said. "He's the fastest I've ever seen."

Despite himself, E.B. chuckled. "And you have seen so many," he said.

"He must be pretty good if he took on two at the same time," Matt suggested.

"There is nothing good about that evil little man," Sue said, hissing the words in a way that showed her revulsion of the man.

"Have you ever shot anybody with your gun?" Green asked.

"Green!" Sue scolded sharply.

"It's all right, Mrs. Fowler," Matt said. "Young boys are curious about such things, I know that."

"So have you?"

"It's not something you ever want to do," Matt replied, being as non-specific as he could.

"But you have shot somebody, I'll bet."

"That's enough, Green," Sue said. "We'll have no more talk about shooting people."

"I'll bet you could beat Butrum. I'll bet you could kill him," Green said.

"Green, I said stop it now, and I mean it!" Sue said. "I'm sorry, Mr. Jensen, I don't know what has gotten into him."

"It's all right. As I said, boys are curious about such things." Matt picked up his hat. "But I really must be going now. And I want to thank you again for a wonderful meal."

Sue began clearing away the table, but E.B. and Green followed Matt outside. Green retrieved Matt's horse, and Matt put the saddle back on, then gave Green a quarter. "Your ma and pa wouldn't take any money for that wonderful meal, but that doesn't mean you can't take a little money for your excellent handling of my horse," he said.

"Gee, thanks!" Green said.

Matt swung into the saddle, then touched the brim of his hat as he looked toward E.B..

"E.B., I thank you again for your hospitality, and do tell Mrs. Fowler of my appreciation for the wonderful meal she cooked," Matt said. "I hope someday that I can repay you in some way."

"One never knows," E.B. said. "You take care now."

Chapter Eighteen

Not too long after Matt left the Fowler place, he saw a gate stretched across the road in front of him. There were two men watching the gate, which was mounted on a pivot so it could be swung open. One of the men stepped out into the road and held out his hand.

"Where are you headed?" he asked.

"Nowhere. Anywhere," Matt said. "Wherever this road leads."

"For you, this road don't lead nowhere beyond this here gate, without you payin' a toll."

"How much is the toll?"

"A dollar."

"Who is collecting the money?"

The two men looked at each other for a moment, then laughed.

"That's a dumb question, mister," the man who had stopped him said. "What's it look like, who is collectin' the money? Me and Carver here." He nodded toward the other gate guard, who was standing just off to one side.

"If you are collecting for the Dakota Territory, I'm afraid I'm going to have to see some authority," Matt said.

"We ain't collectin' for Dakota. We're collectin' for Lord Denbigh, and that's all the authority you need."

"This is a public road."

"Not no more, it ain't. It comes right through the middle of Prestonshire on Elm. That's Lord Denbigh's property, and that makes it his road. If you want to pass through it, you're goin' to have to pay the toll."

"I have no intention of paying a toll to pass on a public road. Open the gate."

"You know what, Bleeker? I think maybe he don't hear so good," Carver said as he reached for his pistol. But when he saw a gun suddenly appear in Matt's hand, he let his own pistol drop back down into its holster. Matt's draw had been so fast that by the time it registered with Carver that Matt was drawing, he had already done so.

"Take off your pistol belts and hand them to me," Matt said. "Both of you."

"Mister, have you gone loco? Do you have any idea who you are up against?"

"I believe this man called you Bleeker, and you said his name was Carver, so, yeah, I know who I'm up against. Now, Mr. Bleeker and Mr. Carver, this is the last time I am going to ask you. Take off your belts and hand them up to me."

"Lord Denbigh ain't goin' to like this. He ain't goin to like it none at all," Carver said.

"Who are you, mister?" Bleeker asked.

"The name is Jensen, Matt Jensen."

"We'll be runnin' into each other again, Jensen."

"I expect we will," Matt said. "Now, take off those gun belts like I said."

Bleeker and Carver removed their gun belts and passed them up to Matt. He looped both of them around the saddle pommel. "Open the gate," he ordered.

With a scowl on his face, Bleeker complied.

"Mister, them guns cost money," Carver said.

"Really? Take the money out of the toll you've collected so far."

Matt slapped his legs against Spirit's sides, and the horse burst forward as if being shot from a cannon. Within less than a minute, he was half a mile down the road.

"Are we goin' after him?" Bleeker asked.

"And do what? We ain't got no guns. He took them, remember? And even if we did, did you see how fast he drew his pistol? I mean, he was sittin' on a horse, but still draw'd that gun faster'n anyone I ever seen. I wouldn't be surprised if he wasn't faster'n Butrum," Carver said.

"I doubt that. I don't think there's anyone faster than Butrum," Bleeker said.

"Yeah? Well, as far as I'm concerned, that's a

question better left decided between Butrum and this feller. I can tell you true, I ain't about to go up against him for no dollar. Especially seein' as it ain't even my dollar we'd be fightin' over," Carver said.

"Yeah, I guess you're right. What did he say his name was?"

"He said his name was Matt Jensen."

"You ever hear of him before?"

"No."

"Me neither. Think we should tell Lord Denbigh about it?"

"Hell, no. You know how he is. If we tell him, he'd more than likely make us pay the dollar."

About one mile beyond where he had been stopped, Matt dropped the pistol belts and guns on the side of the road, then continued on his way. Half an hour later, he saw something that, from this distance, seemed little more than a series of low-rising lumps of clay and rock. As he drew closer, however, the lumps began to take on the shape of houses and buildings, until they finally materialized into a recognizable town. Just on the outside of the town was a sign that read FULLERTON. It gave both the elevation, 1442 feet, and the population, 312.

In his wanderings through the West, Matt Jensen had encountered scores, maybe hundreds of towns like this, so that after a while there was a sameness to all of them. He had never been to Fullerton, but the houses of ripsawed lumber and false-fronted businesses were all familiar to him.

An earlier rain had left the street a quagmire, the mud and horse apples melded together by horse hooves and wagon wheels so that it was now one long, stinking ribbon of slime. There was no rain now and the sun, currently a blazing orb midway through the afternoon sky, beat down upon the manure and the mud, creating a foul-smelling miasma to offend the nostrils and burn the eyes of all who dared to go outside.

On Monroe Avenue, halfway between First and Second Street, Matt saw the office of the newspaper, identified by a sign as the *Fullerton Defender.* Matt rode over to the building, dismounted, then pushed the door open and stepped inside.

"I know I had more capital f's than this," a man was saying as he was searching through his type boxes. "I can't very well set an ad that says window and door frames without the letter f now, can I?"

"You could spell frames with a ph," a woman replied.

"Ha. Door p-h-r-a-m-e-s. Mr. Johnson would love that now, wouldn't he?"

"Here you are, John. Maybe this will help," the woman said, holding out a box.

"F's! Yes! Millie, I love you. I would even marry you if I wasn't already married!"

"What would your wife say about that?" Millie asked.

John smiled. "Oh, I think she would approve."

John and Millie kissed, then, with a start, Millie pulled away. "Oh," she said.

"What?"

"It appears we have company."

John turned toward the front of the room and saw a man standing there, smiling.

"Can I help you, Mister. . ." John started. Then he stopped in mid-sentence. "I remember you. You are Matt Jensen!"

"It's good to see you again, Mr. Bryce." Matt extended his hand.

"Please, it's John, not Mr. Bryce," John said as he shook Matt's hand. "I wasn't sure you would come."

"Why not? You asked me to, didn't you?"

"Yes, it was shameless of me to hold you to a passing remark you made back in Swan, Wyoming, so long ago. But I was desperate enough to eschew all honor."

"Not shameless at all, and it wasn't just a passing remark. I meant it. I am well aware, John, that if it hadn't been for you I might not even be alive today. So whatever I can do for you, I am more than glad to do it."

"Oh, since the last time you saw me, there has been an addition," John said. He held out his hand toward his Millie and, smiling shyly, she walked over to join the two men.

"This is my wife, Millie."

"Oh, after what I just saw and heard, I hope so," Matt teased.

"A bit of foolishness," John said, laughing.

"Mrs. Bryce, it is very nice to meet you," Matt said.

"And I am especially pleased to meet you," Millie said. "John has talked about you. You made quite an impression on him."

"Believe me, he made an even larger impression upon me," Matt replied. "If he hadn't written that story when he did, I might be dead by now."

"I'm glad he was able help you when he did. But I think he was wrong in getting you involved with this."

"Not at all, not at all," Matt replied. "I meant it when I said if there was ever anything I could do for him, I would do it."

"Yes, well, the truth is, I really don't know what you can do," John said. "I mean, being just one man against a veritable army."

"Denbigh has an army, does he?"

"For all intents and purposes he does," John said. "Do you know about him?"

"Only what you said about him in your letter. And I did run into a couple of his men—Bleeker and Carver, I think they said their names were—on the road coming into town."

"Bleeker and Carver, yes, a couple of his worst, though not the worst. I'm sorry about the toll. I'll be glad to pay back the dollar it cost you."

"It didn't cost me a dollar," Matt said.

"What? You mean they didn't charge you a toll?"

"Now that you mention it, I believe they did say

something about a toll," Matt said. "But I convinced them to let me through, anyway."

"You convinced them?" John looked confused for a moment. Then he understood what Matt was saying, and he laughed out loud. "Ha!" he said. "See there, Millie? This is exactly the kind of person we need around here."

"John, don't forget, you just said yourself that Mr. Jensen is just one man up against an army."

"Yes, but from what I know of Matt Jensen, he's not your ordinary one man. Yes, sir, I feel a lot better about the situation now."

"From what you know of him? I thought you only met him that one time," Millie said.

"True, but I've read a great deal about him since then. His name is often in the newspapers, and I am a man who follows the news, as you know."

"I am glad you have come to help us, Mr. Jensen," Millie said. "I just hope we haven't gotten you involved in something that is going to be more than you bargained for in answering John's letter."

"I appreciate your concern," Matt said.

"If you encountered Bleeker and Carver, you already have an idea of what we are up against," John said.

"I also had lunch with a family not too far from here. The Fowlers. Do you know them?"

"E.B. and Millie Fowler, indeed I do know them," John said. "And their son Green. They are as nice a family as you would ever want to meet."

"They told me a little about Denbigh, I expect you will tell me more."

"What do you want to know?"

"You said he has a veritable army working for him. How many men does he have, do you know?"

"I can't quote an exact number for you, but when I said he had an army, I wasn't just talking about the number of men. I mean it is literally an army. He has a lot of rough men, well armed, who don't actually do ranch work. As far as I can determine, their only purpose is just to intimidate the folks in Fullerton, in the valley, and in the whole county. That's why neither the sheriff nor Marshal Tipton will have anything to do with him."

"Does Denbigh do much business with the town?"

"Oh, my, yes. In fact, most of the business the town does is with Denbigh. And because of that, many of the citizens of the town have been perfectly willing to overlook the thing about the toll, afraid they will lose his business. What they don't realize is that because of the toll, he has squeezed out all the other customers, and he can dictate what he will pay for goods and services, which means he can conduct business on his own terms. I have talked to the people about that, but they are too frightened to do anything about it. So I took it upon myself."

"That's why you wrote the letter to me? You were smart to send it to Smoke, by the way. If I hadn't just happened to drop by Sugarloaf when I did, there is no telling when, if ever, the letter would have reached me."

"Yes, but I'm not just talking about the letter. I also put out an extra."

"An extra?"

"Yes. My paper only comes out once a week, but I published a special edition last week so that the paper came out twice—the regular edition and an extra edition."

"I told him not to do that," Millie said. "I was afraid for him."

"Millie, you knew when you married me that I was a journalist."

"Yes, but I thought you would be writing about church socials, weddings, new businesses, that sort of thing. I didn't think you would be declaring war on someone like Nigel Denbigh."

"Be honest, Millie. Did you really think I would just turn my back on it?"

"No," Millie admitted. "I knew that, eventually, you were going to take him up on it. I guess that courage is one of the things that attracted me to you."

"Damn, really? And I thought it was my striking good looks," John said, and all three laughed, somewhat easing the tension.

"I'll show you that extra," John said.

John walked over to a cabinet and pulled out a copy of the newspaper, then brought it back to show to Matt.

EXTRA EXTRA EXTRA EXTRA

Denbigh Hurting Business

CHARGING TOLLS ON PUBLIC ROADS

Stage Service Suffers

These are the times that try men's souls. So wrote Thomas Paine at the founding of our country, in his broadside, The Crisis.

We, the citizens of Dickey County, are facing our own crisis now, having found our once idyllic life threatened by the draconian policies of one who calls himself "Lord" Denbigh. By taking possession of land in such a way as to totally isolate Fullerton, the despot Denbigh is squeezing the life from our community as surely as does a boa constrictor who enwraps its hapless victims within its powerful coils.

Denbigh has seized control of a road that was constructed by the Territory of Dakota as a public thoroughfare along which people should have clear and unfettered access. Now, by means of armed thugs, he demands a toll from honest citizens who seek only to traverse this throughway. This inhibits not only personal travel, but business travel as well. As a result fewer and fewer businessmen are willing to engage in commerce with our town, creating higher costs for the most basic items.

After making a careful study of the law, this newspaper editor has determined that charging a toll for passage on a public road, even though that road might pass through private land, is illegal, and to do so is little more than highway robbery. Were a masked bandit to stop the stagecoach and demand money from the driver and passengers therein, he would be no more a thief than is Nigel Denbigh for extracting this unlawful toll. I call upon Sheriff Hightower of Dickey County to show the courage of his profession and put an immediate stop to this robbery. And I call upon all citizens of Fullerton, indeed, upon all citizens of Dickey County, to refuse to do any business with him. Perhaps, by a unified effort, we can remove the heel of oppression from the necks of our citizens.

"A courageous article," Matt said after reading the story. "What was Denbigh's reaction to it?"

"After the article came out, he sent me a letter, asking me to meet with him."

"And did you meet with him?"

"Yes, but it was a waste of time."

"Why?"

"I had thought by the tone of his letter that we might be able to come to some accommodation. As it turned out, all he actually wanted was to bribe me to stop writing articles critical of him."

John laughed. "In fact, he actually wanted to buy advertisements in the newspaper, extolling his virtues."

"How did he take it when you turned him down?"

"He wasn't very happy about it," John replied. "As I recall, that was when he asked me to leave."

"What about the people in town? How are they reacting to your critical articles? Didn't you say that Denbigh does a lot of business with people in town?"

"Yes, and because of that, I think my articles are making some of the people uncomfortable. But nearly as many appreciate them as are opposed to them."

"And you are going to continue to write articles that are critical of Denbigh?"

"You're damn right I am. That is, as long as I can afford to keep the newspaper going. The problem now is, many of my advertisers have dropped their accounts. They say that they do not want to do anything that would offend Denbigh for fear of losing his business. And without their ads, I may not be able to continue for lack of money."

"How much would it cost for you to continue?"

"I don't know exactly. I can put out a few more editions, but then I will need new newsprint and ink."

"Suppose I buy in as a partner?" Matt suggested. "How much would it cost for me to invest in one fourth of the paper? That would still leave you in control."

"Are you serious?"

"I'm very serious."

"Do you think one hundred twenty-five dollars would be fair?"

"More than fair," Matt said. "I'll give you a hundred and twenty-five dollars for a quarter share of the paper, and another one hundred dollars for operating expenses."

John smiled. "It seems to me like we went through this once before. Only then, it was gold ore you gave me."

"No gold ore this time, just money, I'm afraid," Matt said.

"Just money he says," John said to Millie. "All right, I suppose I can take just money." He and Millie both laughed.

Matt stepped out to his horse, got the money from his saddlebag, then came back in. "I have another suggestion if you are open to it," Matt said as he handed John the money.

"What is your suggestion?"

"Suppose you remain publisher, but hire me to work for you. That will give me an excuse for being here, and I can share the heat on anything that appears in the paper."

"Oh, I don't know. I wouldn't want to put you in danger because of what is essentially my fight," John replied.

Matt laughed.

"What is so funny?"

"John, you invited me here, remember?" Matt asked. "Doesn't that sort of make it my fight?"

Now, John laughed as well. "If you put it that way, I guess you are right," he said.

"Besides, I just bought in to the paper. So in my book, this makes it my fight as well."

"Matt, I have not the words to express my

gratitude. I don't know what I was thinking writing to you as I did, but . . ."

"No but," Matt interrupted. "We are friends. That's all that is needed."

John took Matt's hand into his own. "Thank you," he said. "Thank you so much."

"I'll be in to work tomorrow," Matt said. "In the meantime, I need to find a place to stay while I'm here."

"As I said in my letter, you are welcome to stay on a cot in an extra room at my house."

"No, if this really does develop into some sort of fight, it would better if we weren't staying at the same house. I'll find a hotel."

"I'm afraid our hotel doesn't offer all that much," John said.

"How about Ma Perkins' Boarding House?" Millie suggested.

"Yes," John said. "That would be a great place for him."

"Where is this place?" Matt asked.

"It's just across the street," John said. He pointed. "It's that two-story white house with blue trim."

"Kenny Perkins lives there," Millie said. "So if you need anything, ask him."

"Kenny Perkins owns the house?"

John laughed. "Not exactly. His mother owns the house. Kenny is our paperboy. He is only twelve years old, but he is very resourceful, as you'll see when you meet him."

"All right," Matt said. "I'll give the place a try."

"There is a meeting of the Fullerton Business Association this evening. It's being held in a conference room at the bank. After you get settled in, I'll come by for you. I would like to introduce you to a few others in town."

"All right," Matt agreed. "Just come by for me when you are ready."

Chapter Nineteen

Leaving the newspaper office, Matt rode down to Ma Perkins' Boarding House. The woman who greeted him was very pretty, with blue eyes, high cheekbones, and a light spray of freckles across her nose. There was a young, fresh attractiveness about her, more like spring flowers than an arranged bouquet of roses.

"Yes, sir?" she said.

"I would like to speak to Ma Perkins," Matt said.

"I'm Ma Perkins."

"You?" Matt said, his surprise evident in his voice. "You are Ma Perkins?"

She laughed, and brushed back a fall of auburn hair. "My real name is Lucy," she said. "It's just that when I started my boardinghouse, Kenny suggested I call it Ma Perkins' House. I did, and before I knew it, people were calling me Ma Perkins. What can I do for you, sir?"

"My name is Matt Jensen. John Bryce suggested that I might be able to secure a room here."

"So, Millie and John sent you to me, did they? Well, bless their hearts. They're good people. But I worry about John. I swear, he has more courage than sense, taking on Denbigh like he has. How is it that you know him?"

"I have taken a position at the newspaper with Mr. Bryce," Matt said.

"Is that a fact? My, I had no idea John was looking to increase his staff. But I suppose it is quite a job for him to be running the paper with just nobody but Millie for help."

"I take it then that you have a room I can rent?"

"Yes, indeed, I have room for you," Lucy Perkins said. "Would you like to see it?"

"If you don't mind."

"It's upstairs," Lucy said. "Follow me."

Matt followed Lucy up the stairs, then down the hall to a room that was at the front of the house, looking out onto the street. It was a comfortably appointed room with an iron bedstead, feather mattress, chifforobe, overstuffed chair, table, and lantern.

"Does this meet with your approval?" Lucy asked. Her voice was soft, well modulated, and had a distinct Southern accent. "It will be three dollars a week. I hope that isn't too dear."

"No, I think that is quite reasonable. And it's a very nice room," Matt said. "I'll take it."

"Good, we will be happy to have you as our guest.

Let me tell you about the place. There is a bathing room at the end of the hall, with a tub and a small stove you can use to warm your water. It's the only bathing room in the house, so when you use it, I recommend that you lock the door from inside.

"I furnish breakfast and supper. You are on your own for lunch. Supper is at seven. I know most folks eat at six, but nearly all of my guests work somewhere, and it's sometimes hard for them to get off work and get home in time to have supper at six. I hope that doesn't inconvenience you."

"No, seven o'clock would be fine," Matt said.

"Having just arrived in town, though, you might be hungry now. If you would like, I could have Mrs. Black scare something up in the kitchen for you. She is a wonderful cook."

Had he not enjoyed a good meal at the home of the Fowlers, Matt might have taken Lucy Perkins up on her offer. But he had two weeks of trail dust in his throat as well, so right now, even more than food, was the desire for a cool beer.

"I appreciate that, Mrs. Perkins. But John is going to come by for me in a few minutes. I take it there is some sort of business meeting he wants me to attend."

"Oh," Lucy said with a bright smile. "That would be the Fullerton Business Association. I will be attending that meeting as well. As a matter of fact, I am president of the Association."

"You are the president?"

Lucy laughed at Matt's reaction. "Do you think,

perhaps, that a woman cannot be the president of a business association?"

"No, it's not that," Matt said, trying to recover ground. "It's just that I, well . . ."

"Don't worry about it, Mr. Jensen," Lucy said good-naturedly. "I know it is unusual. Come back downstairs with me to sign the guest book, and I'll give you a key to your room before you leave."

Back downstairs, as Lucy watched Matt sign the guest book, an elderly, overweight, and bald-headed man came in. Looking up at him, Lucy smiled.

"Good afternoon, Mr. Proffer. Did you have a good game of checkers with Mr. Conners?" Then, to Matt, she added, "Mr. Proffer and Mr. Conners are old friends and they meet every day in the general store to play checkers."

"Hrumph," Proffer replied. "Young man, I recommend that you never play checkers with Dilbert Conners. He cheats."

Lucy chuckled. "I take it you lost today."

"Who is this young fella?" Proffer asked.

"This is Mr. Jensen. He is a new resident."

"Do you play checkers, Mr. Jensen?"

"Yes, but I cheat," Jensen said.

"Hrumph!" Proffer replied as he shuffled off to his room.

Lucy tried hard to bury her laugh. "You are awful, Mr. Jensen," she said. "Just awful."

"What did my friend do that is so awful?" John asked, coming into the parlor of the boarding-house at just that moment.

"Hello, John," Lucy said. "Nothing. I was just laughing at something he said to Mr. Proffer, is all."

"Be careful of what you say to Proffer. He's a lawyer, you know, and would sue you at the drop of a hat. Are you ready to go?"

"I am," Matt replied.

"Wait until I get my hat," Lucy said. "If you two don't mind, I will walk down to the meeting with you."

"We will be happy to have your company, Madam President," John said.

In addition to John and Matt, there were seven others in attendance at the business meeting, Lucy Perkins being one of the seven and the only woman. They were sitting around a long table, with Lucy at the head. She began the meeting with a light rap of the gavel on the table.

"Gentlemen, the meeting will come to order," she said. "As you have no doubt noticed, Mr. Bryce has brought a guest. Before I have him introduced, I wonder if I could ask each of you to tell him your name and what you do. Mr. White, we'll start with you."

White was a small, thin man, with a closely cropped mustache and wire-rimmed glasses. He started to stand.

"No need to stand," Lucy said. "We'll do this informally."

"I'm Leland White, I'm a pharmacist, and I own White's Apothecary."

"I'm Otis Miller, I own the bank," the heavyset man sitting next to White said.

"I'm Ernie Westpheling. I own the gunshop." Westpheling was a tall, very dignified-looking man.

"Paul Tobin. I own the Fullerton Livery." Tobin had a very prominent scar that cut, like a purple lightning flash, across his left cheek.

"Jason Scott, Scott Leathergoods." Scott was totally bald.

"Troy Jackson. I'm the blacksmith." Jackson was a very large, very powerfully built man with huge arms and shoulders that strained against the shirt he was wearing.

"Now, Mr. Bryce," Lucy said. "Since all the introductions have been made, suppose you introduce your guest."

"Madam President, gentlemen," John began. "This is Matt Jensen."

"Matt Jensen?" Westpheling said. "Look here, this isn't 'the' Matt Jensen, is it?"

"What do you mean, 'the' Matt Jensen," Scott asked.

"You mean you've never heard of Matt Jensen?"

"I have," Miller said. "You are a gunman, aren't you, Mr. Jensen?"

"Gentlemen, would you please allow me to continue my introduction?" John asked.

When the others quit talking, John nodded at them. "Thank you. As I said, this is Matt Jensen. I wrote to him and asked him to come to Fullerton, because I think we need a man of his caliber and experience."

"Need him to do what?" Leland White asked.

"Specifically, Mr. Jensen will be in my employ. But, given the recent, let us say, adventures of some of Denbigh's men, I think it would be good for the town to have someone like Mr. Jensen around."

"To do what?" Miller asked.

"Just to be a presence," John said.

"Mr. Jensen, I mean no offense by this," Miller said. "But we already have one too many gunmen in this town. If you haven't met him yet, I'm sure you will. His name is Ollie Butrum, and he is pure evil. He is also deadly quick. If I were you, I would leave town right away rather than face such a man."

"Thank you for your concern," Matt said.

"But you have no intention of leaving, do you?" Miller asked.

"I was invited by John Bryce," Matt replied. I will be in town as long as John wishes me to stay."

"John, you said you intended Mr. Jensen to be a presence," White said. "What do you mean by that?"

"You do remember when Denbigh's ruffians tried to destroy the newspaper office, don't you, Leland?"

"Yes."

"With Matt as my employee . . ." John stopped and looked over at Matt before he continued. "The fact is, he isn't exactly an employee. He is more like a partner, since he bought in to the newspaper. And as a partner in the paper, I do not think we need fear any more vandalism."

"I don't like it," White said. "It looks to me like you are declaring war with Denbigh. And you are bringing in the entire town into your personal war."

"That's just it, Leland," John replied. "It isn't my personal war. Can't you see it? Denbigh literally has the entire town under siege."

"I, for one, am glad to have Mr. Jensen around," Westpheling said.

"As am I," Tobin said.

"Count me in," Scott added.

Jackson, the big blacksmith, reached his long arm across the table. "Welcome to Fullerton, Mr. Jensen," he said.

"Leland? Otis?" John said.

Otis Miller, the banker, shook his head. "I don't like him being here, but there's nothing I can do to stop it," he said. "Having this man around is going to cause us trouble. You mark my words. There will be trouble."

After the discussion about Matt, the meeting moved on to other issues, from how they, as businessmen, were going to respond to the city council's proposal to increase the sales tax by a penny on the dollar, to a vote of support of, as well as a donation to, the town fire department's plans to hold a firemen's ball at the end of the month.

When the meeting adjourned, Lucy asked Matt if he would be coming back to the house right away.

"No, I don't think so. I think I'll take a look around the town, just to get myself acquainted," Matt said.

Lucy Perkins chuckled. "That won't take you very long," she said. "Fullerton isn't exactly what you would call a big city."

Leaving the bank, Matt walked south on Monroe, where he encountered such businesses as an apothecary, a leather goods store, a mercantile, and the Morning Star Hotel. Turning west on South-worth Street, he encountered private houses and a church. He turned back north on Fullerton Street, which was lined on both sides with houses. Then from Fullerton, he turned east on Second Street, which brought him back to Monroe, the main street of the town. Back on the main street, he decided to look for a saloon.

The saloon wasn't hard to find. The New York Saloon was the biggest and grandest building in the entire town. He started to step up onto the porch.

A rather small, pale-eyed man was standing just in front of the saloon door. He was wearing a leather vest decorated with silver conchos, a string tie, and a large turquoise-studded silver belt buckle. Matt had to hold back a chuckle, because the man was dressed more like an Eastern dandy's idea of what a Westerner should wear than a real cowboy.

"You're new in town, ain't you, mister?" the little man asked. "When did you get in?"

Matt had already heard Butrum described, so he knew who this was the moment he was addressed. His immediate thought was to tell Butrum it was none of his business when he arrived. But, based upon some of the uneasiness expressed in the meeting of the businessmen earlier, he decided not to be confrontational.

"Today," Matt said.

"Show me your coupon," the little man said.

"What coupon?"

"Don't play dumb with me, mister. You know what coupon I'm talking about. The one you got when you paid your toll on the road. Show it to me."

"Oh, the toll," Matt said. "Well, there's the problem. I decided not to pay the toll."

"You *decided* not to pay the toll?" the little man asked, his voice increasing the volume and pitch. "Who the hell are you to decide not to pay the toll?"

"It doesn't look to me like you and I are going to be friends," Matt replied. "So I see no reason to tell you my name."

"Draw, mist—"

That was as far as the little man got, because though he was quick, Matt was quicker. The difference was, Matt, who by now was standing right in front of him, didn't reach for his own gun. Instead, he brought his right hand around in a backhanded blow that swept the little man off the porch and onto the ground, where he landed in a rather substantial pile of horse apples. The blow had not only stunned the little man, it knocked the pistol from his hand. Matt reached down, picked the pistol up from the porch, then went inside as if nothing had happened. Stepping up to the bar, he swung open the cylinder of the little man's pistol, punched out all the cartridges, then handed the empty revolver to the bartender.

"This belongs to that little fella who was standing out on the front porch," Matt said. "I expect he is going to be coming in here asking for it in a moment or two."

"My God, mister, is this Ollie Butrum's gun?" the bartender asked.

The bartender's question got the attention of everyone in the room, and all conversation came to a halt as they looked toward the tall stranger who had just come in.

One of the most interested of the saloon patrons was sitting in the very back of the room, nursing a drink. He had piercing dark eyes, a hook nose, and a protruding chin, which he was now rubbing absent-mindedly as he studied Matt Jensen.

"I don't know the little fella's name," Matt said. "He didn't give it to me."

"How did you come by his gun?"

"He drew it against me, so I took it away from him," Matt said.

"You took it away from him? Mister, Ollie Butrum has killed at least ten men that I know of. He's little, but he's as quick as a rattlesnake and twice as evil."

"Yes, well, I didn't exactly get the idea that he was a Sunday School teacher."

The bartender and the others in the saloon laughed.

"Sunday School teacher. That's a good one," the bartender said.

"How about a beer?" Matt asked.

"Sure thing, mister," the bartender said, picking up a mug and stepping over to the beer barrel. "And this first one is on the house. Anyone who can take a gun away from Ollie Butrum deserves it."

"Hell, Paul, you always give a free beer to someone who comes into the saloon for the first time," one of the saloon patrons said.

"Now, don't go givin' away my secrets, Stan," Paul said, and the others laughed. Paul drew a beer then handed it to Matt.

"What brings you to Fullerton, Mister . . ." The bartender paused in mid-sentence, waiting for Matt to supply his name.

Matt took a swallow, wondering how he should answer. Already in Colorado, Wyoming, Arizona, and New Mexico, his name was well enough known that he often got a reaction when he said it. He thought that whatever he had to do here, he could do it best if he kept a low profile, but he also had not spent any time in this part of the country, so it was entirely possible that he could say his name without generating any reaction. He decided to risk it.

He lowered his glass. "The name is Jensen. Matt Jensen. I came to Fullerton to take a job. I'm going to be working for the newspaper."

"Is that a fact? John Bryce hire you, did he?" Stan asked.

"Yes."

"What will you be doing?" Paul asked.

"I expect I'll do whatever he needs done—keep the office and the printing press clean, run errands, sell advertising, maybe write an article now and then for him."

Paul laughed out loud.

"What's so funny?"

"A handyman. You took Butrum's gun away from him, but you are going to be a handyman. This is rich. Yes, sir, this is really rich."

"It's honest work," Matt said. "You don't have anything against honest work, do you?"

"No, I don't mean that," Paul said. "It's just that—look out, mister!" Paul suddenly shouted.

Paul's shout wasn't necessary because the innate awareness Matt had developed over the years of putting his life on the line had already warned him. Spinning toward the door, Matt saw Ollie Butrum charging through it with a gun in his hand. Butrum pulled the trigger and the bullet slammed into the bar right next to Matt.

"You son of a bitch! Nobody does that to me!" the gunman shouted. He thumbed the hammer back for a second shot, but before he could pull the trigger, Matt dropped his beer, drew his own pistol, and fired. The .44 slug from Matt's pistol caught the little man in the heart. When the bullet came out through the back, it brought half his shoulder blade with it, leaving an exit wound the size of a twenty-dollar gold piece.

Butrum staggered backward, crashing through the batwing doors and landing flat on his back on the front porch. His body was still jerking a bit, but his eyes were open and unseeing. He was already dead; only the muscles continued to respond, as if waiting for signals that could no longer be sent.

For a long moment, no one spoke. They just stared through the drifting gun smoke in shocked amazement at the body that lay on the floor.

"Looks like I'll be needing another beer," Matt said as he put his pistol back in his holster.

Chapter Twenty

Quickly, the bartender drew another beer and handed to Matt.

"Since I spilled the other one, I guess I'd better pay for this one," Matt said as he put a nickel on the bar.

"Mister, if I was you, I'd drink that beer just real fast, then ride on out of town," the bartender said.

"Why?" Matt asked. "It was self-defense. Everyone in here saw it. I'm not concerned about the law. Besides, I've taken a job here. I'm going to be working at the newspaper, remember?"

"It ain't the law you need to worry about," Stan said. "It's Nigel Denbigh." He pointed toward the body. "Butrum worked for him."

At that moment, a middle-aged, overweight man came into the saloon, wheezing from the effort of having moved so quickly. He had his gun in his hand, but when he saw Butrum sprawled out on the floor, he lowered his gun and just stared for a long moment in absolute shock at the body. The gun was still in Butrum's hand.

The man, who was wearing a badge, looked up, the expression on his face still mirroring his shock.

"Who? Who did this?" he asked.

"I did," Matt said.

"You're under arrest."

"It was self-defense," Matt said.

The marshal shook his head. "Don't be lyin' to me, mister. Butrum was an evil little bastard, I'll grant you that, and more'n likely he needed killin'. But you just can't go around killin' someone in cold blood and sayin' it was self-defense."

"The stranger is tellin' the truth, Marshal Tipton," the bartender said. "Butrum come in here with his gun blazin'. You can see, right here, where his bullet hit the bar. Jensen wasn't doin' nothin' but standin' here real peaceable like, drinkin' his beer and talkin' to us."

"Are you tellin' me that Butrum already had his gun in his hand, blazin' away, you said, and this fella was just standin' here, but somehow he drew his gun and kilt Butrum?"

"That's exactly what I'm sayin'," Paul said.

"And I'm backin' him up, Tipton," Stan said. "I seen ever'thing that happened."

With a sigh, Marshal Tipton put his pistol back in his holster. "Mister, you want to tell me how it was that you could do that? Are you that damn good? Or are you just that damn lucky?"

"I guess it was just luck, Marshal," Matt said self-deprecatingly.

"Well, I can tell you this for sure. Denbigh ain't goin' to like this," the marshal said. "He ain't goin' to like it one little bit."

"You didn't say Lord Denbigh," Matt said.

The marshal looked at Matt with an expression of confusion, and some fear. "Wait a minute! Are you workin' for Denbigh?"

"No. I was just commenting," Matt said. "I never heard of him until today, but from what I have heard, I don't think I would like working for him very much. And I've heard he insists upon being called Lord Denbigh."

"Yeah, well, the sumbitch can insist all he wants. I ain't goin' to be callin' him Lord."

"Ha," Stan said. "You talk big, Marshal Tipton, but I haven't seen you take down Denbigh's tollgate."

"The tollgate is out on Ellendale Road, at least two miles south of town. That means it ain't in my jurisdiction, which means it ain't my job and you know it," Tipton said. He pulled a soiled handkerchief from his pocket and wiped his face. "There's no way I can legally go outside of the town limits. But if he was to put one up here on Monroe, or Southworth, or Fullerton, I'd stop him soon enough."

"I'm sure you would, Marshal, I'm sure you would," Paul said.

Tipton turned toward the bartender and pointed

his finger. "And I ain't a' goin' to be takin' no sass from you neither," he said.

"I didn't mean nothin' by it, Marshal," Paul said. "Hell, you ain't the only lawman in the county that gives Denbigh free rein. None of the other town marshals, nor the sheriff, nor even the U.S. marshals have done anything to stop him."

"This here fella is the only one who has had the gumption to go against him, and he didn't actually go against him, just Butrum," Stan said.

"Yeah," Tipton replied. "Let's get back to this. What is your name, mister? The reason I ask is when Denbigh gets through with you, I don't want to have to strap you to a board and stand you up in the middle of town tryin' to figure out who you are, like we did with those two cowboys."

"The name is Jensen. Matt Jensen."

Normally, when Matt told someone his name he got some kind of response, but as he studied the marshal's eyes for any glimmer of recognition, he saw no response of any kind. The marshal did not recognize the name, and for that Matt was relieved.

"Are you just passing through our town?" Tipton asked.

"No, I plan to stay awhile," Matt said.

The marshal squinted his eyes. "Are you what they call a shootist? Have you come here to make money with your gun?"

"I've come to take a job at the newspaper," Matt said.

"The newspaper?" Tipton said, nearly shouting the word. "Mister, you have just killed one of the deadliest men in all of Dakota, and you tell me you don't do nothin' but work for the newspaper?"

"Nothing but work for the newspaper?" Matt repeated. "Surely, Marshal, you are not unaware of the power and influence a newspaper can and should exercise? The freedom of the press is one of our nation's most powerful freedoms."

"Yeah, well, what I mean is, I know Butrum," Tipton said. "That is, I knew him. And he was an evil bastard, true enough, but I've never know'd him to just come into a saloon and start shootin' like that. Got any idea what might have got him all riled like that?"

"I don't know," Matt said. "It could be that he got upset because I took his gun away from him."

Paul, Stan, and the others in the saloon laughed.

"You took his gun away from him? You expect me to believe that?"

"I did take his gun away from him," Matt said, "but it turns out that he had another one I didn't know about."

"Why did you take his gun away from him?" Tipton said. "No, a better question is, how did you take his gun away from him?"

"I took it away from him because he pointed it at me. I don't like for people to point guns at me. And as to how, when I knocked him down he dropped the gun, so I picked it up, brought it in here, emptied it, and handed over to Paul, the bartender."

"That's right, Marshal," Paul said. He reached under the bar, then picked the pistol up, holding the handle by his thumb and forefinger. "This here is Butrum's gun."

"I'll be damn," Tipton said. "You knocked him down, you say?"

"Yes. When he drew on me."

"Why did he draw on you? Not that a fella like Butrum needed much of reason to draw on anyone."

"He was standing out front when I came up, and he got all upset when I didn't show him the coupon."

"Yes, that would be the coupon you got when you paid a toll at the road," Tipton said. "So, why didn't you show it to him?"

"That was the problem, Marshal. I didn't pay the toll, so I didn't have a coupon to show him."

"Wait a minute," Tipton said. "Are you telling me that when you came through the tollgate, you refused to pay the toll? Denbigh has at least two men, sometimes more, manning that gate. So I'm going to be just real interested in hearing how you got by them."

"I just convinced the two men who were watching the gate that I was not going to pay them, so they let me through."

"That would be Bleeker and Carver," Tipton said. "They are both hard men, Mr. Jensen, but you want me to believe that you were able to talk them into letting you through without paying the toll."

"Maybe I should have made myself more clear," Matt said. "As it so happened, I had a gun in my hand, and they didn't have one in theirs. That might have made it a little easier to convince them."

Tipton sighed, and shook his head. "Jensen, if I was you, I wouldn't be takin' that newspaper job. I'd be ridin' on out of here as quick as I can."

"Why?"

"Because you are trouble, mister," Tipton said. "You refused to pay the toll, and you just killed one of Denbigh's men. He ain't going to like this. No, sir, he ain't going to like this one bit. If you want to stay alive much longer, you'll climb up on your horse and ride out. Only, don't leave by the Ellendale Road."

"Oh, I can't leave town now. Like I told you, Marshal, I have just taken a job with the publisher of your local newspaper. Plus, I have just paid for a week's lodging at a local boardinghouse. Leaving now would not be the honorable thing to do."

"Well, all I can say is, if you really are working at the newspaper, you and John Bryce should get along just fine. Bryce is nothing but a hardhead who seems to enjoy agitating Nigel Denbigh."

"What do you mean by agitating Denbigh? Do you think perhaps it is because John Bryce tells the truth?"

Tipton stroked his chin. "I don't know about

that," he said. "All I know is, he seems to love to cause trouble. It would be far better for everyone if the paper wouldn't be quite so hostile toward Denbigh, and I've told him that too. Maybe Bryce should just publish articles about church socials, ladies' teas, barn dances, and such. I don't know if you seen it when you come into town, but we're havin' us a firemen's ball comin' up soon. What he ought to do is write more about that."

"I'm sure that Mr. Bryce covers all the social events and news of local interest," Matt said. "But I know him, and I know that he is the kind of man who feels that a newspaper should stand for things like truth, justice, and the rights of the citizens of this town to make a fair living, without being held up by an outlaw like Nigel Denbigh."

"An outlaw? Look here, that's pretty serious language, isn't it? It's not like he is robbing banks, or holding up stagecoaches. He is a rancher, the largest and wealthiest rancher in the county."

"He is a rancher who extracts an illegal toll from people who use a public road just because it passes through his land. And since you say that you can't do anything about it because it is out of your jurisdiction, then John Bryce is the only one who is standing up to him."

"Yes, well, that's not very smart of Bryce, if you ask me," Tipton said. "But I reckon that, being as it is his paper, he can pretty much do whatever he wants."

"Marshal, have you seen all you need to see? Can I get this body hauled out of here?" Paul asked.

"Yeah, I've seen ever'thing I need to see. Go ahead, get him down to the undertaker's place," Tipton answered.

"Free drinks for the rest of the night to anyone who will get this little turd's carcass out of here," the bartender offered, and four men hurried over to pick up the body.

"I'll have the magistrate hold an inquest tomorrow," Tipton said. "So's not to have to put you in jail tonight, I'll release you on your own recognizance if you promise to show up."

"I'll be there, Marshal," Matt replied.

Chapter Twenty-one

After Butrum's body was dragged out of the saloon and the excitement of the event died down, Matt took his beer over to a table and sat down. A young boy who was sweeping the floor came over to him.

"I've read about you," the boy said quietly.

"Have you?"

"Yes, sir. I've read all about you and your brother, Smoke Jensen."

Matt didn't correct the boy.

"I read all about you in a book called *Matt Jensen and the Outlaws of Dead End Gulch.*"

Matt smiled. The boy was talking about the penny dreadfuls. And though Matt had not yet been featured in as many of the novels as had Smoke, there were a few about him out now as well.

"That is you, ain't it? I knew it was you as soon as I seen the way you handled Butrum. And I know Butrum was fast, 'cause like the marshal said, he kilt two cowboys here a couple weeks ago, took 'em both on at the same time, and shot 'em both dead."

"That's me," Matt said. "But do me a favor, will you? Don't tell anyone else what you know about me."

A big smile spread across the boy's face. "No, sir, I won't. I know how sometimes folks like you, when you are fighting for truth and justice, have to keep quiet about who you really are."

"I appreciate that," Matt said. "What's your name?"

"Jimmy Smith."

Matt gave Jimmy a quarter."

"What's this for?" the boy asked.

"I want to hire you to work for me, Jimmy," Matt said.

"I can't. I work for Mr. Paul Coker. He's the bartender."

"You can still work for him," Matt said. "The kind of work you will be doing for me is secret work. From time to time, you might hear things that I should know. If you do, I want you to come over to the newspaper office and tell me. I'll give you a quarter every day, and an additional quarter every time you bring me some information. Are you willing?"

"Yes, sir!" Jimmy said, the smile on his face growing even wider.

"We'll keep it our secret," Matt said.

"I will tell no one," Jimmy said.

"Do you see that man sitting alone at that table over in the corner?"

"You mean The Hawk?"

"The Hawk?"

"Yes, sir, well, he ain't been in town very long, so I don't know his real name. The Hawk is just what I call him," Jimmy said. "I call him that 'cause he's got a big nose that looks sort of like a hawk's beak. And he don't never talk to nobody. He just watches."

Matt had noticed him the moment he came into the saloon. This was the same man he had seen walking away from a full glass of whiskey back in Pueblo. He had seen him again on the train, going to Sugarloaf. That he was now here in Fullerton was way beyond mere coincidence.

"I want you to find out what you can about him," Matt said. "But don't let him know what you are doing."

"That's sort of like lawman work, ain't it?" Jimmy asked.

"I suppose it is in a way."

"Then I'll do it," Jimmy promised. "I figure that's going to be my job one of these days."

"Do you now?"

"Yes, sir," the boy said. He smiled proudly. "I don't plan to stay in Fullerton much longer. One of these days soon, I'll leave, and maybe I'll get me a job as a deputy somewhere. What I'd really like to do is become a marshal. Not like Marshal Tipton, I'm talkin' about a United States marshal."

"That's a pretty noble ambition," Matt agreed. "But your mother and dad may want you to wait until you are a little older."

"I ain't got no ma and pa," the boy said. "I never

had no pa. Well, I had one, but my ma never know'd who he was. My ma, she was a—well, she was what they call a—fancy lady, if you know what I mean. But she was a good ma to me, and I ain't none ashamed of her."

"Nor should you be," Matt said.

"Truth to tell, mister, my last name ain't really Smith, it's just one my ma took. She died two years ago when I was twelve."

"Where do you live?"

"Mr. Tobin lets me stay in a nice room over at the stable and charges me nothing because I muck out the stalls for him. And Mr. Coker, he gives me three meals a day because I sweep the floors for him. I have a good life."

Matt thought of his own orphaned boyhood and how he had been little more than a slave to the Soda Springs Home for Wayward Boys and Girls. It would have been much better had he been on his own, like this boy. Others might feel sorry for Jimmy, but Matt knew that the boy was serious when he said he had a good life.

Matt smiled. "I guess you do at that," he said.

"Do you want me to go over there and start spyin' on him now?" Jimmy asked.

"No. He has seen us talking, so if you get too close to him now, he might get suspicious," Matt said.

"Oh, yes, I see what you mean," Jimmy replied. "I guess you have to pay attention to things like this when you are first learnin'."

"And be careful," Matt cautioned.

"Yes, sir, I will be," Jimmy promised. "Oh, oh," he said.

"What?"

"Them three men that just come in? They ride for Denbigh. That's the same man Butrum worked for. I don't reckon they're goin' to be any too happy over Butrum getting' hisself kilt like he done."

"Hey, bartender," one of the three men called. "Where at is Butrum? How come he ain't standin' out on the front porch like he nearly always is?"

"Ha! I'll bet he's upstairs with a whore," one of the others said.

"Are you kiddin'? He's so ugly, not even a whore will have anything to do with him," the third said, and all three laughed.

"What'll it be, gents?" Paul, the bartender, asked.

"Whiskey," the first said. "And you ain't answered my question. Where at is Butrum?"

"He's down at Lisenby's," Paul replied.

"Lisenby's. What's that? Another saloon?"

"Maybe it's a whorehouse for ugly people," the third said, and again all three men laughed.

"It is a mortuary," Paul said.

"A what?"

"It is an undertaker's parlor."

"Well, what the hell is he doing down there?"

"He's dead, cowboy," Stan said from the opposite end of the bar. "When someone is dead, they generally wind up in a mortuary."

"Dead? What the hell do you mean, dead? Who killed him?"

Neither Stan nor Paul answered the question.

"You heard me. Who killed him? Whoever it was had to have shot him in the back, 'cause there ain't no man alive faster."

"Jimmy, you'd better move away from the table," Matt said quietly.

The cowboy pulled his gun and pointed it at the bartender. "I expect you had better tell me right now who killed him, else I'll put a ball in your brain."

"I killed him," Matt said, his words loud and clear.

The cowboy turned toward Matt. "You killed him?"

Matt stood up. "I did," he said.

"What did you do, mister? Shoot him in the back?"

"You're name is Logan, ain't it?" the bartender asked.

"Yeah, Logan, what of it?" Logan replied. He was still glaring at Matt.

"Logan, he didn't shoot Butrum in the back. He took him on, face-to-face. And not only that, Butrum already had his gun in his hand."

"What? You expect me to believe that?" Logan replied.

"Believe it, Logan, because it's true," Stan said.

"I seen it my ownself. Wouldn't believe it if I hadn't seen it," one of the other saloon patrons said. "But what they are tellin' you is true. Butrum come chargin' in here with his gun in his hand. This fella was standin' at the bar drinkin' a beer, but he dropped his beer, drew his gun, and killed Butrum."

"What did you shoot him for?" Logan asked.

"He was pointing a gun at me," Matt said. "I don't like it when people point their gun at me. I don't even like it when someone is holding a gun in front of me, whether they are pointing it at me or not."

Logan looked down at the gun he was holding.

"Like you," Matt continued. "I would feel much better if you would put that gun away."

"Ha! Would you now?" Logan replied.

"Yes, I would."

"What if I decide I don't want to put it away?"

"Then I will kill you," Matt answered easily.

"Are you daft, mister? I'm holding a gun in my hand."

"So was Butrum," Matt answered easily.

"Logan, put the gun away," one of the other two said.

"I ain't puttin' my gun away."

"What if he starts shootin', and winds up shootin' all of us?"

"That's it! Caleb, you and Ben pull your guns too. I don't care how fast he is, he can't kill all three of us."

"What if he kills just one of us?" Caleb asked.

"Yeah, that's what I'm talkin' about. He probably can't get more'n one of us before we get him."

"Which one?" Ben asked. "Which one of us is willin' to be the one that gets hisself kilt for the other two?"

"Put your gun away now," Matt said. Although he was standing, facing Logan, he had not drawn his gun, nor had he made any move toward it.

Logan hesitated for another moment, then slipped his gun back into its holster.

"Yeah, well, all right, I can't see gettin' into a fight over Butrum," Logan said. "There didn't none of us like that little son of a bitch away. Come on," he said to the others. "Let's go over to the Mex place. Hell, I like tequila better anyway."

"We just got here," Ben said.

"I'm goin' with Logan," Caleb said. "If you want to stay in here all by yourself, you go ahead."

"No," Ben said. "I'm comin' too."

Without another word, the three men turned and left the saloon. There had been a collective holding of breath by everyone in the saloon, and now, as one, they let it out, followed by several loud exclamations.

"Damn! If that don't beat all I ever seen! He was standin' there without a gun in his hand, and bluffed down three armed men."

"I don't think it was a bluff," Stan said. "I think he would have killed them if they had tried anything."

"What are you talking about? Logan already had his gun in hand. And maybe Logan ain't as fast as

Butrum was, but he is pretty damn fast. I've seen him shoot."

"He wasn't bluffing," Stan said again resolutely.

All the other patrons turned to look at Matt, but he had already retaken his seat at the table, and he was just sitting there, staring into his beer.

"Damn. He wasn't bluffing, was he?" someone said.

Chapter Twenty-two

Matt met the other residents of Ma Perkins' Boarding House at breakfast the next morning. Mr. Proffer was the only other male resident. Miss Grimes was a schoolteacher, Mrs. Mouser and Mrs. Gibson were, like Lucy Perkins, widows, though they were much older.

Kenny had already heard the news of Matt shooting Butrum, and he kept looking at Matt across the breakfast table.

"Is it true?" Kenny asked. "Did you really do it?"

"Is what true?" Lucy asked. "Kenny, don't be rude to our guests."

"I'm not bein' rude, Ma," Kenny said. "I think it's great, if it's true."

"If what is true?"

"When I went down to help Jimmy put out the feed in the livery stable this morning, he said that Mr. Jensen shot Butrum last night."

"Kenny, what a thing to say!" Lucy said.

"It's true, Ma. Jimmy seen it."

"Jimmy saw it," Miss Grimes corrected.

"He told you too?"

"I was correcting your grammar," the school-teacher said.

"To hear Jimmy tell it, it must have been somethin' to see," Kenny said. "According to Jimmy, Butrum come into, uh, I mean came into the saloon with his gun in his hand, blazing away. His first shot missed Mr. Jensen, but Mr. Jensen drew his gun and shot back and didn't miss. Jimmy said he had never seen anyone draw his gun as fast as Mr. Jensen drew his."

Throughout Kenny's dissertation, Matt said not a word. Instead, he just picked up his cup of coffee and took a swallow.

"Very good coffee, Mrs. Perkins," Matt said, aware that she and everyone else at the table were now staring at him. He put the coffee cup down.

"Is the boy telling the truth?" Proffer asked. "Did you kill Butrum last night?"

"Yes," Matt said. "Mrs. Perkins, I'm sorry if this distresses you. I'll move out as quickly as I can."

"If you make him move out, I will move out as well," Proffer said quickly.

"Nonsense," Lucy said. "Neither of you need move out. If Mr. Butrum was shooting at you, of course you had no choice but to defend yourself. And though I never met Mr. Butrum, I did read about him in the newspaper. I know that he has killed at least three men within the last month. I am not normally given to such sentiments, but in his case, I would say good riddance."

"Will there be a hearing?" Proffer asked.

"Yes, I am to present myself to the marshal's office at ten this morning."

"You may not know this, Mr. Jensen, but I am a retired lawyer," Proffer said. "I would be glad to accompany you to the hearing, just to make certain that you are treated fairly. And I will do so pro bono."

"Pro bono?" Kenny asked.

"It means he would do it for free," Matt explained. He looked over at Proffer. "I would love to have you accompany me," he said. "But I intend to pay for your services."

There was no courtroom as such, so the hearing was held in the marshal's office, presided over by James Cornett, the city magistrate. Because of the lack of room, the only ones allowed in were those whose testimony would have direct bearing on the outcome of the case. That included those saloon patrons who were eyewitnesses. Matt asked for, and received permission for, Julius Proffer, duly licensed and a member of the bar, to be present as his counselor. Cornett agreed.

The hearing took less than half an hour, and the magistrate ruled that the shooting was justifiable.

"I got no reason to hold you, Jensen," Marshal Tipton said, "so I ain't goin' to." He raised his finger to make a point. "But I am goin' to be keepin' an eye on you. You say you're workin' for the newspaper, but I've got the idea in my mind that

you ain't just a handyman. I figure if you're workin'
for John Bryce, he has somethin' else in mind. So
I'm tellin' you right now, don't you be makin' no
trouble for Nigel Denbigh. I don't need it, and this
town can't afford it."

"I'll keep that in mind," Matt said.

When Matt returned to the newspaper office,
John showed him a broadsheet.

"I've put out another extra," John said. "What do
think?"

"We have been doing a newspaper in this town
for over two years," Millie said. "In all that time, not
one extra, but this is the second extra this month."

"Do you think this story doesn't deserve an
extra?" John asked.

Millie smiled, then walked over to her husband
and leaned up to kiss him on the cheek.

"I think it absolutely deserves an extra," she said.
"I was just making an observation."

Matt took the broadsheet from John.

EXTRA EXTRA EXTRA EXTRA

Deadly Encounter

SHOOTOUT AT NEW YORK SALOON

Butrum Killed

Olliver Butrum, a killer employed by
Nigel Denbigh and, in the opinion of this

editor, Satan's surrogate, was himself killed yesterday when he attempted, yet again, to ply his deadly avocation. Witnesses stated that Butrum rushed into the New York Saloon with wild and flashing eyes, his mouth contorted with anger, and with a blazing pistol in his hand.

His target was Matt Jensen, a man who was standing at the bar enjoying a beer. What happened next sent Butrum to his Maker with what had to be the biggest surprise of his life. Confident in his own ability to dispense death by the adroit use of his pistol, Butrum encountered a man who was more than his equal. Matt Jensen, witnesses report, stood calmly as the bullets flew, drawing his own revolver in the blink of an eye and discharging it with deadly effect. Butrum went down with a .44-caliber ball lodged in his heart.

As Nigel Denbigh's employee, Butrum's only job was to intimidate and, if necessary, kill in the enforcement of Denbigh's illegal collection of tolls on the Ellendale Road. Butrum was quite good at his job and, within the month instant, sent three innocent men to their graves.

Although the death of anyone should not be applauded, there are times when it is difficult not to be grateful for the demise of evil, even if that evil is incarnate in the form of a human being. Ollie Butrum was just such an incarnation and this is such a time.

Matt read the story, then handed the paper back to John. "Denbigh is not going to like the story much," he said. He chuckled. "Which is why I like it."

"Yes, well, it never hurts to tweak the beard of the giant when you can," John replied.

"Denbigh ain't got no beard."

Both Matt and John turned toward the front door of the newspaper office, where they saw Jimmy Smith, the young man who worked both in the saloon and at the corral.

"I know he has no beard. It's a metaphor," John said.

"I know what a metaphor is. Miss Grimes taught us. It's like calling someone a snake, when he ain't really a snake," Jimmy said.

"Very good, Jimmy, very good," John said. "Now, what can I do for you?"

"I need to talk to Mr. Jensen," Jimmy said. "Only, it has to be a secret."

"Does it have to do with the arrangement we have?" Matt asked.

"Yes, sir."

"It's all right. You can talk in front of Mr. Bryce."

"The fella you was askin' about? The one sittin' at the table last night?"

"Yes, what about him?"

"His name is Lucas Meacham," Jimmy said.

"So that's Lucas Meacham," Matt said.

"You mean you know him?"

"I've heard of him," Matt said. "I've heard nothing good about him, but I have heard of him. He is what they call a regulator, someone who hunts wanted men for the reward. He seems to have followed me here," Matt said. "Though I have no idea why. There is no paper out on me."

"Is this Meacham fellow going to be trouble?" John asked.

"Let's just say that he might be the joker in the deck."

Matt pulled a quarter from his pocket and handed it to Jimmy. "Thank you, Jimmy, that was good work."

"Thank you, sir," Jimmy replied, smiling happily as he pocketed the coin. "Oh, I know something else too," he said.

"About Meacham?"

"No, sir, this ain't nothin' to do with what we was talkin' about. This is about somethin' else, somethin' Kenny Perkins told me."

"What would that be?" Matt asked.

"Kenny's ma is hopin' you'll go to the firemen's ball come this Saturday."

John laughed out loud.

"Are you?" Jimmy asked.

"We'll just have to see, won't we?" Matt replied.

"You didn't tell Jimmy that, did you?" Lucy Perkins asked her son, her voice rising in exasperation.

Kenny had just returned home after delivering the extra edition of the *Defender*, and casually mentioned to his mother that he had told Jimmy

Smith about her expressed interest in Matt Jensen attending the firemen's ball, which would be held the coming Saturday night.

"Please don't tell me that you told him that," Lucy said.

"But Ma, you said that yourself. I heard you tellin' Mrs. Bryce that you hoped Mr. Jensen would go to the firemen's ball."

"That was strictly between Millie and me," Lucy said. "It was nobody else's business, not your business, and certainly not Jimmy Smith's business."

"But Jimmy is my best friend," Kenny said. "I tell him everything."

"He may be your best friend, but he isn't mine. You can tell him anything you want about yourself, but I don't want you blabbing to him, or to anyone else, things about me."

"I'm sorry, Ma," Kenny said contritely.

Lucy sighed, then walked over, put her arms around her son, and pulled her to him.

"You are a good boy, Kenny," she said. "I know it has been hard on you without your father. It's been hard on me as well, but you have been such a big help to me. I don't know if I could make it without you."

"Are you going?" John asked. Jimmy had already left, and John and Matt were cleaning the press after the extra run.

Matt laughed. "You are as nosy as Jimmy."

"Of course I'm nosy, I'm a newspaperman," John said. "It is my profession to be nosy. What do you think of her?"

"You mean what do I think of *Ma* Perkins?" Matt accented the word "Ma," and John laughed out loud.

"Yeah, Millie and I had a good laugh thinking about that. No doubt when you heard her name was Ma Perkins, you were expecting some fat old lady."

"I will admit I was surprised when she answered the door," Matt said. "You are right, she is not someone I would think of as 'Ma.' She is an uncommonly handsome woman."

"She is a very good woman too," John said. "A lot of women would not have had the gumption to stay if they lost their husband the way she lost Emil."

"What happened?"

"Emil worked with dynamite. Evidently, there was a bad fuse or something, because the instant he held a match to it, the stick blew. That set off all the other sticks, and Emil was killed."

"That's a shame."

"Yeah. But like I said, she has really been strong. Her strength is to be expected, though, since she comes from a good family. Her father owns a plantation in Mississippi, and was a brigadier general in the Confederate Army. Her husband, Emil, was a good man who met her when he came down to Mississippi after the war. He was a Yankee civil engineer, so her father didn't approve, but she defied her father, married Emil for love, and came out here with him when he took a job with Peabody Mining Company."

"Is she doing all right with the boardinghouse?"

"It's not just the boardinghouse, you know," John said. "She also owns the Coffee Cup Restaurant, and the Fullerton Ladies Emporium. That's how she wound up as president of the Fullerton Business Association. And Kenny, the boy that works for me? He's a regular entrepreneur. In addition to delivering papers for me, he mows lawns in the summer, shovels snow in the winter, cuts and delivers firewood, and helps Jimmy out at the livery stable. Yes, sir, that boy is going to be a wealthy man someday."

In the New York Saloon, Lucas Meacham sat at his usual table in the back of the room, listening to the patrons who had witnessed the shooting yesterday regale those who hadn't seen it, with the story, told and retold, until eventually it became so embellished as to bear little resemblance with the facts.

"'No man relieves me of my pistol and lives! Die, you impudent dog!' Butrum shouted as he pushed through the doors, a blazing gun in each hand, and a knife clinched in his teeth."

Unexplained was how Butrum could have shouted such a challenge while clutching a knife in his teeth.

"*'You have met your match, Ollie Butrum. You will take your supper in hell!' Matt Jensen replied as he drew both guns and returned fire, his bullets finding their mark.*"

Meacham shook his head in disgust as he saw Matt Jensen being promoted to the status of hero right in front of him. At least the story, as reported in the Extra edition the Perkins kid had brought to the saloon earlier, more closely adhered to what actually happened.

Looking up from the story, he saw Logan, Caleb, and Ben coming into the saloon. The only reason he knew their names was because he heard them spoken last night. He'd also learned last night that these three men worked for Denbigh.

Seeing them gave him an idea, and getting up from his table, he walked up to the bar.

"Gentlemen, if you would join me at my table, I'll pay for your drinks," Meacham said.

"You'll buy the drinks?" Logan said. "Hell, yeah, we'll join you."

Paul poured whiskey for the three men and Meacham paid for them. The four men returned to Meacham's table.

"I don't like to look a gift horse in the mouth, mister, but why did you buy us drinks?"

"You three men ride for Denbigh, don't you?"

"Yeah," Caleb said. "Only, he don't like to be called that. He likes to be called Lord Denbigh."

"Why do you ask?" Ben wanted to know.

"Have you been back out to the ranch since last

night? What I'm asking is, have you told him about Butrum?"

The three looked at each other. Then Logan spoke for them. "No, we ain't told him yet," Logan said. "It ain't nothin' we're lookin' forward to doin', so we was kind of hopin' he'd find out about it on his own."

"Suppose I tell him for you," Meacham suggested.

"What? Why would you want to do that?"

"I have my reasons," Meacham answered.

Logan smiled broadly and looked at the other two riders. Then he reached his hand across the table to shake with Meacham.

"Mister," he said. "We'd be pleased to let you tell Lord Denbigh about Butrum gettin' hisself killed last night."

Meacham had not been specific with the three riders as to why he wanted to be the one to tell about Butrum. But he believed it was possible that Butrum getting killed may have just elevated his own position with Denbigh. It was time that he rode out to have another visit with the man.

Chapter Twenty-three

As Lucas Meacham approached the tollgate, he thought about telling them that, like them, he was working for Denbigh. If he didn't tell them, they would charge him a dollar every time he rode through, and that could get expensive.

Meacham smiled at the thought. What did he care how much it cost him, as long as he got every dollar back? And then he had an idea. What if he claimed more trips through the gate than he actually made?

No. That wasn't such a good idea. If Denbigh found out what he was doing, it could mess up the entire thing. He was going to make enough money just by killing Matt Jensen. But if he hadn't known before, he knew now that killing Matt Jensen wasn't going to be easy.

Bleeker came out to meet Meacham as he approached the gate.

"Well, now, seems to me like you just come

through here yesterday. What's the matter, you don't like Fullerton?"

"Just take my dollar and keep your mouth shut," Meacham said.

"Mister, I don't know who you are," Bleeker began, but he stopped in mid-sentence when he saw how quickly Meacham drew his pistol.

"You've got two choices, mister," Meacham said. "You can take my dollar and keep your mouth shut, or you can. . ." Meacham swung his pistol toward Carver when he saw Carver trying to sneak out his own gun. "I wouldn't," he said.

Carver moved his hand away from his gun.

"What do I have to do to make you take my dollar?" Meacham asked.

"Don't go gettin' a burr under your saddle, mister, I didn't mean nothin' by it," Bleeker said. He took the dollar proffered by Meacham. "Open the gate, Carver, let this gentleman through."

"Just be glad Butrum ain't here," Carver said. "He ain't as nice as we are."

"Butrum is dead," Meacham said as he rode through the open gate.

"What? How? When?"

Carver's shouted question was ignored.

"Is Lord Denbigh expecting you, sir?" Tolliver asked when he answered the door pull ring.

"No."

"Wait here, I will see if he will grant you an audience."

"Tell him Butrum is dead," Meacham said.

"Oh, dear, that is news," Tolliver said.

Meacham chuckled. "I must say, you don't seem all broke up over it."

"I cannot lie, sir," Tolliver replied. "I cannot work up any degree of distress over his demise. Wait here, please."

"How did it happen?" Denbigh asked a moment later, when Meacham was shown into his study.

"Jensen killed him."

"Was the contest fair?"

"It wasn't fair at all."

"I didn't think so. Butrum was exceptionally skilled in the use of his pistol, could withdraw it from its holster quite quickly, and discharge it with extreme accuracy. I can understand how someone would have to take unfair advantage in order to best him."

Meacham shook his head. "You got it all wrong. It wasn't fair because Butrum already had his gun out and fired first. He missed, and before he could fire a second time, Jensen drew his gun and killed him."

"That is hard to believe," Denbigh said.

"It's not hard to believe at all. Matt Jensen is known all over the West. Nobody outside of Dakota Territory ever heard of that little turd you hired."

"It wouldn't have happened if you had done

your job," Denbigh said. "I hired you to kill Jensen and you haven't done it. Now I am out my best man."

"He wasn't your best man," Meacham said.

"Oh? And who is?"

"I am."

"But you don't work for me. I have contracted with you to do one thing, and you have not done that."

"I'm going to do it, but the conditions have changed," Meacham said.

"You have already changed the conditions once," Denbigh said, obviously irritated by the way the conversation was going. "I will not raise the agreed-upon amount."

"No need to," Meacham replied. "I'll still kill him for three thousand dollars, just like we agreed. But I also want to work for you full time. I want to take Butrum's place."

"I thought you were quite the paladin, roaming the West in pursuit of desperadoes for the reward money."

"I'm tired of that," Meacham said. "Most of the time, you don't get more'n a couple hundred dollars for it, and sometimes you don't get nothin' at all. I'm lookin' for a job that can use my particular skills and will let me settle down."

"I see. And how good are your particular skills?" Denbigh asked.

"They are good enough."

"So you say. Suppose we arrange a demonstration?"

"All right. Want me to shoot a flower, the way you did?"

"Not quite," Denbigh said. "I will come up with a way for you to display your prowess."

"Tell me what you want, and I'll do it."

Five minutes later Denbigh, Meacham, Tolliver, and several others from the household were out on the well-kept lawn, standing next to the exquisite flower garden of Denbigh Manor. Tolliver's face was pale with fright. His right arm was extended to his side, and he was holding a whiskey glass.

"Now, when I say drop it, you drop it," Meacham said. "I will shoot the glass before it hits the ground."

"Not good enough," Denbigh said.

"What do you mean?"

"You will, no doubt, begin your draw as soon as you tell Mr. Tolliver to drop the glass. That gives you an advantage. I propose that you say nothing. Allow Mr. Tolliver to drop the glass in his own time. Then, once you see the glass leave his hand, you can draw and shoot. If you are successful, then I will believe that your skills are certainly adequate for the task."

"I don't know. Something like that might make me hurry the shot. I could wind up hitting your man, instead of the glass."

"Oh, my!" Tolliver said.

Denbigh had brought his own dueling pistol out,

loaded and capped. He now raised his pistol and pointed it at Meacham.

"Don't worry, Mr. Tolliver," Denbigh said. "If Mr. Meacham's bullet so much as nicks you, I will kill him."

"What?" Meacham said. "If I hit him, it won't be my fault! You are the one who changed the rules on me."

"Oh, it doesn't matter whose fault it will be," Denbigh said. "My declaration stands. If you so much as nick Mr. Tolliver with your bullet, I will kill you."

"What kind of demonstration is that?" Meacham asked.

"Quite a good one, I would imagine," Denbigh replied. "If you think about it, this very effectively duplicates the condition of a real encounter, because now, as in the case of an actual quarrel, your own life is in danger. You do have the choice now of backing out if you wish. But if you do back out, I must warn you now that any and all business arrangements we may have discussed will be considered null and void."

"Null and void? What does that mean?"

"It means that our heretofore-agreed-upon contract pertaining to Matt Jensen is no more. No matter whether you fulfill the contract or not, I will pay you nothing."

"And if I do the demonstration?"

"If you do it successfully, then our agreed-upon contract will still be in force, and, you will be the newest, and most highly compensated, employee of my fiefdom. So, which will it be, Mr. Meacham? Will you make the try, or not?"

"I'll do it," Meacham said.

"Good for you," Denbigh replied. Aiming the pistol at the side of Meacham's head, he cocked it, the hammer making a click as it came back and locked into place.

"Do you have to point that thing right at my head?" Meacham asked.

"Indeed I do."

Meacham cleared his throat, then pulled his pistol from the holster to loosen it, before dropping it back. He held his hand, slightly cupped, just over the holster. He bent slightly at the knees, and just as slightly, leaned forward.

"I'm ready," he said.

"Mr. Tolliver, you may drop the glass at anytime you wish."

Tolliver gritted his teeth and closed his eyes.

"And don't worry. You will not be struck by an errant shot for, should that occur, I will kill him."

For a long moment, there was an eerie tableau vivant in the garden. In the stable, a horse whickered; overhead, a crow called; and a freshening breeze created a whisper in the leaves of the aspen trees and caused the windmill blades to begin spinning.

Then, with a grimace, Tolliver dropped the glass. As quick as thought, Meacham drew and fired. The glass was shattered.

"Ahh!! I'm shot, I'm shot!" Tolliver shouted.

At Tolliver's yell, Meacham looked toward Denbigh, and was relieved to see the Englishman smile and lower his pistol.

"You aren't shot, Mr. Tolliver," Denbigh said. "That's merely shattered glass. Mr. Meacham was brilliant. I believe he has adequately proven his expertise to me."

"Am I hired?" Meacham asked.

"Yes, indeed, Mr. Meacham. You are hired."

Chapter Twenty-four

"John, Mr. Jensen, you might want to come see this," Millie said.

Matt was in the back of the newspaper office with John, trying to learn the workings and mechanisms of the Washington Hand Press, the machine with which the *Fullerton Defender* was printed. Millie was out front, sweeping the porch.

"What is it?" John asked, starting toward the front door.

"It's Denbigh."

At the south end of town, Matt saw five riders coming in, one rider in the lead, then four behind him riding two abreast. Behind the four riders was as elegant a coach as Matt had ever seen. It was pulled by four white horses, driven by a liveried driver. The coach itself was green, the wheels were yellow, and there was a large crest on the door.

The coach was followed by six more riders in three ranks of two.

"John, you asked about Lucas Meacham?" Matt asked.

"Yes."

"There he is," Matt said, pointing to the rider who was leading the others. "Have you ever seen him before?"

"No, I haven't," John said. "Not only have I never seen him with Denbigh, I've never even seen him in town before. He must be new."

"New to you, but not to me," Matt said. "I've been seeing him for several days, now."

As the coach passed the newspaper office, Matt saw its occupant looking toward him with great interest.

"That," John said, "is Nigel Denbigh."

The hollow, clopping of hoofbeats from seventeen horses filled the street with sound, and much of the town turned out to watch the parade.

"Does he always make such an arrival?" Matt asked.

"He always arrives by coach, and he always has a group of men who come with him," Millie said. "I don't know that I've ever seen this many before. I guess he has brought more than usual for the funeral."

"The funeral?"

"Millie ran into Fay Lisenby at the mercantile. Her husband is the undertaker, and she told Millie that Denbigh wanted a big funeral for Butrum."

"Has anyone else who works for him ever died or been killed? What I'm asking is, is this unusual?"

"I don't know that anyone who worked for him died or was killed before now," John said. "That said, this is still a very unusual event. Butrum wasn't that well liked of a man." He made a scoffing sound that might have been a laugh. "What am I talking about? Butrum was hated. Nobody ever had one good thing to say about him, not even the others who rode for Denbigh. You have to wonder why Denbigh would even bother to have a funeral for him."

"To send me a message, I suspect," Matt replied.

"You think he knows about you already?" John asked. "Wait, what am I saying? Of course he knows about you. Everyone in town, probably in all of Elm Valley, knows by now that you killed Butrum. And my bet is, they are all cheering the fact."

"Maybe I'll just make it easier for him to know me," Matt suggested.

"What do you mean?"

"I'm going to the funeral."

"I don't know how you can conduct a funeral for that man," Millie said to her father. "He was pure evil."

"All have sinned and fallen short of God, daughter," Reverend Landers replied. "And I would preach a funeral for him if I were asked, but I have already been told that there will be no funeral per se, in that no prayers will said and no words will be spoken. Denbigh wanted to hold the service, such as it is, in the church, but I told him that, without words being spoken, there would be no service in the church."

"Good for you," Millie said, hugging her father. "Why is it that the only two men who will stand up to Denbigh are my father and my husband?"

"I don't think we are the only two, Millie," John said. "Seems to me as if Matt has already started."

"Oh," Millie said. "Yes, I guess you are right at that."

Butrum's body lay in state at the Lisenby Undertaker Parlor, displayed in a black lacquer coffin that was extensively decorated with silver trim. The top half of the lid was open so that anyone who wished could view his body. The death grimace on his pasty face made him even uglier in death than he had been in life. Because he was so small, his burial suit had to be cut to fit, and it made him look more like a grotesque gargoyle than a human being.

Quite a few citizens of the town came, some because they did business with Denbigh and thought it would be to their advantage to come, but most out of a sense of morbid curiosity. As they filed by the open coffin to look down at the pale face of the deceased, someone would occasionally, more out of habit than conviction, cross himself, then walk away. The expression on the faces of most, however, showed no sympathy for the man, and a few even showed satisfaction that he was dead.

Matt stood in the back of the room and watched

as residents of the town filed by, never once venturing up toward the coffin. He recognized Logan, Caleb, and Ben, Denbigh's men who'd happened into the saloon shortly after he had killed Butrum, as well as Carver and Bleeker, the two men he had encountered at the tollgate on the road into town. He could tell that they recognized him as well, but neither of them approached him, nor did he see either of them say anything to Denbigh about it. He was sure that they'd never even told Denbigh about their encounter. He saw Logan point him out to two other men who had ridden into town with Denbigh's entourage.

"That's Slater and Dillon," John whispered, indicating the two men that Logan was talking to. "They are every bit as evil as Butrum was. I just don't think they are quite as good with a gun."

Although Matt didn't see anyone else point him out specifically, he knew that word had spread because at one time or the other, he saw every one of Denbigh's men take a glance his way. Usually, though, when he looked back, they looked away, unwilling to meet his gaze.

"Ladies and gentlemen, if you would kindly step back from the bier, we can load the coffin into the hearse and proceed to the cemetery for the interment," Lisenby said.

The visitors began filing out of the room where the body had been displayed, while six of the men who had come to town with Denbigh acted as pallbearers, picking up the coffin and carrying it out to a glass-sided hearse, its ebony wood glistening in the morning sun. Four white horses stood in harness, each horse draped with a purple pall, their manes adorned by a black feather plume.

Matt saw Meacham say something to Denbigh. Denbigh nodded, then approached Matt.

"Mr. Jensen, I believe?" Denbigh asked in his clipped British accent.

"That's right."

"I am . . ."

"I know who you are, Denbigh," Matt said.

Denbigh winced at being addressed in such a way, but he said nothing about it. "I am informed that you are the one who killed Mr. Butrum,"

"I am."

"I am also told that a hearing found that the shooting was justified."

"It did."

"Nevertheless, whether justified or not, I must say that you certainly have a great deal of cheek. I mean, here you are, present for the funeral services of the very man you killed."

"You're calling this a funeral, are you?"

"Yes, of course. What would you call it?"

"Seems to me like it is more of a burying than a funeral. At least from what I have noticed," Matt said.

"What do you mean? I have bought and paid for the finest coffin one can buy. And, as you can see, he is being transported to his final resting place in style." Denbigh indicated the hearse that was even now receiving the coffin of the late Ollie Butrum.

"Excuse me, Lord Denbigh," Lisenby said, calling over to him from his position at the back of the hearse. "Will you be present for the interment?"

"No," Denbigh replied. "I shall leave that in your capable hands."

"Very good, sir."

"You aren't going to the cemetery to see your friend buried?" Matt asked.

"He was my employee, not my friend," Denbigh said.

"As I said, it isn't much of a funeral," Matt repeated.

"So, it is a service you want, is it? And would you have a vested cleric reading words and telling lies about what a noble life Mr. Butrum lived?"

"Are you saying he did not live a noble life?"

"You met him briefly," Denbigh said. "Did he seem all that noble to you?"

"I would say—no," Matt replied.

Quite unexpectedly, Denbigh laughed out loud, his laugh totally incongruous in the setting. In fact, some of the attendees, who had left the viewing room and were now watching the coffin being loaded onto the hearse, looked toward him in shock.

"Oh, my, I seem to have upset some of the locals who, no doubt, feel that I am not showing the proper respect for the late Mr. Butrum."

This time it was Matt's turn to laugh. "I doubt any of them are that concerned about it. In fact, I would say that most of them are glad to see him gone."

"Do you believe you did the town a favor by dispatching Mr. Butrum?"

"I think that would be the consensus," Matt replied.

"Consensus? My, that's quite a word for someone like you to use. Are you an educated man, Mr. Jensen?"

"It depends on your definition of the term education," Matt said. "I have some formal schooling, though most of my education was outside the classroom. But it was intense, thorough, and has been much more applicable to my life than would be a degree from some university."

"What you are saying is, you can track a bear, but you know nothing of Chaucer."

Matt began to quote:

> *"When priests fail in their saws,*
> *And lords turn God's laws*
> *Against the right;*
> *And lechery is held as privy solace,*
> *And robbery as free purchase,*
> *Beware then of ill!*
> *Then shall the Land of Albion*
> *Turn to confusion,*
> *As sometime it befell."*

Denbigh applauded, clapping his hands lightly. "Hear, hear, Mr. Jensen, you do know Chaucer. Is it limited to Chaucer's *Prophecy*?"

"I've read *The Canterbury Tales*, and a few others of his works."

"I must say, I am impressed."

"Easily so, I would surmise."

"Yes, well, perhaps another day we can discuss English literature. In the meantime, I would be interested in what exactly brought on the confrontation between you and Mr. Butrum?"

"He wanted to see proof that I had paid the toll."

"A simple enough request. Why didn't you show him the coupon?"

"I had no coupon, because I paid no toll."

"I see," Denbigh said. "They tell me that Mr. Butrum came after you with his gun already in his hand. And you, or at least so they say, were standing there holding a beer in your hand. Yet despite that, you were able to drop the beer, withdraw your pistol from it sheath, and fire, all before he could shoot a second time. Is that true?"

"It must be true if that's what you heard," Matt said.

"You don't strike me as a man who is easily lied to."

Denbigh nodded. "Very astute of you, Mr. Jensen. Very astute," he said.

"I hear that you have taken a position with the newspaper."

"I have."

"You are a man who is obviously good with a pistol, and despite a lack of formal education, you show a surprising acquaintance with Chaucer, but you would take a job with a small-town newspaper?"

"It is honest employment."

"Surely, your salary is paltry. How would you like to come work for me? I would put you in charge of all my associates. I think you would be surprised and well satisfied with the compensation I can offer."

"From what I noticed when you rode into town, you already have someone in charge."

Denbigh smiled. "You must be talking about Mr. Meacham. Have you ever met him?"

"I've seen him around. I've never met him."

"I'm sure the two of you could work well together, but let's rectify the fact that you have never met, shall we?" Denbigh said. He held his hand up toward Meacham and motioned him to come over.

"This is Lucas Meacham," Denbigh said when Meacham joined them. "Mr. Meacham, this is Matt Jensen."

Meacham started to stick out his hand, but when he saw that Matt was not going to reciprocate, he pulled it back.

"We've met," Meacham said.

"No, we haven't," Matt replied. "Though you have been following me for the last several days."

"I wasn't following you," Meacham said. "I was coming here to take a job with Lord Denbigh."

"Would that be the job he just offered me?" Matt asked.

Meacham glanced over quickly toward Denbigh. "Is that true?" he asked.

Denbigh chuckled. "Worry not, my dear fellow.

It was merely a matter of banter," he said. "Your job, as long as you perform it adequately, is secure."

"What exactly is that job, Mr. Meacham?" Matt asked.

"To take care of things," Meacham answered.

"The way Butrum took care of things?"

Meacham smiled. "Turns out he wasn't all that good at it, was he?"

"Shall we get under way, Mr. Meacham?" Denbigh asked.

"Yes, sir," Meacham said. Then to Matt, he said, "I have a feeling that we're goin' to meet again."

"I have that feeling as well," Matt said.

Meacham nodded, then turned and walked away.

Matt watched while Denbigh climbed into his coach, then as Meacham mounted and took his position in front of the others, who, in military precision, formed into columns to escort the coach. At a signal from Meacham, the coach, and all the men who had accompanied Denbigh, left, once again filling the street with the echo of horses' hooves.

John Bryce had purposely held himself apart from the conversation of Matt and Denbigh, as well as Matt and Meacham. Now he walked over to join Matt.

"You said you have heard of him," John said, nodding toward Meacham.

"Yes, I've heard of him."

"Is he going to be trouble for us?"

"I imagine that is his intention," Matt replied without elaboration.

Lisenby stood alongside the elegant, glass-sided hearse until Denbigh and the others had departed. Then he called out to one of his men, who was waiting back in the barn.

"Bring up the wagon."

A well-weathered wagon, its sun-bleached wood gray and splitting, emerged from the barn, drawn by a single mule. The driver of the wagon, the driver of the hearse, and Lisenby took the coffin, closed now, from the hearse and set it, none too gently, into the back of the wagon.

"Dewey, get the hearse back in the barn. Mick, the grave is already open and Al is out there. Take this carcass out there and get it planted."

As Dewey drove the hearse back to the barn, Mick drove the wagon down the street toward the cemetery with one of its wheels squealing in protest as it made its solitary journey.

"How was the funeral?" Millie asked when Matt and John returned to the newspaper office.

"No tears," John answered.

"Did you expect them?"

"Not really. What is that?" John asked, noticing a story Millie had just finished setting.

"It's a story about the Firemen's Ball this Saturday night."

Because it was already set to print, the typeface from John's perspective was backward. Nevertheless, he was able to read it as quickly and easily as the average person could after it was already printed.

"Good story," John said. "Two m's, one t in commitment," he pointed out.

"Aahh, I knew better than that," Millie said. She made the correction. "Are you going, Mr. Jensen? It sounds like it is going to be fun."

"Oh, yes," Matt replied. "I don't want to miss this."

Chapter Twenty-five

To show that he was a magnanimous man, Denbigh let it be known that on Saturday night he would open the tollgate free of charge to anyone who wanted to come to town to attend the Firemen's Ball. As a result of his action, small ranchers and farmers, and their families, doubled the population of Fullerton on the night of the ball.

The firemen were using the ball as a means of raising money to buy a new pumper. In order to make certain that the people got their money's worth, they hired a band all the way from Bismarck. Making the trip in a rented carriage the Fullerton Fire Department supplied them, they arrived in mid-afternoon, and went straight to the hotel ballroom to set up.

Green Fowler and several of his friends, boys that he went to school with, were looking upon the afternoon and evening as a great party, and it was a party not only for the young people but for the adults.

Even before the dance started, the band began practicing, and the high skirling of the fiddle, the low thump of the bass viol, and the melodic strum of the guitar could be heard out in the street. Monroe Avenue had been thoroughly cleaned of horse droppings, and now resembled a carnival midway. There were booths where women were displaying their quilting projects, and Kenny Perkins, ever the entrepreneur, had spent the last two days prior to the dance making doughnuts, tarts, cookies, and fudge. Today, he had a booth where he sold the confections, as well as coffee and lemonade. For the occasion, he had hired Jimmy Smith and Becky Carson, one of his classmates, to help him.

Green and the other boys were running up and down the street, darting in and around the booths. One of them suggested that they play the game of "Shooting Ollie Butrum," and they did so with relish, Green winning the coveted role of portraying Matt Jensen because he had actually met him.

At Ma Perkins' Boarding House, the boarders were all gathered around the supper table when Lucy came into the dining room, obviously dressed for the dance.

"Mrs. Black has baked a wonderful apple pie tonight," she said. "And Mrs. Mouser has graciously offered to serve."

"My, oh, my, Mrs. Perkins, if you don't look lovely

tonight," Proffer said. "Why, if I were thirty years younger, wouldn't I be squiring you."

"Why, thank you, Mr. Proffer," Lucy said, beaming at the compliment.

"Where is Mr. Jensen?" Mrs. Gibson asked. "I thought he would dine with us, tonight."

"I believe John and Millie Bryce invited him for dinner," Lucy said.

"Well, I am sure he will be at the dance. Please tell him we missed him tonight," Mrs. Gibson said.

"If I see him, I certainly shall," Lucy said.

The ball was well under way, and Matt was standing against the back wall enjoying the music and the movement and swirl of the women in their butterfly bright dresses, and of the men, uncomfortable in their unaccustomed suits as they danced. He watched as one of the cowboys walked over to the punch bowl, took a quick look around the room, then, as unobtrusively as possible, poured whiskey into the bowl. Matt chuckled, because this was the third cowboy within the last fifteen minutes to make such an addition to the fruit punch.

He saw Lucy Perkins the moment she came in. She was clearly the most beautiful woman in the room, and though Millie had told Matt that Lucy was thirty-one years old, which was three years younger than Matt, she did not look a day over twenty-one. Lucy was greeted warmly by several of the men and women, and after returning their greetings, she walked over to the punch bowl, where she picked up a stem of crystal. Matt reached her just as she picked up the ladle.

"I wouldn't drink that if I were you," he said.

"Oh, tish," Lucy said, flashing a big smile. "You think I don't know it has been spiked? This isn't the first ball I've ever attended, you know."

Lucy turned to Matt and saluted him with a full glass. "It's so nice to see you here, Mr. Jensen," she said.

Lucy took a swallow of her drink, then immediately lowered the glass and coughed. Putting the glass down on the table, she made a fist, then hit herself in her bare chest, just above the cleavage her dress displayed.

"Oh, my!" she gasped. "What is in that? Kerosene?"

Matt laughed. "You can't say I didn't warn you," he said.

Lucy joined in the laugh. "No, I can't say that," Lucy agreed.

"Ladies and gents, choose your partners and form your squares!"

Lucy looked at Matt expectantly and, with a smile, Matt held out his hand.

"Shall we dance, Mrs. Perkins?"

"Must you call me Mrs. Perkins?" she asked.

"Do you prefer Ma?"

Lucy laughed out loud, and clasped her hand to her mouth. "How about Lucy?" she suggested.

"Lucy it is," Matt replied.

"Thank you, Matt, I would love to dance."

They danced two more squares before six of Denbigh's men rode up. All six were armed when they stepped up to the table to buy their tickets.

"Gentlemen, if you are going to come in here, you are going to have to leave your guns outside," the fireman who was manning the front door said.

"I don't take my gun off for anyone," Meacham said.

"That's fine, sir. If you want to keep your gun, you may keep it," the fireman said politely. "You just can't come in here with it."

Seeing that there appeared to be some disturbance at the front door, Matt, John, and one of the other fireman walked over to see what was going on.

"Any trouble, Carl?" John asked the fireman at the door.

"These gentlemen don't seem to want to check their guns," Carl replied.

"Meacham, isn't it?" John said to Meacham.

"That's right," Meacham replied.

"Mr. Meacham, as I am sure you can tell by looking around this room, nobody is armed," Carl, the fireman at the door said. "That means you are in no danger here. I see no reason for you and your men to be armed."

"What about Jensen here?" Meacham asked. "I've never known him to be without his gun."

Without saying a word, Matt opened his jacket to show that he wasn't armed.

"All right, boys, give up your guns," Meacham said to the others as he unbuckled his gun belt and handed it to the fireman who was sitting at the table. He forced a smile. "We do want to be sociable, after all."

Meacham, Slater, Dillon, Wilson, Bleeker, and Carver gave up their guns, then the six of them moved on into the ballroom. For the first few minutes, there was an uneasiness in the room. All knew that these men worked for Denbigh, and Slater, Dillon, and Wilson were frequent troublemakers when they came to town.

"Well, come on!" Slater shouted. "This is supposed to be a dance, ain't it? How can you dance without music?"

Walter Bowman, the fire chief, nodded at the band leader, and with a few stomps of his foot and nods of his head, the music started once again. Within a few minutes, the dancing resumed, everyone got back into a good mood, and the six interlopers were forgotten.

Unable to get any of the ladies of the town to dance with them, Slater, Dillon, and Wilson cavorted around in their own square, and while they were disruptive with their loud laughter, and sometimes intrusive with their wide turns, they weren't causing enough trouble to make it uncomfortable for others at the dance.

Meacham made no effort to dance. Instead, he stood to one side, leaning back against the wall, observing. Bleeker and Carver discovered the spiked punch, and they quickly ensconced themselves by the punch bowl, where they did little but drink and exchange obscene observations about the women who were present. That might not have caused any trouble at all, had Matt not overheard one of their comments when he came to the table to get coffee for himself and Lucy.

"They say that Perkins woman runs a boarding-house," Bleeker said to Carver. "Ma Perkins', they call it. But look at her. Does she look like someone who runs a boardinghouse?"

"Ha!" Carver replied. "Boardinghouse, is it? It's a whorehouse just as sure as a gun is iron, and she is the chief whore."

"Of course she is," Carver said. "Look at her. You can tell she is a whore just by lookin' at her."

"What do you say that after this dance is over, we drop by her whorehouse and do some business with her?" Bleeker said.

Matt put both cups down and stepped up to the two men.

"Excuse me. I wonder if I could ask you two men to step outside?"

Matt's sudden appearance surprised the two men, neither of whom had noticed him approach the coffee table.

"What do you want us to go outside for?" Bleeker asked.

"Because I heard what you two said about Mrs. Perkins, and I don't like it."

"Calling her a whore, you mean?" Bleeker replied

with a chuckle. "Seeing as you are probably samplin' some of her services, I don't know why you would get all upset over it."

"Step outside," Matt said again.

"Why should we?"

"Because I'm going to have to whip your ass, and I don't want to create a disturbance in here," Matt said.

"Now which ass are you going to whip?" Bleeker asked. "Because maybe you didn't notice, but there are two of us and only one of you. And you ain't wearin' no gun this time."

"I know that it isn't fair," Matt replied. "I mean, being that there are only two of you. But life isn't fair, and sometimes that's just the way it is."

A big grin spread across Bleeker's face and he turned to Carver.

"Well, now, what do you think, Carver? Looks to me like he is challengin' both of us at the same time. Christmas is coming early this year. What do you say we go outside with this fella and teach him a lesson or two?"

"But quietly," Matt said. "I see no need for disturbing the others at their fun."

"You mean you don't want your whore to see you get beat, don't you?" Carver said.

"Let's go," Bleeker said. "This is going to be fun."

Matt followed the two men outside, but as soon as they reached the street, both of them turned and made swipes at him with knives. Their quick turn, and the fact that both were carrying knives, caught Matt by surprise.

"I thought this was to be a fistfight," Matt said.

"Yes, well, life is just full of surprises, ain't it?" Bleeker said as he made another swipe toward Matt. The two men handled their weapons skillfully, but again, Matt managed to avoid the blades.

"Ha!" Bleeker said. "You took away our guns, but you didn't say nothin' about knives, did you?"

Carver feinted and as Matt jumped away from him, Bleeker swung his knife in a low vicious arc. Despite the quickness of Matt's reaction, Bleeker's flashing blade opened a wound in his side, and Matt staggered back.

Bleeker moved in again, trying to take advantage of Matt's wound, but to his surprise, Matt sent a booted foot at the Y of Bleeker's legs. When Bleeker dropped his knife and grabbed his groin, Matt slammed his fist into Bleeker's neck, crushing his larynx.

Bleeker fell to the ground, even as Matt picked up the knife and turned to face Carver. Seeing what happened to Bleeker, and now realizing that he was alone, Carver turned and ran, leaving his partner writhing and choking to death on the ground behind him.

Matt was in no condition to give chase; in fact, he was in no condition to continue the fight, and he was glad Carver had run. He felt the nausea rising up in him. Bile surged in his throat and he threw up in the street. Dizzy and weak, he staggered back to the hotel, then stepped into the ballroom.

"Mr. Jensen!" Carl called. "Mr. Jensen, what happened?"

At the loud and concerned shout of the fireman, the dance caller stopped, the squares ceased their movement, and even the music, after a few more ragged bars, fell silent. Everyone stared at Matt with curiosity. Then, seeing blood spilling through the fingers of the hand he held clasped over his wound, some of the other women screamed.

"Matt!" Lucy called out loudly.

Matt felt the room spinning, then a weakness, then nothing.

Chapter Twenty-six

When Matt opened his eyes, he was lying in bed in the room he had rented from Lucy Perkins. He felt a slight pressure around his middle and lifting his head from the pillow, saw that he was wearing a bandage that had been wrapped all the way around his body. For just a moment, he wondered what he was doing here, and why he was wrapped in a bandage. Then he remembered the fight he had had with two of Denbigh's men.

Damn. He had been in this position before when a man named Clyde Payson had hired two Mexican assassins to kill him. They had come at him with knives in the night, and though he had been badly cut in that fight, as he had in this one, he had left one of them dead and the other blind.[3]

---

[3] *Matt Jensen: The Last Mountain Man*

He wondered if the cut he'd received this time had cut across the old scar.

Matt tried to get up, but when he swung his legs over the side of the bed, he felt an overwhelming wave of dizziness, and he knew that he wasn't going to be able to stand up.

The door to his room opened, and Lucy came in.

"What are you doing sitting up?" she asked sternly. "The doctor said you were to remain flat on your back for at least five days. It has been only three days."

"Three?" Matt said. "I've been in bed for three days?"

"Yes."

Suddenly, Matt realized that, except for the bandage wrapped around his middle, he was naked. And the bandage concealed nothing.

"Damn!" he said, and he got back into bed and under the sheet so quickly that he got dizzy again. He put his hand to his forehead, as Lucy chuckled.

"It serves you right, trying to get up by yourself," she said. "And don't worry about me seeing anything. Who do you think has been changing your bandage every day?"

"I'm hungry," Matt said.

"Well, blessed be, I've been waiting three days to hear you say that," Lucy said. "You lost a lot of blood, and Dr. Purvis said I should give you beef broth to restore it. But, try as I might over the last three days, I couldn't make you take anything except a little water. I'll get you some broth."

"Forget the broth, how about a steak?" Matt said.

"You'll like this broth," Lucy promised. "I already have some ready."

Lucy left, then returned in just about a minute, carrying a tray with a bowl and a spoon. She put the tray on a table and moved the table closer to the bed.

The broth was rich, with a very appetizing aroma, and when Matt looked at it, he saw that it was augmented with noodles.

"I don't see how the noodles can hurt you," Lucy said. "And since you haven't eaten in three days, you probably need something a little more substantial than just broth."

"Uhmm," Matt said after he took his first bite. "Lucy, these noodles are delicious!"

"I'm glad you like them," Lucy said. "Mrs. Black didn't make these. I made them myself. I learned how to cook them from my mammy."

Matt chuckled. "Your mammy. That's right, John did say you were a Southern lady."

"Oh, and the worst kind," Lucy teased. "I'm a Southern lady who married a Yankee." She poured a glass of red wine and handed it to him. "The doctor said that red wine would help too."

"What about beer? Did he say beer would help?"

"I think we'll just go with the wine," Lucy said.

"Won't you join me?" Matt asked.

Lucy smiled and poured another glass for herself. "I thought you would never ask," she said.

Prestonshire on Elm

"Tell me, Mr. Meacham," Denbigh said as he held a brandy snifter in his hand. "What do you know of psychology?"

"Psychology? I've never even heard of that word. What does it mean?"

"It is the study of the human mind, and how the mind works," Denbigh said. "Herr Wilhelm Wundt has established a laboratory in Germany and is discovering some fascinating aspects of how the mind works."

"I see," Meacham said.

Denbigh chuckled. "You don't see at all, do you?"

"No, sir, I don't reckon I do."

"I bring the subject of psychology up, Mr. Meacham, because we are about to do something that will have a whole effect that is greater than its parts."

Meacham's face was still a blank.

"Never mind. I will explain so that even you can understand. The largest rancher around, other than myself, of course, is Ian McCann. If something were to happen that would cause McCann to cease operation, I believe it would have a great psychological effect on all the others. They would see that if the biggest among them is not safe, then neither will they be."

"Do you want me to kill him?" Meacham asked.

"No," Denbigh replied. "Though I must say I am heartened by your eagerness to perform such a task, should I ask it of you. It won't be necessary to kill him, only to dishearten him. Are you willing to do that?"

"You're the boss," Meacham said. "I'm willing to do whatever you want."

Leo McCann was in the bunkhouse with Curly Dobbins and Slim Toomey. Curly was playing a guitar, and Slim was accompanying him with a Jew's harp. Leo was stamping his foot and clapping his hands, enjoying the impromptu performance, when Slim lowered the Jew's harp and walked over to look through the window.

"What the hell?" he said.

Curly quit strumming the guitar, and the music fell silent. "What is it?" he asked. "What do you see out there?"

"Lights," Slim said. "I see a lot of lights."

"Lights? What? Lanterns? Candles? What are you talking about?"

"I don't know, I'm not sure. I'm going outside to take a better look."

"I'll come with you," Curly said, laying the guitar down, then stepping out onto the porch of the bunkhouse with his friend.

Leo went out onto the porch with the two men who rode for his father. As he stepped outside, he saw what Slim had seen, nearly a dozen lights. But even before he had time to wonder what he was seeing, he started wondering why he was seeing it. Each light was a burning torch, carried by a horseman, and now the horses were thundering down Crowley's Ridge, heading straight for the ranch buildings.

"Son of a bitch! It's Denbigh's men!" Slim shouted. "They're comin' to burn us out! Boy, get our guns! They're just inside the door!"

Leo stepped back into the bunkhouse and grabbed a pistol from each of the holsters that were hanging from a peg, then hurried back outside and handed them to Curly and Slim.

Slim got off one shot, Curly didn't even do that, before a fusillade came back from the riders. Curly and Slim both went down, while Leo, unhit, dived off the porch, then crawled around behind it.

The riders started shooting through the windows of the main house, a couple of them taking great delight in shooting holes through the stained-glass transom that was the pride of Leo's mother. Then, one by one, they rode right up to the house and tossed their burning torches, some of them through the windows, others onto the roof. Not until the house was heavily involved in flames did they turn and, with laughter as from hell, rode away at the gallop.

"Ma! Pa!" Leo shouted. He was concerned about Slim and Curly, but more concerned about his parents, who he knew to be still in the house. He started toward the house, but before he got there, he saw his mother and father come running out the front door. They hurried down the porch steps, then ran over to Leo, who embraced his mother.

"Who did this? Who did this terrible thing?" Cora McCann asked.

"I seen 'em," Leo said. "I seen all of 'em." Leo looked at his father, whose skin now glowed orange in the reflected light of the fire. "It was Denbigh's men, Pa," he said. "I recognized a bunch of them."

"Curly? Slim?" Ian said.

"They was both shot. They're layin' there on the porch of the bunkhouse."

Ian hurried over to his two men, then knelt beside them. It took but a cursory examination to see that both were dead.

"What are we goin' to do, Pa?" Leo asked.

Ian stood up and looked back at the house, which was now totally enveloped in flame.

"It's too late for the house," Ian said. "But we might be able to save the other buildings if I can get help here quickly enough."

"You stay with Ma," Leo said. "I'll go get help."

The Fowler Ranch

E.B. Fowler had guests for dinner, and Sue had gone all out for the occasion. She baked a ham, made two pies, and had decorated the house with wildflowers.

Their guests were their nearest neighbors, Ralph and Amanda Putnam and their daughter Helen. The Putnams were farmers rather than ranchers, but Ralph had been one of the men who had gone with E. B. Fowler, Ian McCann, and the others in the unsuccessful attempt to force their way through Denbigh's tollgate.

They had just finished their dinner and were in the parlor talking.

"Do you know anything about this fella Matt Jensen?" Ralph asked.

"Why?" Sue asked quickly. "I know he was hurt the other night at the dance. He hasn't died, has he?"

Ralph shook his head. "No, I was in town this morning, and I saw Doc Purvis. He said Jensen is coming along."

"Oh," Sue said. "That's good. For a moment, you frightened me. I thought he might have died."

"Why are you so concerned about him? Do you know him?"

"We sort of know him," E.B. said. "He stopped by here on his way into town the first day."

"What kind of man is he?"

"He's very nice, pleasant, well spoken," E.B. said.

"He had lunch with us," Sue added.

"He may be pleasant and well spoken, but he has been here less than two weeks and he's already killed two men," Ralph said.

"Ralph, that isn't fair," E.B. said. "Both cases were self-defense."

"Yes, so they say."

"Do you have any reason to doubt it?"

"You don't think he killed Butrum because—" Ralph paused in mid-sentence.

"Because what?"

"I don't know. Maybe he wanted to take Butrum's place? It would be a good way of getting it."

"You mean work for Denbigh?" E.B. asked.

"Yes."

"No, he would never do that. He has taken a job with John Bryce, and you know how Bryce feels about Denbigh. Anyone who has ever read the *Defender* knows how Bryce feels about Denbigh."

"Yeah, I guess so."

"Sue, this cake is wonderful," Amanda Putnam said, changing the subject.

"Thank you, it's a recipe I got from Cora McCann."

Green and Helen were over in the corner, playing a game of checkers.

"Look how well they get along together," Amanda Putnam said. "Like brother and sister."

"Ha! Better than that," Sue said. "I had a brother, and we fought like cats and dogs."

"Who knows, maybe they will get married someday and can join our properties together," E.B. said.

"And which would it become, E.B.? A bigger ranch or a bigger farm?" Ralph asked.

E.B. laughed. "Either way, maybe they could compete with Prestonshire on Elm."

"Not likely. Denbigh isn't going to stop until he owns the whole valley," Putnam said.

"Please, let's not spoil a perfectly lovely evening

talking about Nigel Denbigh," Sue pleaded. "I don't care to hear his name again."

"I agree," Amanda said. "We hear enough about that monster as it is. There is no need to let him destroy our evening."

E.B. held up his hand. "All right," he said. "You have my solemn oath that I won't mention that son of a bitch's name again."

"E.B.!" Sue scolded. "Your language!"

"Well, what else could I say, Sue? You said I couldn't mention his name again."

Ralph laughed out loud. "I think he got you there, Sue."

Suddenly, someone burst through the front door, startling everyone with his unexpected entrance. His clothes were dirty and torn. His face was scratched by brush, his hat was gone, and he was bent over with his hands on his knees, breathing hard. It was Leo McCann, Ian's son. E.B., Ralph, Sue, and Helen went over to him.

"Leo, what in heaven's name is it?"

"Mr. Fowler! Mr. Putnam!" Leo said, gasping for breath. "You gotta come! You gotta come quick!"

"Come where, son? You have to tell us what is going on."

"Our ranch has been hit!" Leo said. "Curly and Slim have both been shot dead."

"What?" Sue gasped.

"And they've set fire to the ranch. Our house is burnin' down, Mr. Fowler. I expect it's purt' nigh burnt to the ground by now!"

"Who would do such a thing?" Helen asked.

"It was Denbigh, ma'am," Leo replied.

"You saw Denbigh?" E.B. asked.

"No, sir, I didn't see Denbigh, but it was him that done it all right, 'cause I seen a lot of his men that I recognized. Slater, Dillon, Wilson, Carver, and that new fella he has workin' for him. Meacham, I think his name is."

"Pa, come out on the porch! I can see the fire from here," Green called back into the house.

E.B. and the others ran out onto the front porch, where they could see a red glow in the night coming from the direction of the McCann ranch.

For a moment, everyone just stood there, mesmerized by the scene. Then, E.B. gathered his senses. "Come on!" he shouted. "If we get over there in time, we might be able to save some of it! Sue, you gather all the buckets you can find. I'll hitch up the wagon."

"I've got some more buckets back over at my house," Putnam said. "I'd better go get them."

"Do that, I'll meet you there," E.B. said as he started toward the barn. "Green!"

"Yes, Pa?"

"You saddle Rhoda—no, wait, better make it Patch, he's stronger and faster. Ride as fast as you can and go to as many farms and ranches as you can get to. Tell them what is happening and tell them to meet us at McCann's."

"All right," Green said. He was disturbed by the fact that the house of one of their neighbors was being burned down, but excited over the prospect of riding Patch. He was not only going to ride his father's favorite horse, he was going to ride him at full speed.

"Which way you goin' first, Green?" Leo asked.

"I'll go east," Green said. "Startin' with Mr. Byrd's house."

"All right, I'll go north, starting with Mr. Donovan's place."

Even before E.B. had the wagon hitched up and brought around to the front of the house, Green and Leo left, both riding at a full gallop.

Sue ran out of the house carrying six empty buckets that she threw in the back of the wagon. No sooner was she in her seat than E.B. snapped the reins against the back of the team and the wagon lurched forward, reaching full speed quickly.

By the time they arrived, a few others, who were closer to the McCann Ranch and had seen the fire, were there also. A bucket brigade had already started with a line of men passing buckets filled from the well toward the men nearest the fire, while a line of women passed the empty buckets back for refill. E.B. and Sue added their buckets and joined in, just as the Putnams arrived.

Chapter Twenty-seven

The next morning, the cool morning air was redolent with the smell of smoke and charred wood as the sun peeked up over the eastern horizon. More than a dozen wagons were parked in the soft, morning light, and in the wagons, nestled among the quilts and blankets, slept the very young children of the families that had come to help fight the fire. By light of day, the damage done by the fire could be clearly seen. The house had burned all the way to the ground, and was now nothing more than smoldering ashes. The stained-glass transom that was one of the hallmarks of the house was now a slag of melted and discolored glass. The bodies of Dobbins and Toomey, McCann's only two cowboys, were lying on the porch of the bunkhouse, covered by a single sheet. The smokehouse, granary, bunkhouse, and barn had not burned because they had been protected from the flames by the efforts of those who had come to fight the fire.

Cora McCann was showing signs of exhaustion and, like everyone else, was covered with soot and smoke. She sat on the porch of the bunkhouse, holding a picture frame in her hands.

"It's a picture of my mama and daddy," Cora said sadly. The picture was of a man sitting on a chair and a woman standing behind him with her hand on his shoulder, both staring stoically at the camera. "It is all I have left of them, and it was the first thing I saved."

Nearly all of the McCanns' furniture had been destroyed in the fire, but a few things had been rescued, and they formed a pathetically small pile on the ground at the end of the bunkhouse porch. Within the ashes of the once-beautiful house, the belongings not saved were blackened and twisted beyond recognition, though standing out un-damaged, almost defiantly, in the midst of what had been the kitchen, sat the cast-iron stove. Leo was poking around through the ashes, and he opened the oven door.

"Ma!" he shouted. "The biscuits!"

"What biscuits?"

Leo pulled out a tray, upon which stood two dozen perfectly baked biscuits. He took a bite of one, then laughed. "They're still good!"

"How could that be? I didn't even bake them," Cora McCann replied. "I just had them in the oven ready to bake this morning."

"That's how it happened," E.B. explained. "The heat from the house burning was enough to bake them, but the oven protected them from being burned."

"You want one, Ma?" Leo asked.

Cora shook her head. "No, pass them around to the others. As hard as everyone worked all night, some of the folks are sure to be hungry."

Because only the very young took biscuits, there were enough to go around. They ate with relish, but the adults and the older children who had worked side by side with the adults through the long night were too tired to participate in the impromptu breakfast. They were also saddened by the death of the two young cowboys who had worked for McCann, as well as for the loss of the McCanns' house.

"How many were there?" E.B. asked Ian. This was the first chance they had to really talk about it, because the entire night had been passed in the effort to protect the other buildings.

"There were at least nine or ten," Ian said. "I didn't get a real good count."

"Leo said he recognized some of them," E.B. said.

"Yeah," Ian said. "It was some of the same ones we run into the day we tried to go through the tollgate. Slater, Dillon, Wilson, Bleeker . . ."

E.B. shook his head. "No, it couldn't have been Bleeker. Bleeker got himself killed, remember?"

"You're right. It was the other one who mans the tollgate. What is his name?"

"Carver," Leo answered.

"Yes, Carver. And that new fella that Denbigh

hired was with them. Fact is, he was leading them. I can't think of his name, but he was the fella that came to the dance and didn't do nothin' but lean up against the wall the whole time and stare at people."

"That would be Lucas Meacham," E.B. said.

"Yes, Meacham. He was with them too."

"This has gone too far," Louis Killian said. "If the sheriff won't do anything, then maybe we need to go to the federal government."

"What can they do?" Putnam asked. "We aren't even a state. They barely know that we exist."

"I know who can help," E.B. said.

"Who?"

"Matt Jensen."

"Why would he help? And what could he do anyway?" McCann asked. "He got himself cut up in a knife fight the night of the dance, remember? He's half dead."

"Ralph saw Doc Purvis yesterday morning," E.B. said. "Doc said Jensen was comin' along just fine."

"Still, he is just one man."

"He doesn't have to be one man," E.B. said.

"What do you mean?"

"The idea you had the other day of all of us getting together to try and force our way through the tollgate was a good one, but it didn't go far enough. It could be that Frank Tanner was right."

"What are you saying? That we should go to war against Denbigh?"

"Yes, that is exactly what I am saying. With someone like Matt Jensen to lead us."

"Do you think he would?"

"Yes, I think he would. He is working for the newspaper, and we already know that John is a fighter," E.B. replied. "Hell, I wouldn't be surprised if John hadn't invited Jensen to come for this very reason. Remember, he killed Ollie Butrum in a face-to-face gunfight, and he fought Bleeker and Carver barehanded when both of them had knives. You know how that came out. He killed Bleeker and he ran Carver off."

"All right, E.B.," McCann said. He looked over at Cora, who was still staring at the picture she was holding; then he looked at his two cowboys, lying dead on the porch beside her. "When we go into town to bury Curly and Slim, we'll have a talk with this Jensen fella and see what he has to say."

Ma Perkins' Boarding House

If anyone had asked Lucy about Matt, she could have testified that he was very much alive and very well. It was before dawn and he was still asleep when Lucy slipped out of Matt's bed. Her clothes were lying on a chair next to the dresser, and for a moment she considered just darting down the hall to her own room naked, just as she had done a few times after a very late night bath. But, there was always the chance that one of her guests might step out of his or her room, so she decided it would be safer if she put her clothes on before she left the room.

As soon as she was dressed, she leaned over and kissed Matt gently on the cheek, then felt a warmth as she recalled their time together last night. Matt stirred slightly, but didn't awaken, and Lucy opened the door quietly, then closed it just as quietly as she stepped out into the hall.

"Ma?" Kenny said.

Kenny's unexpected appearance startled her and she jumped.

"Oh!" she said.

"Are you all right?" Kenny asked.

"Yes, you startled me, is all. My goodness, the sun isn't even up yet! What are you doing up so early?"

"Me'n Jimmy's goin' fishin'," Kenny said. "Did you just come out of Mr. Jensen's room?"

Lucy breathed a sigh of relief that she was completely dressed.

"Well, yes, as a matter of fact, I did."

"What were you doing in there?"

"That's really none of your business, Kenny, but I heard him call out," she said. "I thought maybe his wound had opened up again, so I stepped into his room to check on him."

"Oh, yeah, I didn't think of that. Is he all right? Do you need me to stay home from fishing?"

"No need for you to stay home. Mr. Jensen is fine. He's sound asleep. He must have been dreaming or something. Where are you going?"

"Brewer's Pond," Kenny said. "Jimmy said there's lots of perch there. Maybe I can catch enough for you to have fried fish for supper. Do you think Mr. Jensen likes fried fish?"

"I'm sure he does, honey. Almost everyone likes fried fish."

"Especially the way Mrs. Black makes it," Kenny said. "She makes the best fried fish in the whole world."

"You mean you don't like it when I cook?"

Kenny looked shocked. "No, Ma, no, I don't mean that. I mean, Mrs. Black, she can cook fish and all, but you are the one who is really the best cook in the world."

Lucy chuckled, and ran her hand through her son's hair. "I was just teasing you," she said. "You don't have to say I'm the best cook just because I'm your mama. But it's a good thing to be nice to your mama. Run along now, and have a good time."

Chapter Twenty-eight

E.B., Sue, and Green were returning to their own house after spending the entire night fighting the fire at the McCann ranch. All three were in the wagon, though Patch, the horse Green had ridden to arouse the other farmers and ranchers, was tied onto the back.

The morning sun beat down upon the wagon, giving back both heat and the distinct smell of weathered wood. Sue was beside E.B., her head nodding as she dozed where she sat. Green had stretched out in the back of the wagon and was sound asleep. Even E.B. was experiencing long periods of time when his eyes were closed, but the team knew the way back home and as they plodded along, the hollow clopping sound of the hoofbeats served as a serenade.

Suddenly, three men appeared in the road in front of the wagon, causing the team to stop abruptly. The rapid stop jerked both E.B. and Sue awake.

E.B. recognized all three of them as being Denbigh's men, but he could only recall the names of two of them, Meacham and Slater.

"Well, now, look what we have here. A nice little farmer's family out for a morning ride. What are you doing out on the road so early, farmer?" Meacham asked.

"I'm a rancher, not a farmer," E.B. answered.

"Hey, Slater, Wilson, you think having a couple of milk cows makes a man a rancher?" Meacham asked the two men with him, and they both laughed.

"You didn't answer my question, farmer. What are you doing out on the road so early?"

"Not that it is any of your business, but we spent the night helping Mr. McCann fight the fire at his ranch."

"Oh? McCann have a fire over at his place, did he?"

"Come to think of it, you sorry son of a bitch, I suppose it is your business, since you are the one who set the fire and killed his two riders."

Meacham's eyes narrowed. "I don't appreciate being called a son of a bitch," he said.

"Is that a fact? Well, I'm sure that Mr. McCann didn't appreciate having his house burned down either. Now get out of my way."

A cold smile started at Meacham's lips, but didn't make it all the way to his eyes. He shook his head.

"We're not going anywhere until you pay the toll."

"What are you talking about? I've paid the damn toll every time we have gone into Fullerton. There is no tollgate here. I'm going home now, and I'll be damn if I pay the toll to go back to my own house."

By now Green was awake, and he was on his knees behind his mother and father.

"What's going on, Pa?" Green asked.

"Nothing is going on," E.B. answered. Then he directed his attention back to Meacham and the other two men. "Get off the road. Get out of my way," he demanded.

"Now, Mister . . ."

"His name is Fowler," Slater said. "E.B. Fowler. He lives about a mile and a half south of here."

"Thank you," Meacham said. "Now, Mr. Fowler," Meacham continued. "You know as well as I do how this is going to turn out. No matter how much you argue with me, it's all going to end the same way. You are going to pay me two dollars, one for you, one for your wife. I won't charge you anything for the boy. When you do that, I'll let you through."

"Get out of the way," E.B. said again.

Meacham held up his hand. "I'll tell you what. Just to show you the kind of generous man I am, I won't even charge you for your wife. I'll just charge you one dollar."

"Look, Meacham, I don't have any money with me, so I couldn't pay you a dollar even if I wanted to," E.B. said. "We left home in the middle of the night to fight a fire, not to go into town to go shopping."

"That's all right, we can work something out," Meacham said. He leered at Sue. "That is, if that pretty little wife of yours is willing to cooperate."

"What? What do you mean? What are you talking about?" E.B. asked angrily.

"Well, now, come on, Mr. Fowler, I'm sure you've been around," Meacham said. "You've seen ways women have of making money. There are three of us here. If your woman plays her cards right, you'll not only get your toll paid, why, you can even come away with a dollar or two."

"Shut your mouth, you filthy son of a bitch!" E.B. shouted. "On second thought, I'll shut it for you!"

E.B. had a shotgun under the seat and he reached down to grab it, catching Meacham and the other two riders by surprise. He swung it around and fired, and though he hoped to hit Meacham, Meacham managed to dodge out of the way just in time. The load of buckshot caught Slater in the chest, knocking him from his horse.

E.B. never had the satisfaction of seeing that, though, because even as he was firing, so was Meacham. Meacham's bullet hit E.B. in the middle of his forehead, knocking him over the seat and into the back of the wagon. He lay there with a black, oozing hole in his forehead, and his eyes open, but unseeing.

"You killed him!" Sue screamed.

"I didn't have no choice," Meacham replied. "He killed Slater, and he would've killed me if he could."

It wasn't until then that Sue saw three or four little wounds on Meacham's face. Though he had escaped the bulk of the shot, a few on the periphery of the shot pattern had hit him in the cheek, and he was now bleeding from the wounds. He took out a handkerchief and began dabbing at the small punctures.

"Meacham, Slater is dead!" Wilson said.

"I know the son of a bitch is dead. I'm here too, you know," Meacham replied irritably. He glared at Sue as he continued to dab at the wounds on his face. Finally, he waved his hand.

"Go on," he said. "Get on out of here."

Green crawled over into the seat, picked up the reins, and slapped them against the back of the team, driving them away as his mother sat, weeping, by his side.

Hiding behind a berm that surrounded Brewer's Pond and butted up against the road where the shooting had just taken place, Kenny Perkins and Jimmy Smith had seen the whole thing.

"You . . ." Kenny said under his breath and, angrily, he started over the berm, only to be pulled back by Jimmy.

"Get back down here and be quiet!" Jimmy hissed. "You want to get us both killed?"

"But did you see what he did?"

"I saw it."

Acquiescing to Jimmy's demand, Kenny remained quiet, and they watched as Green drove the buckboard away.

"What are we going to do about Slater?" Wilson asked.

"Throw his carcass over the back of his horse,"

Meacham replied. "We'll take him back to the ranch and let Denbigh do whatever he wants with him."

"You mean Lord Denbigh, don't you?" Wilson asked.

Meacham glared at Wilson, but didn't respond. Wilson dismounted, then, struggling some because Meacham offered no help, he draped Slater's body across the horse.

Kenny and Jimmy remained put until Meacham and Wilson were out of sight.

"Let's go," Jimmy said.

"Go where?"

"Back into town. Mr. Jensen told me to keep him informed about things. I believe this is something he will want to hear about."

When Matt went in to work at the newspaper office that morning, he was greeted effusively by both John and Millie Bryce.

"How are you feeling?" John asked.

"Fully recovered," Matt replied.

"Good, good, you would be surprised at how many people have stopped by to ask about you," John said. "You got here just in time. I'm doing another editorial about Denbigh. And I'm going to send this one straight to the governor."

"Have you sent any of your previous articles to the governor?" Matt asked.

Millie laughed.

"What are you laughing about?" Matt asked.

"He has sent every article he has ever written about Denbigh to the governor."

"And the governor has never responded?"

"Not yet," John said.

"Not yet, he says," Millie said. "My husband is the eternal optimist."

"Mr. Jensen! Mr. Bryce!" Jimmy shouted as he and Kenny rushed in through the front door at that moment. "It was awful! You should've seen it!"

"What?" John asked. "What are you talking about?"

"Meacham killed Mr. Fowler," Jimmy said.

"Oh, my God!" Millie said. "Are you sure?"

"Yes, ma'am. Me and Kenny—uh, Kenny and I," he corrected, "seen the whole thing."

"What happened?" Matt asked.

Jimmy told the story of the encounter he and Kenny had witnessed on the road next to Brewer's Pond. Whenever there was a break in the narrative, Kenny would jump in with his own observations.

"And you say that E.B. killed Slater?" John asked.

"Yes, sir, he pulled his shotgun out from under his seat and shot Slater, then Meacham shot him," Jimmy said.

"It's going to be another case of justifiable homicide, isn't it?" Millie asked. "The sheriff isn't going to do a thing about it."

Chapter Twenty-nine

Three days later, a joint funeral was held for E.B. Fowler, Curly Dobbins, and Slim Toomey. Reverend Landers offered to do a separate funeral service for E.B., but Sue said that the three men had died on the same day, fighting the same evil, and she thought E.B. would be proud to be buried with Dobbins and Toomey.

Every farmer and rancher in the valley came into Fullerton for the funeral, and there were so many that the church could not hold them all. As a result, the funeral was held outside on the church grounds. After the funeral and the interment, everyone returned to the church grounds, where they had dinner and expressed their condolences, not only to Sue and Green for their loss, but also to the McCanns for the loss of their friends and the loss of their house.

Marshal Tipton was present for the funeral and

the meal, but he was growing uncomfortable at the repeated demands that he do something.

"I can't do anything about it and you know it," Tipton said. "It happened outside of town. I have no authority to make any arrests outside the city limits. Besides, from what the two boys said, Fowler fired first, which means even if I did have the authority to act, I couldn't do anything."

"What about Curly and Slim? They didn't fire first. They were defending McCann's house," John said.

"It's the same thing. McCann's ranch is outside of the town limits. There is nothing I can do. That's the sheriff's responsibility, not mine," Tipton said.

The Fowler Ranch

"You're sure there's nobody here?" Wilson asked.

"Nobody here," Carver answered. "They all went into town for the funeral."

"Burn it."

Carver put his fingers to his mouth, then let out a piercing whistle. Getting the attention of the two men down by the house, he waved at them. They waved back, then lit a couple of torches and threw them onto the shake roof. Within moments, the Fowler house was on fire.

The same thing was happening at the Byrd, Donovan, Killian, Jennings, and Putnam houses so that, by two o'clock that afternoon, while all the valley farmers and ranchers were in town, their houses had been burned, or were being burned, to the ground.

Meacham carried the report back to Denbigh.

"Excellent," Denbigh said. "Excellent work."

"M'lord!" Tolliver said. "Are you saying that every house of every farmer and rancher in the entire valley has been burned?"

"Indeed Mr. Tolliver. Upon my orders," Denbigh replied.

"But why, sir? Why would you do such a horrible thing?" Tolliver asked, aghast.

"Careful, Tolliver, remember your place!" Denbigh chastised sternly.

"But m'lord," Tolliver started, only to be interrupted by Denbigh's raised finger.

"Tolliver," Denbigh said, purposely calling him only by his last name. "Your family has been in service to my family for over one hundred years. I would think that such a long relationship would have inculcated some loyalty. I am not used to, nor will I accept, having my actions criticized, or even questioned, by an inferior."

"Yes, m'lord," Tolliver said, lowering his head in submission.

"However, because of that long relationship, I will share my reasoning with you. It is not necessary that I share it, you understand, but I shall do so nevertheless.

"It is my intention to build a great fiefdom, incorporating all the small ranches and farms in the valley. In exchange for rebuilding all the houses, I will demand title to the land. They can continue to live there, but all of them will be working for me."

"You would make serfs of them?"

"Exactly."

"But, m'lord, there is no serfdom society in America."

"Maybe it is time we established one," Denbigh said. "After all, it works very well in England. Why wouldn't it work here? And if you think about it, I am really doing all these people a favor. They would be much better off serving me—no more worry about crop failures or cattle dying. You do see that, don't you, Mr. Tolliver?"

"Yes, m'lord," Tolliver said quietly.

Fullerton

Dennis Donovan was helping some of the women clean up from the dinner after the funeral. He had just put a box of dishes into the back of his buckboard when he saw someone that he recognized as a Denbigh rider approaching. He went out to meet him.

"What are you doing here?" Donovan asked angrily. "Did you come to gloat over killing three of our men, and burning Ian McCann's house down?"

"No. I need to talk to Matt Jensen."

"What do you need to talk to him for?"

"Please, it's important."

Donovan thought about it for a second, then shrugged. "All right, come on, I'll take you to him."

Matt, John Bryce, Curt Jennings, and several

others, including both the mayor and Marshal Tipton, were still engaged in conversation, still trying to decide the best way to handle Denbigh, when Donovan came up to them with his visitor in tow.

"Matt, this here fella wants to talk to you," Donovan said. "But you better watch out because, though I don't know his name, I do know that he rides for Denbigh."

"Rode for Denbigh, not anymore," the man said. "Mr. Jensen, my name is Caleb Jenkins. I don't know whether or not you remember me, we met on the night that you, uh, that is, on the night that Butrum got hisself kilt."

Matt thought of the three cowboys who had braced him that night, and he remembered that one of them was named Caleb.

"I remember you," Matt said. "What can I do for you?"

"I, uh . . ." Caleb looked around at all the other men, then swallowed nervously. "I don't know how to tell you this," he said.

"How about you just come out and say it?" John suggested.

Caleb held up his hands, palms out, as if pushing himself away from the others. "I want you to know, I want you all to know, I didn't have nothin' to do with it," he said. "And when I heard what all Meacham and the others done, what Denbigh had them do, well, I just couldn't take it no more. I decided I needed to get out of there, but before

I leave, I figure I owe it to all of you to tell you what happened."

"Get on with it, Jenkins," Donovan said. "What are you talking about? What happened?"

"Your house has been burned down. That's what happened," Caleb said.

"What? You son of a bitch!"

"I didn't have nothin' to do with it, I told you that!" Caleb said, stepping back away from Donovan.

"Let him talk, Dennis. I have a feeling there is more," John said.

Caleb cleared his throat, then nodded. "Yes, sir. There is more," he said. "There's lot's more."

"What else is there?"

"It ain't only this feller's house that's been burned," Caleb said.

"Who else's house did they burn?" Byrd asked.

"They burned your house too," Caleb said.

"Mine? How do you know my house was burned? You don't even know who I am, do you?"

"No, sir," Caleb replied, "but it don't matter none that I don't know your name. I know your house was burned 'cause all of 'em was."

"What?" John gasped. "Are you saying all the houses were burned?"

Caleb nodded. "Yes, sir, that's what I'm sayin' all right. Denbigh know'd that all of you would be in town for the funeral, so he told Meacham to take some men and burn down every house in the valley. So, that's just exactly what Meacham done."

The news spread quickly around the grounds,

and men began to shout and curse as the women began to weep.

"The sheriff will for sure have to act now," Dr. Purvis said.

"No, he won't. You know Hightower as well as I do, and you know that that cowardly son of a bitch will find some reason not to do anything," Jennings said.

"Well I'm not going to stand around palavering about it," Killian said. "I'm going to go out and check my house."

"No, don't do that," Matt said.

"What do you mean, don't do that? Don't you understand? It's my house."

"I know that it is your house, and I know that all of you are probably anxious to go check on your homes, but I'm going to ask you to trust me for a while," Matt said. "I want you to stay in town, find someplace for your wives and children to be for the night."

"What do you mean, stay in town for the night?" Jennings asked. "How do we know you are not in cahoots with Denbigh? He burned our houses while we were in town. Who knows what he might do next?"

"Jennings, do you really think Matt is in an alliance with Denbigh?"

"I don't know," Jennings replied. "I don't know anything about him."

"Have you seen Butrum around lately?"

"Butrum? No, he's dead, he . . ." Jennings paused in mid-sentence, then looked at Matt for a long moment. "Wait a minute. You are the one who killed him, aren't you?"

"That's right, he is the one who killed him," John said, answering for Matt.

"All right, maybe you aren't in cahoots with Denbigh. But why do you say we should stay in town tonight?" Jennings asked.

"Because I think it is time we did something about Denbigh once and for all," Matt said. "I want everyone to meet me in front of Ma Perkins' Boarding House in an hour."

"Uh-huh, and what do you have in mind? Are you going to plead our case to the sheriff?"

"No," Matt said. "We aren't going to need the sheriff for this. We're going to take care of it ourselves."

"What do you mean, take care of it ourselves?" Killian asked.

"Just what it sounds like," Matt said. "For those of you who are willing to do it, we are going to take the fight to Denbigh."

"Now you're talking," Donovan said. "Yes, sir, taking the fight to that son of a bitch is what we should have done a long time ago."

"Ma Perkins' Boarding House, one hour from now," Matt said. "Now, you had better find someplace for the women and children to spend the night."

"Let me have your attention for a moment!" Reverend Landers called out. "If any of you are unable to find shelter for the night, you are welcome to stay in the church!"

"Thanks, Parson," someone called back.

"John, come with me," Matt said as he started walking quickly away from the church grounds. Behind them, all the men had scattered to gather their families and to find shelter for them for the night.

"Matt, I'm all for this taking care of it ourselves," John said as they walked briskly. "But I can't help but wonder what happens afterward. There have been vigilante groups before in the Dakota Territory, and the governor has not looked upon them all that favorably. As a matter of fact, he hanged the leader of a vigilante group just six months ago."

"We won't be vigilantes," Matt said.

"What will we be?"

"We'll be the posse of a United States deputy marshal."

"How?"

Matt took a star from his shirt pocket, showed it to John, then returned it. "I didn't know exactly what I was getting into by coming up here," he said. "So when I came through Denver, I stopped to see a U.S. marshal friend of mine and got myself deputized."

One hour later, Matt stood on the front porch of the boardinghouse looking out over those who had answered his call. Lucy had Mrs. Black make a lot of coffee, and now she and Millie Bryce were passing out coffee to the men who were gathered on her front lawn. Kenny protested giving the coffee away free, suggesting that he could make a lot of money selling it, but he backed down when Lucy explained that, in this small way, they were making their own contribution to the fight.

"Gentlemen, I trust that all of you have found a place of shelter for the night," Matt said. "I want you to get a good night's sleep, because tomorrow morning we are going out to Prestonshire to arrest Denbigh, Meacham, Wilson, Carver, and anyone else who we find that was involved in killing Curly and Slim and in burning the houses."

"What do you mean we are going to arrest them?" Byrd said. "How are we going to do that? Not even Tipton can do that."

"That's because Tipton is a city marshal," Matt said. "And we—that is, all of you who will raise your right hand to be deputized—will be deputy U.S. marshals. Our authority has no boundaries."

"Deputy U.S. marshals. Who are we going to get to deputize us?"

Once again, Matt took the star from his pocket, but this time he didn't return it. This time he pinned it onto his shirt.

"Raise your right hands," he said. "Repeat after me. I do solemnly swear that I will faithfully execute all lawful orders given me by the deputy U.S. marshal in charge of this posse."

The men repeated the oath.

"We will meet here again tomorrow morning at eight o'clock," Matt said.

Present at the meeting, but not participating, was Marshal Tipton. When the meeting broke up, he stepped up onto the porch to talk to Matt.

"Are you really a U.S. marshal?" he asked.

"I'm a deputy marshal."

"Why didn't you come tell me that as soon as you came into town?"

"I believed that it was to my advantage to keep it secret until necessary for me to show the badge."

"You have no intention of arresting Denbigh, do you? You plan to take your army out there and kill him, don't you?"

"That is not true, Tipton. I have every intention of arresting him."

"What if he won't let himself be arrested?"

Matt raised the coffee cup to his lips, then took a swallow before he replied.

"Then it may be that I will have to kill him," Matt said. "Either way, he has collected his last toll, burned his last house, and killed his last man."

Chapter Thirty

When Tolliver heard the pull bell ring late at night, he got out of bed, put on his housecoat, lit a candle, then walked through the house to the front door. Opening the door, he was surprised to see Marshal Tipton.

"Marshal Tipton? Isn't it a little late to be calling, sir? Lord Denbigh has already retired for the night."

"Wake him up, Tolliver, this is important," Tipton said.

"I don't know, sir. He can be quite irritable when disturbed after he has gone to bed."

"Better to be irritated than dead, isn't it? Wake him up," Tipton demanded.

"Very well, sir. Come with me. You can wait in the parlor."

Tolliver led Tipton into the parlor, where he lit a candelabrum to provide some light. Then he left the parlor to go to Denbigh's bedroom. He tapped lightly on the door.

"Yes," Denbigh said from inside. "I heard the door pull. What is it, Mr. Tolliver?"

"Marshal Tipton is here to see you, sir," Tolliver said. "He said that it is a matter of some importance."

Tipton was sitting in a leather chair staring at the points of light atop each candle when Denbigh came in.

"Mr. Tipton, I trust that you have a very good reason for disturbing me in my slumber?" Denbigh said, the tone of his voice displaying his displeasure.

"Is saving your life important enough?" Tipton replied.

"What are you talking about?"

"Did you burn all the houses in the valley today?"

"Are you going to try and claim some jurisdiction over that now?" Denbigh asked.

"No. But the ranchers and farmers whose houses you burned are planning on coming out here after you tomorrow."

"Let them come," Denbigh said. "They will be nothing but a disorganized mob. My men will dispatch them quite easily."

"They aren't disorganized," Tipton said. "They are being led by Matt Jensen."

"Jensen is leading them?" At that news, Denbigh showed a little more concern.

"Yes."

"Well, what are you doing out here? If you know

about this, why don't you stop it? You certainly have jurisdiction over them. A vigilante mob is against the law, isn't it? Even in a place as bereft of civilization as the Dakota Territory?"

"I have no jurisdiction over them."

"What do you mean, you have no jurisdiction? They are in town, aren't they?"

"I don't have jurisdiction because they aren't a vigilante mob. They are a deputy U.S. marshal's posse. As it happens, Matt Jensen is a deputy U.S. marshal, which means his authority supersedes mine."

"I see. Tell me, when is this supposed to happen?"

"They will gather at eight o'clock in the morning, then come out here. I'd say you need to be ready for them by no later than a quarter till nine."

"All right, thank you, Mr. Tipton. I will be prepared for them."

"I'd better get back to town."

"Yes, you do that. No, wait a minute. It might be best if you don't go back to town at all."

"Why not?"

"They are going to gather at eight in the morning, you say?"

"That's their plan."

"Forewarned is forearmed," Denbigh said. "I am not going to wait out here for them. I am going to take the battle to them. I will be coming into town tomorrow with twenty men. We will strike as they are organizing. They won't know what hit them, and the battle will be over before it even started. You need to be out of town when that happens, just so there is no question as to where your loyalties lie."

"Yeah," Tipton said. "Yeah, I guess maybe you are right. I think I'll ride on down to Ellendale tonight to have a talk with the sheriff about the situation here in the valley."

"I'll have Mr. Tolliver show you out," Denbigh said. Picking up a small bell from the table beside him, he shook it, and the resultant tinkling summoned Tolliver.

"Yes, m'lord?"

"Show the marshal out, please. Then summon Mr. Meacham for me."

"Yes, m'lord."

After Tolliver summoned Meacham, he stood just outside in the parlor listening to them talk as they discussed the next day. Then, half an hour after Meacham left, Tolliver opened the door slightly to Denbigh's room. He could tell by the heavy and rhythmic breathing that Denbigh was asleep.

Not until then did Tolliver go out to the barn, where, in the dark because he didn't want to take a chance of anyone seeing a light, he saddled a horse and rode away into the night.

There was no one manning the tollgate, so Tolliver was able to pass through without arousing any interest or concern as to what he was doing out on the road this late. It was after eleven when he reached town.

As he rode down Monroe, the hollow clopping of the hoofbeats sounded exceptionally loud in the still of the night and he began having second thoughts. What exactly did he have planned?

He answered his own question. He had nothing planned.

Then, seeing that the only lit up building in the entire town was the saloon, he rode to it, dismounted, tied off his horse, and stepped inside. The saloon wasn't entirely filled at this hour of the night, though there were more people than he would have imagined. Looking around, he saw several faces he could recognize, though no one he could call by name.

It was Dennis Donovan who saw him first.

"I'll be damned," Donovan said.

"What is it?" Jennings asked. Jennings was sitting at the table with Donovan as the two men shared a bottle of whiskey that sat between them.

Donovan pointed to Tolliver, who was standing nervously just inside the door. "Ain't that the guy who works for Denbigh? His servant or something?"

"Yeah, I think it is," Jennings said.

Donovan got up and walked over to him. "What are you doing here, mister?" he asked.

"I am looking for Mr. Jensen," Tolliver said.

"Did you expect to find him here?"

"I don't know," Tolliver said. "I don't have any idea

where to find him. I was hoping he might be here, or that someone here might help me find him."

"You ain't welcome here, mister. You need to go on back to Denbigh where you belong," Donovan said angrily.

"Please, sir, if you would direct me to Mr. Jensen, I would be most grateful."

"The only thing I'm going to do for you is direct your ass out of here," Donovan said. "And if you don't leave now, I'll mop up the floor with you."

"Strike me if you must, sir, but after you finish, please, I must speak with Mr. Jensen," Tolliver repeated.

Tolliver offered no resistance, and closed his eyes to accept whatever blows Donovan intended to deliver.

"Wait a minute, Dennis," Jennings called out to him. Jennings walked over to join them. "If he's willing to take a beating, maybe he has a good reason for wanting to see Jensen."

Donovan paused for a moment, then called over to the bartender who, like everyone else in the saloon, had stopped to watch the interplay between the two men.

"Paul, do you know where Jensen stays?"

"Yeah, he has a room at the boardinghouse," the bartender answered. "The same place where you boys had your meeting tonight."

"I thought maybe he did, but I wasn't sure," Donovan replied. He looked back at Tolliver. "All right, come with me. I'll take you to Jensen."

* * *

When Denbigh and twenty of his men approached Fullerton at eight-thirty the next morning, they expected to arrive in town by surprise, then ride up to the boardinghouse, where they would catch the valley farmers and ranchers by surprise. But the surprise was theirs for they saw stretched across the road in front of them, and extending for several feet to either side, an obstruction that would deny passage to their horses. Behind the crossed and sharpened log battlements was a barricade constructed of boxes, barrels, and logs. Protruding over the top of the barricade were a dozen or more rifles.

"Whoa! What the hell!" Wilson shouted as he and the others riding with Denbigh came to a quick halt. "What is that?"

"It is nothing you need worry about," Denbigh said.

"It don't look like nothin' to me," Wilson said.

"Me neither," Carver added.

"Forward, men, don't weaken now," Denbigh said.

"Forward? Into that?" Wilson said. "Are you crazy?"

"I have gone to great lengths to recruit only the most skilled gunmen in the territory," Denbigh said. "Are you telling me now that you are afraid to go against a bunch of farmers and small ranchers? At the first shot, they will run."

"I don't think so," Wilson said, shaking his head. "I was at Shiloh. Wasn't nobody there but farmers and such. And they didn't run. I'm gettin' out of here."

"No, you ain't," Meacham said, pulling his gun and pointing it at Wilson.

"You watch me," Wilson said. Turning his horse, he started to ride away, but before he had gone no more than a few feet, Meacham fired. His bullet caught Wilson in the back, just between his shoulder blades, and it exited from his chest. Slater fell from his horse, dead before he hit the ground.

The other men riding with Denbigh broke into a gallop then, running away. Meacham raised his pistol to fire again, but Denbigh stopped him.

"No need to do that," he said. "Killing them won't bring them back."

Now, only Meacham and Denbigh remained, and they dismounted and continued to stare toward the fortifications that had been erected overnight.

Matt Jensen appeared then, climbing down from the barricade and walking toward the two men.

"Give it up, Denbigh," Matt said. "I'll see that the two of you get a fair trial."

Denbigh applauded sarcastically.

"Very good, Jensen, very good!" he said. "But I thought you were coming after me. How did you know we would be coming after you?"

Tolliver appeared then, standing on top of the barricade.

"I'm afraid I told them, m'lord," Tolliver said.

"You? Mr. Tolliver, you would betray the trust

that has existed between our families for over one hundred years?"

"I am not betraying that trust, m'lord," Tolliver said. "Your own family charged me with the responsibility of seeing that you did nothing to disgrace the Denbigh name. I am afraid I have been remiss in that duty, but there came a time when I could not let this go any further."

At that moment, and quite unexpectedly, Jimmy Smith came riding up the road behind Denbigh and Meacham. Jimmy was carrying a string of fish he had caught that morning. Because he had spent the night camped out on Brewer's Pond, he had no idea of the events that had transpired in the town during his brief absence.

More curious than frightened, he continued to ride forward.

"Jimmy, go back!" Matt called, but it was too late.

Moving quickly, Meacham jumped behind Jimmy's horse, then pulled the boy down. Wrapping his left arm around Jimmy's neck, Meacham managed to keep Jimmy between him and Matt. Meacham's right hand held his pistol against the side of Jimmy's head.

"Well now, Mr. Jensen," Denbigh said. "It would seem that there has been a change in our situation."

"What do you say, Jensen?" Meacham said. "Are you going to ask me to let the kid go? Are you going to try to convince me that the kid has nothing to do with this?"

Matt glared at Meacham, but said nothing.

"Undo your gun belt," Meacham said. "Let it fall to the ground."

Matt continued to glare at Meacham, but he made no move to comply with Meacham's demand.

"Do it!" Meacham shouted, and to emphasize his order, he pulled the hammer back on the pistol he was holding against Jimmy's head.

Slowly, deliberately, Matt unbuckled his gun belt and let it fall.

By now, everyone who had taken up arms behind the barricade was standing on top, watching the drama unfold before them.

"Now what?" Matt asked. "As you can see, you aren't going anywhere. Your men have left you. Your time is over."

"Oh, I think not," Denbigh said. "These people have no homes to return to. I will provide them with homes, bigger and better than the ones they had before. I think we will be able to establish a relationship that is beneficial to us all. Of course, in order to assure that nirvana, I am going to have to take you out of the picture."

"Oh? And just how do you plan to do that?" Matt asked.

"By engaging you in an affair of honor," Denbigh said.

"What are you talking about?" Matt asked.

"We are going to have a duel, you and I, Mr. Jensen," Denbigh said. Reaching into his saddlebag, he removed a wooden box. He opened the box and pulled out two dueling pistols.

"When I say duel, that is exactly what I mean. Not the kind of crass gunmanship by which you bested Mr. Butrum. This will be a gentleman's duel, fought with the weapon of a gentleman—a single-shot, beautifully balanced pistol."

As he was talking, he was also loading the two pistols, then, once loaded, he held both of them out by the barrel, presenting the butts toward Matt.

"To show you that I have engaged in no chicanery in the charging of the pistols, you may choose whichever one you wish," he said.

Matt selected one of the pistols, then checked to see that the cap was in place.

"Very good," Denbigh said. "Now, since this is an affair of honor, we shall require seconds. Mr. Bryce! I take it you are there, somewhere among those standing on the barricade."

"I'm here," John replied.

"You will be Mr. Jensen's second. Mr. Tolliver, you will be my second."

"What does a second do?" John asked.

"As seconds, it should have been we who loaded the weapons," Tolliver said. "And, according to that same code, we should try and arrange some accommodation between the parties that would prevent the duel from occurring in the first place."

"Very good, Mr. Tolliver, you know the code duello. But then, I was certain that you would.

However, do not be concerned if all the niceties aren't observed. You see, a duel is between two gentlemen of equal birth. Mr. Jensen, being a commoner, should not even be afforded this honor. However, I am a man of magnanimity, so I am extending him this privilege."

Matt looked at the pistol in his hand as if it were something foreign and incomprehensible.

"Mr. Jensen, you seem uncomfortable with your weapon," Denbigh said. "Would you rather use your own Colt?"

"Yes," Matt replied.

Denbigh laughed. "I'm sure you would. But I intend to make a gentleman of you, if it kills you." He laughed again, harder this time. "If it kills you," he said again.

"Are you planning on talking all day?" Matt asked.

"No," Denbigh said. "The only thing left to say is to explain the rules to you. We will stand back to back, then we will walk off twenty paces. Mr. Meacham shall count the paces. Upon the count of twenty, we will both turn and fire. Then, after you are killed, Mr. Meacham will maintain custody of the boy until we are safely out of here."

"Suppose I don't want to do this?" Matt said.

"I'm going to kill you, Mr. Jensen, one way or the other," Denbigh said. "At least this way, you will have a chance. Not much of a chance, to be sure, but you will have a chance. Now, shall we proceed?"

Matt and Denbigh stood back to back, holding

their right arms crooked, so that the pistols were pointing straight up.

"Mr. Meacham, if you would, please, begin your count."

"One," Meacham started, and as he counted, Matt and Denbigh paced away from each other, the distance between them opening appreciably. There was not a sound from any of the men who were standing on the barricade, watching.

At the count of twenty, both men turned. Denbigh pointed his gun toward Matt and fired, but Matt, in violation of the code of dueling, dropped to one knee so that the heavy ball whistled harmlessly by his head. Matt aimed, not at Denbigh, but at Meacham who, while watching the duel, had presented more of himself than before. Even so, it was a small target, but it was all the target Matt needed. The .58-caliber ball hit Meacham in his right eye, then burst through the back of his head carrying with it, blood, bone, and brain detritus. Jimmy Smith was free.

Denbigh, who was also wearing a pistol, drew his gun and aimed it at Matt, but before he could pull the trigger, the sound of another shot rent the air.

Denbigh was struck in the chest, and he clasped his hand over the wound, then pulled it away and watched as his blood filled the palm. Looking toward the man who had fired the shot, he saw Tolliver holding a smoking pistol.

"*Et tu, Brute?*" he asked with his dying breath.

One week later

Matt was standing in front of the newspaper office. Spirit was saddled and ready to go, and John, Millie, Lucy, Kenny, and Jimmy were with him.

"As the new owner of Prestonshire, Mr. Tolliver has removed the tollgate, and has promised to rebuild every house that was burned," John said.

"It's obvious that Tolliver is a decent man," Matt said. "And a lucky break that he is the one who inherited the ranch."

"More than just a lucky break," Matt said. "It's a matter of family inheritance. Turns out that Tolliver and Denbigh shared the same father, and though he could not pass on his name or title, the old man did see to it that Tolliver was in the will, if anything happened to Denbigh."

"I wonder if Tolliver knew that when he shot Denbigh," Millie said.

"Doesn't matter," Matt said. "The killing was obviously justified. And the result is positive for everyone." He laughed "Especially for me."

"Matt, will we ever hear from you again?" Lucy asked.

"Good-bye, Matt," John said. Then to the others, "Come on folks, he needs to get started."

"No need to rush him off," Millie said, but John interrupted her with a pointed glance toward Lucy.

"Oh, yes," Millie said. "Come along Kenny, Jimmy. Let them say good-bye in private."

Lucy waited until John and the others had disappeared back into the newspaper office. "What

I should have said, I suppose, is will I never hear from you again?" she told Matt.

"Never is a mighty long time, Lucy," Matt said.

"It wouldn't work, you know," Lucy said.

Matt didn't have to ask what wouldn't work. He knew exactly what she was talking about.

"I have businesses to run, a son to raise," she went on. "And I can't see you playing checkers with Mr. Proffer."

"He wouldn't play with me anyway. I cheat, remember?"

Lucy laughed. "Yes, I remember. And speaking of remembering, thank you, Matt. You have given me memories that will last a lifetime."

"Lucy, I . . ."

"No," Lucy said. "Please, just get on your horse and go now, while I still have my composure."

Matt swung into the saddle and looked down at her. She wasn't crying, though he could see a glistening of tears in her eyes.

"It wouldn't work," she said again. "But, oh, isn't it lovely to contemplate?"

Before Matt could answer, Lucy turned away from him, then walked quickly into the newspaper office.

Matt clicked at Spirit, and started the long ride to Ellendale. He saw clouds building up in the west. No doubt, there would be rain.

THE LAST GUNFIGHTER SERIES BY
WILLIAM W. JOHNSTONE

THE MOUNTAIN MAN SERIES BY
WILLIAM W. JOHNSTONE

Available Wherever Books Are Sold!

Visit our website at **www.kensingtonbooks.com**